THE WERE-WOLF AND OTHERS

The Hippocampus Press Classics of Gothic Horror Series

Edited by S. T. Joshi

The Were-Wolf and Others

The Weird Writings of Clemence Housman

Edited by S. T. Joshi

Hippocampus Press

New York

Published by Hippocampus Press
P.O. Box 641, New York, NY 10156.
www.hippocampuspress.com
All rights reserved.

First Edition
1 3 5 7 9 8 6 4 2

ISBN: 978-1-61498-378-1

Contents

Introduction

We are deeply indebted to Elizabeth Oakley's *Inseparable Siblings* (2009)[1] for what little information is known about Clemence Housman, the author of *The Were-Wolf,* a classic treatment of this venerable motif of weird fiction. Of the three siblings of this talented family who attained celebrity, Clemence was the least-known in her lifetime, by her own choice: her writing occupied only about two decades of her long life, and although she gained notoriety for social and political activism, her overall reputation pales in comparison with her brothers, A. E. and Laurence Housman. But in the field of weird fiction, she stands preeminent among this trio.

Clemence Housman was born on 23 November 1861, the third child of Edward Housman and Sarah Jane Williams. Edward was the son of a vicar, and Sarah Jane was the daughter of the Reverend John Williams, so it is not surprising that fervent Christian belief was central to the lives and minds of their entire family, especially Clemence's. She was preceded in birth by Alfred Edward (1859) and Robert (1860), and was followed by Katherine (1862), Basil (1864), Laurence (1865), and George (1869). For much of this period the family lived at Perry Hall, in the town of Bromsgrove, Worcestershire, in west-central England, not far from the Welsh border. The family suffered a variety of health difficulties in the 1860s; Sarah Jane, weakened by her frequent pregnancies, died on 26 March 1871. Alfred and Clemence were particularly affected by her death; but whereas Alfred eventually renounced his Christian faith (as is evident in his grimly pessimistic poetry), Clemence's faith was renewed, and she took to heart her mother's dying

---

1. Elizabeth Oakley, *Inseparable Siblings: A Portrait of Clemence and Laurence Housman* (Studley, UK: Berwin Books, 2009). Further references will occur in the text.

wish to look after her younger brother Laurence. She carried out this adjuration for the whole of her life.

Edward, a solicitor, suffered business setbacks that, in 1872, caused him to move his family out of Perry Hall and into a residence nearby called the Clock Tower—a seventeenth-century manor house that was owned by another member of the family. In 1878 the family returned to Perry House, as Edward's brother Joseph rescued him from his financial difficulties. In 1873 Edward married his first cousin, Lucy Housman, and she became a beloved stepmother to his seven children. The boys of the family were sent to Bromsgrove School; no formal schooling was given to the two girls, but Lucy read to them frequently and they read much on their own. Clemence later confessed to have been markedly influenced by Charles Kingsley's children's book *The Heroes* (1855), a series of stirring accounts of (male) heroes out of Greek mythology. Her brother Laurence maintained that Clemence "had an inborn appetite which she has never lost for heroes and heroines in suffering for the sins of others" (Oakley 20)—a strikingly apt description of the basic thrust of her literary work.

But Clemence was also attracted to the world of art. She had appreciated the wood engravings (a process distinct from woodcuts) in the *Graphic,* a popular London magazine. In 1878 Clemence and Kate began attending the Bromsgrove School of Art, one of many such schools across Great Britain that were designed to promote home-grown art and design. The next year she won a prize in geometry. She also took to assisting her father in his solicitor's office, gaining valuable knowledge about law and taxation that she would put to unconventional use later on in life.

Although the eldest son, Alfred Edward, surprisingly failed his exams at Oxford in 1881, he nevertheless went on to become a distinguished professor of Latin at Cambridge. For all the celebrity of his later poetry, he remains one of the great classical scholars of his or any other day. Laurence, who also exhibited substantial talent in both art and literature, went to London in 1883 to be a commercial artist. Clemence accompanied him, determined to fulfill her chosen career goal as a wood engraver. At first they lived with Alfred, but had little to do with him. It was at this time that Alfred became romantically involved with a man, revealing his sexual orientation to his siblings for the first time; Laurence also later revealed that he was gay.

Clemence took specialized courses in wood engraving at two different institutions, the Kennington Art School and the South Lambeth School. It was then that she began selling her wood engravings to an array of magazines—including the *Graphic,* the very periodical that had inspired her interest a decade earlier. Regrettably, a few years later technological advances rendered the art of wood engraving largely obsolete as a commercial enterprise, although Clemence continued to practice it on her own. She illustrated some of Laurence's early books.

But literary work was never far from her mind. In 1890 she published *The Were-Wolf* in the Christmas 1890 issue of *Atalanta,* a magazine for girls. It was published in book form by John Lane (The Bodley Head) in 1896, after Laurence had encouraged the publisher to take on the project. The year 1896 was something of an *annus mirabilis* for the Housman siblings, as this was when the first edition of A. E. Housman's *A Shropshire Lad* appeared, as well as a volume of Laurence's poetry, *Green Arras.* A. E.'s verse cycle was immediately hailed as a poetic triumph; less attention was paid to the other two volumes, although Clemence's book did garner a number of favorable reviews.

Clemence went on to write the delicately weird novel *The Unknown Sea;* it was published by Duckworth in 1898. This book did not fare so well with reviewers, as several criticized the tortuous language Clemence used in writing it, rendering parts of it opaque. But it is unquestionably a powerful work fusing supernaturalism and Christianity, and deserves a wider audience. Elizabeth Oakley (60) reports that Clemence had been working for fourteen years on her second novel, *The Life of Sir Aglovale de Galis* (1905), meaning that she had begun work on it around the time she wrote *The Were-Wolf.* This lengthy elaboration of a minor episode in Sir Thomas Malory's *Le Morte d'Arthur* was not at all well received, and this hostile reception may have contributed to her effective abandonment of writing for the remainder of her life.

Meanwhile, Clemence (and Laurence as well) had found a new interest that occupied much of their lives over the next decade or more— woman suffrage. The quest to grant women the right to vote had essentially begun after the passing of the first Reform Bill in 1832, when women were explicitly barred from voting. The campaign endured all manner of setbacks and opposition from conservative politicians and the general public (male and female), but its advocates were relentless. Clemence participated in an unsuccessful attempt on 30 June 1908 to deliver a resolution on the subject to the House of Commons. She and Laurence both worked on embroidering huge banners for the cause.

At this time the movement was split between two factions—a somewhat more moderate group that advocated peaceful persuasion, and a more radical group (led by Emmeline Pankhurst and her two daughters) who believed that actual violence was the only way to shake up the establishment, even if meant a short-term discrediting of their cause. Clemence and Laurence largely identified with the former group. They ran an organization called the Suffrage Atelier. Clemence, becoming somewhat more bold, helped to form the Woman's Tax Resistance League in 1909. The principle of refusing to pay taxes because women did not have "representation" in Parliament was explicitly taken from the "no taxation without representation" canard of the American Revolution; it was also a clever way of embarrassing the government, as the news reports of respectable middle-class women sent to jail created much bad publicity. Clemence herself went to jail for five days in 1911 over her failure to pay property taxes. After her release, the government quietly dropped the case.

Clemence—who was largely being supported by Laurence, chiefly from his steady job as an art critic for the *Manchester Guardian* (1895–1914), as well as the sales of some of his more popular books—resigned from the Woman's Tax Resistance League in 1914, soon after the outbreak of World War I. The war forced the issue of woman suffrage to go into abeyance, as all public and governmental attention was fixed on the winning of the war. Otherwise, Clemence's and Laurence's life in London was one of contentment, as Clemence enthusiastically took to gardening, playing the piano, and cooking. She was of a quiet and subdued temperament, but her work on woman suffrage indicated that she could be passionate about issues she cared about. The cause finally prevailed on 10 January 1918, when Parliament passed a limited woman suffrage act; it was expanded in future years.

Around this time Clemence and Laurence finally left London for a house in New Milton, Hampshire. Then, in 1924, they moved into a house in the small town of Street, Somerset, in southwest England. The house was designed by Laurence, and Clemence worked extensively on the gardens. Just before her move she published her final work, the story "The Drawn Arrow," appearing in an anthology published in 1923. But the story had apparently been written years earlier and published in a magazine—an appearance that has not been located. The life of the two siblings was comfortable, especially during the early 1930s, when Laurence's series of plays about Queen Victoria proved immensely popular and lucrative.

By this time tragedy inevitably descended upon the family. George Housman had died in 1901, while serving in the Boer War; Roger died in 1905. A. E. Housman died in 1936; Laurence became his literary executor. Their lives were disrupted by the outbreak of World War II: Laurence, in spite of his detestation of Hitler and Mussolini, continued to advocate pacifism, as he had done in the previous world war; Clemence was not quite so ardent on the subject during this conflict. She suffered a stroke in 1944 that required the attendance of a nurse for a time, but she made a full recovery. But then her sister Katherine (Kate) died in 1945. Clemence suffered a far more severe stroke in 1953 that largely incapacitated her, so that she was unable to appreciate the reprint of *Sir Aglovale* by Jonathan Cape in 1954, as arranged by Laurence. She died on 6 December 1955, and Laurence followed her on 20 February 1959.

The Were-Wolf is a remarkable novella by any standards. The werewolf motif can be traced all the way back to classical antiquity: there are brief allusions to the myth in Virgil's *Eclogues* (39 B.C.E.) and Ovid's *Metamorphoses* (c. 2–17 C.E.); the most famous passage is an episode in Petronius' *Satyricon* (c. 55 C.E.). And although there are, as Stefan Dziemianowicz has noted,[2] other instances in medieval literature, in modern weird fiction we have to look to two tales that appeared in quick

---

2. Stefan Dziemianowicz, "The Werewolf," in S. T. Joshi, ed., *Icons of Horror and the Supernatural* (Westport, CT: Greenwood Press, 2007), 2.653–87.

succession, Sutherland Menzies's "Hugues, the Wer-Wolf" (1838), and Captain Frederick Marryat's "The Werewolf"—a chapter from his novel *The Phantom Ship* (1839) that has frequently been reprinted as a separate narrative. The most extensive treatment during this time was George W. M. Reynolds's *Wagner, the Wehr-Wolf* (1846).

What distinguishes Clemence Housman's novella, of course, is that her werewolf is female. It is true that the wolf in Marryat's "The Werewolf" is also a woman—significantly named Christina—but it is unlikely that the story exercised any significant influence on Housman's work. Her werewolf is named White Fell, indicating both her snowy complexion and her baleful nature: the archaic adjective "fell" means "savage" or "destructive"—a definition that fully applies to her, leading the protagonist to refer to her explicitly as a "Fell Thing." The name of the hero, Christian, can hardly be an accident. A conscious echo of the allegorical hero of Bunyan's *The Pilgrim's Progress* (1678), Christian must sacrifice himself to protect the life of his brother, Sweyn (who indeed becomes a "swain" eagerly courting the fetching White Fell, oblivious to the clear signs of her sinister supernatural powers). It is here that, as Housman makes a bit too explicit at the end, Christian demonstrates that he "had been as Christ, and had suffered and died to save him from his sins." Like Christ, Christian is the prototypical scapegoat—an innocent, taking on the sins of others to preserve their moral purity.

The Unknown Sea is a longer and more complex work, but its basic thrust is largely the same. Here again we have a protagonist named Christian, and his character is etched more carefully and lovingly in the course of the narrative. He falls under the sway of Diadyomene, an elusive figure he finds on a remote island near his coastal village, where he is a poor fisherman tending to his elderly parents. Is she a supernatural entity—perhaps a mermaid of some sort? It would appear so, although Housman is exquisitely subtle in resisting any overt demonstrations of her non-human nature. Her name is a neo-Greek coinage of uncertain signification. Suffice it to say that she may be a pre-Christian—and, indeed, an anti-Christian—creature, as indicated by her pungent cross-examination of the simple-minded Christian in regard to the paradoxes of the Holy Trinity.

The scenario is rendered more complex by the appearance of Christian's cousin Rhoda. His parents wish her to marry Christian, but she quickly becomes aware that his heart is given to another, and she declines his proposal. As Oakley states, "It is she who understands his spiritual struggle better than anyone else, and aids him in the tasks he performs to save Diadyomene's soul" (55). For Diadyomene does have a soul, and Christian helps her to regain it at the end of the novel—at the cost of his life, just as his namesake in *The Were-Wolf* did.

The Unknown Sea is a remarkable novel: on the very borderline of the weird, it is written in a dense and at times perplexing prose idiom—partly archaic, partly a product of Housman's poetic usage—that can at times render certain sentences or whole passages difficult to follow; but the overall message—Christian's love of an entity who may herself symbolize the sea in all its complex moods—is manifest. It is a lost classic of our field.

"The Drawn Arrow" is not explicitly weird, unless we assume that it is set in an imaginary realm, as indeed it appears to be. One wonders if this tale of a king seeking to regain his kingdom was influenced by Lord Dunsany. In his celebrated play *King Argimēnēs and the Unknown Warrior* (first performed in 1910; included in *Five Plays,* 1914) Dunsany features an overthrown king whose memorable first line is: "This is a good bone; there is juice in this bone."[3] Housman appears to echo this in the initial utterance of her king: "The half of my kingdom would I give for one draught of water." Whatever the case, there is once again a wistful and prose-poetic quality to this tale that allows it to enter the weird, as it were, through the back door.

The resurrection of the work of Clemence Housman began when Alden H. Norton reprinted *The Were-Wolf* in her anthology *Masters of Horror* (1968).[4] It has since been widely reprinted—but almost never with the illustrations that Laurence Housman made, which his sister then rendered into wood engravings. It has been translated into French, German, and other languages. *The Unknown Sea* has been reprinted in

---

3. Lord Dunsany, *Five Plays* (London: Grant Richards, 1914), 59.

4. The novella was first reprinted in Frederick de Berard's *Classic Library of Famous Literature, Volume 5: Weird Tales* (1899).

various shoddy public domain editions. This is the first collected edition of Housman's entire supernatural work (her Arthurian novel *Sir Aglovale* has no weird elements), and it is time that this heir of Ann Radcliffe, Mary Shelley, Rhoda Broughton, Amelia B. Edwards, and so many other female writers of Gothic fiction receives her due as a pioneering contributor to the genre.

—S. T. JOSHI

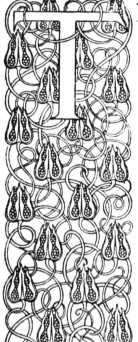he Were-Wolf

The Were-Wolf

To the Dear Memory of E. W. P.

"You will think o' me sometimes, my dear?"

he great farm hall was ablaze with the fire-light, and noisy with laughter and talk and many-sounding work. None could be idle but the very young and the very old: little Rol, who was hugging a puppy, and old Trella, whose palsied hand fumbled over her knitting. The early evening had closed in, and the farm-servants, come from their outdoor work, had assembled in the ample hall, which gave space for a score or more of workers. Several of the men were engaged in carving, and to these were yielded the best place and light; others made or repaired fishing-tackle and harness, and a great seine net occupied three pairs of hands. Of the women most were sorting and mixing eider feather and chopping straw to add to it. Looms were there, though not in present use, but three wheels whirred emulously, and the finest and swiftest thread of the three ran between the fingers of the house-mistress. Near her were some children, busy too, plaiting wicks for candles and lamps. Each group of workers had a lamp in its centre, and those farthest from the fire had live heat from two braziers filled with glowing wood embers, replenished now and again from the generous hearth. But the flicker of the great fire was manifest to remotest corners, and prevailed beyond the limits of the weaker lights.

Little Rol grew tired of his puppy, dropped it incontinently, and made an onslaught on Tyr, the old wolf-hound, who basked dozing, whimpering and twitching in his hunting dreams. Prone went Rol beside Tyr, his young arms round the shaggy neck, his curls against the black

jowl. Tyr gave a perfunctory lick, and stretched with a sleepy sigh. Rol
growled and rolled and shoved invitingly, but could only gain from the
old dog placid toleration and a half-observant blink. "Take that then!"
said Rol, indignant at this ignoring of his advances, and sent the puppy
sprawling against the dignity that disdained him as playmate. The dog
took no notice, and the child wandered off to find amusement elsewhere.

The baskets of white eider feathers caught his eye far off in a distant
corner. He slipped under the table, and crept along on all-fours, the or-
dinary commonplace custom of walking down a room upright not being
to his fancy. When close to the women he lay still for a moment watching, with his elbows on the floor and his chin in his palms. One of the
women seeing him nodded and smiled, and presently he crept out behind her skirts and passed, hardly noticed, from one to another, till he
found opportunity to possess himself of a large handful of feathers.
With these he traversed the length of the room, under the table again,
and emerged near the spinners. At the feet of the youngest he curled
himself round, sheltered by her knees from the observation of the others, and disarmed her of interference by secretly displaying his handful
with a confiding smile. A dubious nod satisfied him, and presently he
started on the play he had devised. He took a tuft of the white down,
and gently shook it free of his fingers close to the whirl of the wheel.
The wind of the swift motion took it, spun it round and round in widening circles, till it floated above like a slow white moth. Little Rol's eyes
danced, and the row of his small teeth shone in a silent laugh of delight.
Another and another of the white tufts was sent whirling round like a
winged thing in a spider's web, and floating clear at last. Presently the
handful failed.

Rol sprawled forward to survey the room, and contemplate another
journey under the table. His shoulder, thrusting forward, checked the
wheel for an instant; he shifted hastily. The wheel flew on with a jerk,
and the thread snapped. "Naughty Rol!" said the girl. The swiftest wheel
stopped also, and the house-mistress, Rol's aunt, leaned forward, and
sighting the low curly head, gave a warning against mischief, and sent
him off to old Trella's corner.

Rol obeyed, and after a discreet period of obedience, sidled out
again down the length of the room farthest from his aunt's eye. As he

slipped in among the men, they looked up to see that their tools might be, as far as possible, out of reach of Rol's hands, and close to their own. Nevertheless, before long he managed to secure a fine chisel and take off its point on the leg of the table. The carver's strong objections to this disconcerted Rol, who for five minutes thereafter effaced himself under the table.

During this seclusion he contemplated the many pairs of legs that surrounded him, and almost shut out the light of the fire. How very odd some of the legs were: some were curved where they should be straight, some were straight where they should be curved, and, as Rol said to himself, "they all seemed screwed on differently." Some were tucked away modestly under the benches, others were thrust far out under the table, encroaching on Rol's own particular domain. He stretched out his own short legs and regarded them critically, and, after comparison, favourably. Why were not all legs made like his, or like *his?*

These legs approved by Rol were a little apart from the rest. He crawled opposite and again made comparison. His face grew quite solemn as he thought of the innumerable days to come before his legs could be as long and strong. He hoped they would be just like those, his models, as straight as to bone, as curved as to muscle.

A few moments later Sweyn of the long legs felt a small hand caressing his foot, and looking down, met the upturned eyes of his little cousin Rol. Lying on his back, still softly patting and stroking the young man's foot, the child was quiet and happy for a good while. He watched the movement of the strong deft hands, and the shifting of the bright tools. Now and then, minute chips of wood, puffed off by Sweyn, fell down upon his face. At last he raised himself, very gently, lest a jog should wake impatience in the carver, and crossing his own legs round Sweyn's ankle, clasping with his arms too, laid his head against the knee. Such act is evidence of a child's most wonderful hero-worship. Quite content was Rol, and more than content when Sweyn paused a minute to joke, and pat his head and pull his curls. Quiet he remained, as long as quiescence is possible to limbs young as his. Sweyn forgot he was near, hardly noticed when his leg was gently released, and never saw the stealthy abstraction of one of his tools.

Ten minutes thereafter was a lamentable wail from low on the floor, rising to the full pitch of Rol's healthy lungs; for his hand was gashed across, and the copious bleeding terrified him. Then was there soothing and comforting, washing and binding, and a modicum of scolding, till the loud outcry sank into occasional sobs, and the child, tear-stained and subdued, was returned to the chimney-corner settle, where Trella nodded.

In the reaction after pain and fright, Rol found that the quiet of that fire-lit corner was to his mind. Tyr, too, disdained him no longer, but, roused by his sobs, showed all the concern and sympathy that a dog can by licking and wistful watching. A little shame weighed also upon his spirits. He wished he had not cried quite so much. He remembered how once Sweyn had come home with his arm torn down from the shoulder, and a dead bear; and how he had never winced nor said a word, though his lips turned white with pain. Poor little Rol gave another sighing sob over his own faint-hearted shortcomings.

The light and motion of the great fire began to tell strange stories to the child, and the wind in the chimney roared a corroborative note now and then. The great black mouth of the chimney, impending high over the hearth, received as into a mysterious gulf murky coils of smoke and brightness of aspiring sparks; and beyond, in the high darkness, were muttering and wailing and strange doings, so that sometimes the smoke rushed back in panic, and curled out and up to the roof, and condensed itself to invisibility among the rafters. And then the wind would rage after its lost prey, and rush round the house, rattling and shrieking at window and door.

In a lull, after one such loud gust, Rol lifted his head in surprise and listened. A lull had also come on the babel of talk, and thus could be heard with strange distinctness a sound outside the door—the sound of a child's voice, a child's hands. "Open, open; let me in!" piped the little voice from low down, lower than the handle, and the latch rattled as though a tiptoe child reached up to it, and soft small knocks were struck. One near the door sprang up and opened it. "No one is here," he said. Tyr lifted his head and gave utterance to a howl, loud, prolonged, most dismal.

Rol's Worship

Sweyn, not able to believe that his ears had deceived him, got up and went to the door. It was a dark night; the clouds were heavy with snow, that had fallen fitfully when the wind lulled. Untrodden snow lay up to the porch; there was no sight nor sound of any human being. Sweyn strained his eyes far and near, only to see dark sky, pure snow, and a line of black fir trees on a hill brow, bowing down before the wind. "It must have been the wind," he said, and closed the door.

Many faces looked scared. The sound of a child's voice had been so distinct—and the words "Open, open; let me in!" The wind might creak the wood, or rattle the latch, but could not speak with a child's voice, nor knock with the soft plain blows that a plump fist gives. And the strange unusual howl of the wolf-hound was an omen to be feared, be the rest what it might. Strange things were said by one and another, till the rebuke of the house-mistress quelled them into far-off whispers. For a time after there was uneasiness, constraint, and silence; then the chill fear thawed by degrees, and the babble of talk flowed on again.

Yet half-an-hour later a very slight noise outside the door sufficed to arrest every hand, every tongue. Every head was raised, every eye fixed in one direction. "It is Christian; he is late," said Sweyn.

No, no; this is a feeble shuffle, not a young man's tread. With the sound of uncertain feet came the hard tap-tap of a stick against the door, and the high-pitched voice of eld, "Open, open; let me in!" Again Tyr flung up his head in a long doleful howl.

Before the echo of the tapping stick and the high voice had fairly died away, Sweyn had sprung across to the door and flung it wide. "No one again," he said in a steady voice, though his eyes looked startled as he stared out. He saw the lonely expanse of snow, the clouds swagging low, and between the two the line of dark fir-trees bowing in the wind. He closed the door without a word of comment, and re-crossed the room.

A score of blanched faces were turned to him as though he must be solver of the enigma. He could not be unconscious of this mute eye-questioning, and it disturbed his resolute air of composure. He hesitated, glanced towards his mother, the house-mistress, then back at the frightened folk, and gravely, before them all, made the sign of the cross. There was a flutter of hands as the sign was repeated by all, and the dead silence was stirred as by a huge sigh, for the held breath of many was freed as though the sign gave magic relief.

Even the house-mistress was perturbed. She left her wheel and crossed the room to her son, and spoke with him for a moment in a low tone that none could overhear. But a moment later her voice was high-pitched and loud, so that all might benefit by her rebuke of the "heathen chatter" of one of the girls. Perhaps she essayed to silence thus her own misgivings and forebodings.

No other voice dared speak now with its natural fulness. Low tones made intermittent murmurs, and now and then silence drifted over the whole room. The handling of tools was as noiseless as might be, and suspended on the instant if the door rattled in a gust of wind. After a time Sweyn left his work, joined the group nearest the door, and loitered there on the pretence of giving advice and help to the unskilful.

A man's tread was heard outside in the porch. "Christian!" said Sweyn and his mother simultaneously, he confidently, she authoritatively, to set the checked wheels going again. But Tyr flung up his head with an appalling howl.

"Open, open; let me in!"

It was a man's voice, and the door shook and rattled as a man's strength beat against it. Sweyn could feel the planks quivering, as on the instant his hand was upon the door, flinging it open, to face the blank porch, and beyond only snow and sky, and firs aslant in the wind.

He stood for a long minute with the open door in his hand. The bitter wind swept in with its icy chill, but a deadlier chill of fear came swifter, and seemed to freeze the beating of hearts. Sweyn stepped back to snatch up a great bearskin cloak.

"Sweyn, where are you going?"

"No farther than the porch, mother," and he stepped out and closed the door.

He wrapped himself in the heavy fur, and leaning against the most sheltered wall of the porch, steeled his nerves to face the devil and all his works. No sound of voices came from within; the most distinct sound was the crackle and roar of the fire.

It was bitterly cold. His feet grew numb, but he forbore stamping them into warmth lest the sound should strike panic within; nor would he leave the porch, nor print a foot-mark on the untrodden white that declared so absolutely how no human voices and hands could have approached the door since snow fell two hours or more ago. "When the wind drops there will be more snow," thought Sweyn.

For the best part of an hour he kept his watch, and saw no living thing—heard no unwonted sound. "I will freeze here no longer," he muttered, and re-entered.

One woman gave a half-suppressed scream as his hand was laid on the latch, and then a gasp of relief as he came in. No one questioned him, only his mother said, in a tone of forced unconcern, "Could you not see Christian coming?" as though she were made anxious only by the absence of her younger son. Hardly had Sweyn stamped near to the fire than clear knocking was heard at the door. Tyr leapt from the hearth, his eyes red as the fire, his fangs showing white in the black jowl, his neck ridged and bristling; and overleaping Rol, ramped at the door, barking furiously.

Outside the door a clear mellow voice was calling. Tyr's bark made the words undistinguishable.

No one offered to stir towards the door before Sweyn.

He stalked down the room resolutely, lifted the latch, and swung back the door.

A white-robed woman glided in.

No wraith! Living—beautiful—young.

Tyr leapt upon her.

Lithely she baulked the sharp fangs with folds of her long fur robe, and snatching from her girdle a small two-edged axe, whirled it up for a blow of defense.

Sweyn caught the dog by the collar, and dragged him off yelling and struggling.

The stranger stood in the doorway motionless, one foot set forward, one arm flung up, till the house-mistress hurried down the room; and Sweyn, relinquishing to others the furious Tyr, turned again to close the door, and offer excuse for so fierce a greeting. Then she lowered her arm, slung the axe in its place at her waist, loosened the furs about her face, and shook over her shoulders the long white robe—all as it were with the sway of one movement.

She was a maiden, tall and very fair. The fashion of her dress was strange, half masculine, yet not unwomanly. A fine fur tunic, reaching but little below the knee, was all the skirt she wore; below were the cross-bound shoes and leggings that a hunter wears. A white fur cap was set low upon the brows, and from its edge strips of fur fell lappet-wise about her shoulders; two of these at her entrance had been drawn forward and crossed about her throat, but now, loosened and thrust back, left unhidden long plaits of fair hair that lay forward on shoulder and breast, down to the ivory-studded girdle where the axe gleamed.

Sweyn and his mother led the stranger to the hearth without question or sign of curiosity, till she voluntarily told her tale of a long journey to distant kindred, a promised guide unmet, and signals and landmarks mistaken.

"Alone!" exclaimed Sweyn in astonishment. "Have you journeyed thus far, a hundred leagues, alone?"

She answered "Yes" with a little smile.

"Over the hills and the wastes! Why, the folk there are savage and wild as beasts."

She dropped her hand upon her axe with a laugh of some scorn.

"I fear neither man nor beast; some few fear me." And then she told strange tales of fierce attack and defence, and of the bold free huntress life she had led.

Her words came a little slowly and deliberately, as though she spoke in a scarce familiar tongue; now and then she hesitated, and stopped in a phrase, as though for lack of some word.

She became the centre of a group of listeners. The interest she excited dissipated, in some degree, the dread inspired by the mysterious voices. There was nothing ominous about this young, bright, fair reality, though her aspect was strange.

Little Rol crept near, staring at the stranger with all his might. Unnoticed, he softly stroked and patted a corner of her soft white robe that reached to the floor in ample folds. He laid his cheek against it caressingly, and then edged up close to her knees.

"What is your name?" he asked.

The stranger's smile and ready answer, as she looked down, saved Rol from the rebuke merited by his unmannerly question.

"My real name," she said, "would be uncouth to your ears and tongue. The folk of this country have given me another name, and from this" (she laid her hand on the fur robe) "they call me 'White Fell.'"

Little Rol repeated it to himself, stroking and patting as before. "White Fell, White Fell."

The fair face, and soft, beautiful dress pleased Rol. He knelt up, with his eyes on her face and an air of uncertain determination, like a robin's on a doorstep, and plumped his elbows into her lap with a little gasp at his own audacity.

"Rol!" exclaimed his aunt; but, "Oh, let him!" said White Fell, smiling and stroking his head; and Rol stayed.

He advanced farther, and panting at his own adventurousness in the face of his aunt's authority, climbed up on to her knees. Her welcoming arms hindered any protest. He nestled happily, fingering the axe head, the ivory studs in her girdle, the ivory clasp at her throat, the plaits of fair hair; rubbing his head against the softness of her fur-clad shoulder, with a child's full confidence in the kindness of beauty.

White Fell had not uncovered her head, only knotted the pendant fur loosely behind her neck. Rol reached up his hand towards it, whispering her name to himself, "White Fell, White Fell," then slid his arms round her neck, and kissed her—once—twice. She laughed delightedly, and kissed him again.

"The child plagues you?" said Sweyn.

"No, indeed," she answered, with an earnestness so intense as to seem disproportionate to the occasion.

Rol settled himself again on her lap, and began to unwind the bandage bound round his hand. He paused a little when he saw where the blood had soaked through; then went on till his hand was bare and the cut displayed, gaping and long, though only skin deep. He held it up towards White Fell, desirous of her pity and sympathy.

At sight of it, and the blood-stained linen, she drew in her breath suddenly, clasped Rol to her—hard, hard—till he began to struggle. Her face was hidden behind the boy, so that none could see its expression. It had lighted up with a most awful glee.

Afar, beyond the fir-grove, beyond the low hill behind, the absent Christian was hastening his return. From daybreak he had been afoot, carrying notice of a bear hunt to all the best hunters of the farms and hamlets that lay within a radius of twelve miles. Nevertheless, having been detained till a late hour, he now broke into a run, going with a long smooth stride of apparent ease that fast made the miles diminish.

He entered the midnight blackness of the fir-grove with scarcely slackened pace, though the path was invisible; and passing through into the open again, sighted the farm lying a furlong off down the slope. Then he sprang out freely, and almost on the instant gave one great sideways leap, and stood still. There in the snow was the track of a great wolf.

His hand went to his knife, his only weapon. He stooped, knelt down, to bring his eyes to the level of a beast, and peered about; his teeth set, his heart beat a little harder than the pace of his running insisted on. A solitary wolf, nearly always savage and of large size, is a formidable beast that will not hesitate to attack a single man. This wolf-track was the largest Christian had ever seen, and, so far as he could judge, recently made. It led from under the fir-trees down the slope. Well for him, he thought, was the delay that had so vexed him before: well for him that he had not passed through the dark fir-grove when that danger of jaws lurked there. Going warily, he followed the track.

It led down the slope, across a broad ice-bound stream, along the level beyond, making towards the farm. A less precise knowledge had doubted, and guessed that here might have come straying big Tyr or his like; but Christian was sure, knowing better than to mistake between footmark of dog and wolf.

Straight on—straight on towards the farm.

Surprised and anxious grew Christian, that a prowling wolf should dare so near. He drew his knife and pressed on, more hastily, more keen-eyed. Oh that Tyr were with him!

Straight on, straight on, even to the very door, where the snow failed. His heart seemed to give a great leap and then stop. There the track *ended.*

Nothing lurked in the porch, and there was no sign of return. The firs stood straight against the sky, the clouds lay low; for the wind had fallen and a few snowflakes came drifting down. In a horror of surprise, Christian stood dazed a moment: then he lifted the latch and went in. His glance took in all the old familiar forms and faces, and with them that of the stranger, fur-clad and beautiful. The awful truth flashed upon him: he knew what she was.

Only a few were startled by the rattle of the latch as he entered. The room was filled with bustle and movement, for it was the supper hour, when all tools were laid aside, and trestles and tables shifted. Christian had no knowledge of what he said and did; he moved and spoke mechanically, half thinking that soon he must wake from this horrible dream. Sweyn and his mother supposed him to be cold and dead-tired, and spared all unnecessary questions. And he found himself seated beside the hearth, opposite that dreadful Thing that looked like a beautiful girl; watching her every movement, curdling with horror to see her fondle the child Rol.

Sweyn stood near them both, intent upon White Fell also; but how differently! She seemed unconscious of the gaze of both—neither aware of the chill dread in the eyes of Christian, nor of Sweyn's warm admiration.

These two brothers, who were twins, contrasted greatly, despite their striking likeness. They were alike in regular profile, fair brown hair, and deep blue eyes; but Sweyn's features were perfect as a young god's, while Christian's showed faulty details. Thus, the line of his mouth was set too straight, the eyes shelved too deeply back, and the contour of the face flowed in less generous curves than Sweyn's. Their height was the same, but Christian was too slender for perfect proportion, while Sweyn's well-knit frame, broad shoulders, and muscular arms, made him pre-eminent for manly beauty as well as for strength. As a hunter Sweyn was without rival; as a fisher without rival. All the country-side acknowledged him to be the best wrestler, rider, dancer, singer. Only in speed could he be surpassed, and in that only by his younger brother. All others Sweyn could distance fairly; but Christian could outrun him easily. Ay, he could keep pace with Sweyn's most breathless burst, and laugh and talk the while. Christian took little pride in his fleetness of foot, counting a man's legs to be the least worthy of his members. He had no envy of his brother's athletic superiority, though to several feats he had made a moderate second. He loved as only a twin can love—proud of all that Sweyn did, content with all that Sweyn was; humbly content also that his own great love should not be so exceedingly returned, since he knew himself to be so far less love-worthy.

Christian dared not, in the midst of women and children, launch the horror that he knew into words. He waited to consult his brother; but Sweyn did not, or would not, notice the signal he made, and kept his face always turned towards White Fell. Christian drew away from the hearth, unable to remain passive with that dread upon him.

"Where is Tyr?" he said suddenly. Then, catching sight of the dog in a distant corner, "Why is he chained there?"

"He flew at the stranger," one answered.

Christian's eyes glowed. "Yes?" he said, interrogatively.

"He was within an ace of having his brain knocked out."

"Tyr?"

"Yes; she was nimbly up with that little axe she has at her waist. It was well for old Tyr that his master throttled him off."

Christian went without a word to the corner where Tyr was chained. The dog rose up to meet him, as piteous and indignant as a dumb beast can be. He stroked the black head. "Good Tyr! brave dog!"

They knew, they only; and the man and the dumb dog had comfort of each other.

Christian's eyes turned again towards White Fell: Tyr's also, and he strained against the length of the chain. Christian's hand lay on the dog's neck, and he felt it ridge and bristle with the quivering of impotent fury. Then he began to quiver in like manner, with a fury born of reason, not instinct; as impotent morally as was Tyr physically. Oh! the woman's form that he dare not touch! Anything but that, and he with Tyr would be free to kill or be killed.

Then he returned to ask fresh questions.

"How long has the stranger been here?"

"She came about half-an-hour before you."

"Who opened the door to her?"

"Sweyn: no one else dared."

The tone of the answer was mysterious.

"Why?" queried Christian. "Has anything strange happened? Tell me."

For answer he was told in a low undertone of the summons at the door thrice repeated without human agency; and of Tyr's ominous howls; and of Sweyn's fruitless watch outside.

Christian turned towards his brother in a torment of impatience for a word apart. The board was spread, and Sweyn was leading White Fell to the guest's place. This was more awful: she would break bread with them under the roof-tree!

He started forward, and touching Sweyn's arm, whispered an urgent entreaty. Sweyn stared, and shook his head in angry impatience.

Thereupon Christian would take no morsel of food.

His opportunity came at last. White Fell questioned of the land-marks of the country, and of one Cairn Hill, which was an appointed meeting-place at which she was due that night. The house-mistress and Sweyn both exclaimed.

"It is three long miles away," said Sweyn; "with no place for shelter but a wretched hut. Stay with us this night, and I will show you the way to-morrow."

White Fell seemed to hesitate. "Three miles," she said; "then I should be able to see or hear a signal."

"I will look out," said Sweyn; "then, if there be no signal, you must not leave us."

He went to the door. Christian rose silently, and followed him out.

"Sweyn, do you know what she is?"

Sweyn, surprised at the vehement grasp, and low hoarse voice, made answer:

"She? Who? White Fell?"

"Yes."

"She is the most beautiful girl I have ever seen."

"She is a Were-Wolf."

Sweyn burst out laughing. "Are you mad?" he asked.

"No; here, see for yourself."

Christian drew him out of the porch, pointing to the snow where the footmarks had been. Had been, for now they were not. Snow was falling fast, and every dint was blotted out.

"Well?" asked Sweyn.

"Had you come when I signed to you, you would have seen for yourself."

"Seen what?"

"The footprints of a wolf leading up to the door; none leading away."

It was impossible not to be startled by the tone alone, though it was hardly above a whisper. Sweyn eyed his brother anxiously, but in the darkness could make nothing of his face. Then he laid his hands kindly and re-assuringly on Christian's shoulders and felt how he was quivering with excitement and horror.

"One sees strange things," he said, "when the cold has got into the brain behind the eyes; you came in cold and worn out."

"No," interrupted Christian. "I saw the track first on the brow of the slope, and followed it down right here to the door. This is no delusion."

Sweyn in his heart felt positive that it was. Christian was given to day-dreams and strange fancies, though never had he been possessed with so mad a notion before.

"Don't you believe me?" said Christian desperately. "You must. I swear it is sane truth. Are you blind? Why, even Tyr knows."

"You will be clearer headed to-morrow after a night's rest. Then come too, if you will, with White Fell, to the Hill Cairn; and if you have doubts still, watch and follow, and see what footprints she leaves."

Galled by Sweyn's evident contempt Christian turned abruptly to the door. Sweyn caught him back.

"What now, Christian? What are you going to do?"

"You do not believe me; my mother shall."

Sweyn's grasp tightened. "You shall not tell her," he said authoritatively.

Customarily Christian was so docile to his brother's mastery that it was now a surprising thing when he wrenched himself free vigorously, and said as determinedly as Sweyn, "She shall know!" but Sweyn was nearer the door and would not let him pass.

"There has been scare enough for one night already. If this notion of yours will keep, broach it to-morrow." Christian would not yield.

"Women are so easily scared," pursued Sweyn, "and are ready to believe any folly without shadow of proof. Be a man, Christian, and fight this notion of a Were-Wolf by yourself."

"If you would believe me," began Christian.

"I believe you to be a fool," said Sweyn, losing patience. "Another, who was not your brother, might believe you to be a knave, and guess that you had transformed White Fell into a Were-Wolf because she smiled more readily on me than on you."

The jest was not without foundation, for the grace of White Fell's bright looks had been bestowed on him, on Christian never a whit. Sweyn's coxcombery was always frank, and most forgiveable, and not without fair colour.

"If you want an ally," continued Sweyn, "confide in old Trella. Out of her stores of wisdom, if her memory holds good, she can instruct you in the orthodox manner of tackling a Were-Wolf. If I remember aright, you should watch the suspected person till midnight, when the beast's form must be resumed, and retained ever after if a human eye sees the change; or, better still, sprinkle hands and feet with holy water, which is certain death. Oh! never fear, but old Trella will be equal to the occasion."

Sweyn's contempt was no longer good-humoured; some touch of irritation or resentment rose at this monstrous doubt of White Fell. But Christian was too deeply distressed to take offence.

"You speak of them as old wives' tales; but if you had seen the proof I have seen, you would be ready at least to wish them true, if not also to put them to the test."

"Well," said Sweyn, with a laugh that had a little sneer in it, "put them to the test! I will not object to that, if you will only keep your notions to yourself Now, Christian, give me your word for silence, and we will freeze here no longer."

Christian remained silent.

Sweyn put his hands on his shoulders again and vainly tried to see his face in the darkness.

"We have never quarrelled yet, Christian?"

"*I* have never quarrelled," returned the other, aware for the first time that his dictatorial brother had sometimes offered occasion for quarrel, had he been ready to take it.

"Well," said Sweyn emphatically, "if you speak against White Fell to any other, as to-night you have spoken to me—*we shall.*"

He delivered the words like an ultimatum, turned sharp round, and re-entered the house. Christian, more fearful and wretched than before, followed.

"Snow is falling fast: not a single light is to be seen."

White Fell's eyes passed over Christian without apparent notice, and turned bright and shining upon Sweyn.

"Nor any signal to be heard?" she queried. "Did you not hear the sound of a sea-horn?"

"I saw nothing, and heard nothing; and signal or no signal, the heavy snow would keep you here perforce."

She smiled her thanks beautifully. And Christian's heart sank like lead with a deadly foreboding, as he noted what a light was kindled in Sweyn's eyes by her smile.

That night, when all others slept, Christian, the weariest of all, watched outside the guest-chamber till midnight was past. No sound, not the faintest, could be heard. Could the old tale be true of the midnight change? What was on the other side of the door, a woman or a beast? he would have given his right hand to know. Instinctively he laid his hand on the latch, and drew it softly, though believing that bolts fastened the inner side. The door yielded to his hand; he stood on the threshold; a keen gust of air cut at him; the window stood open; the room was empty.

So Christian could sleep with a somewhat lightened heart.

In the morning there was surprise and conjecture when White Fell's absence was discovered. Christian held his peace. Not even to his brother did he say how he knew that she had fled before midnight; and Sweyn, though evidently greatly chagrined, seemed to disdain reference to the subject of Christian's fears.

The elder brother alone joined the bear hunt; Christian found pretext to stay behind. Sweyn, being out of humour, manifested his contempt by uttering not a single expostulation.

All that day, and for many a day after, Christian would never go out of sight of his home. Sweyn alone noticed how he manœuvred for this, and was clearly annoyed by it. White Fell's name was never mentioned between them, though not seldom was it heard in general talk. Hardly a day passed but little Rol asked when White Fell would come again: pretty White Fell, who kissed like a snowflake. And if Sweyn answered, Christian would be quite sure that the light in his eyes, kindled by White Fell's smile, had not yet died out.

Little Rol! Naughty, merry, fair-haired little Rol. A day came when his feet raced over the threshold never to return; when his chatter and laugh were heard no more; when tears of anguish were wept by eyes that never would see his bright head again: never again, living or dead.

He was seen at dusk for the last time, escaping from the house with his puppy, in freakish rebellion against old Trella. Later, when his absence had begun to cause anxiety, his puppy crept back to the farm, cowed, whimpering and yelping, a pitiful, dumb lump of terror, without intelligence or courage to guide the frightened search.

Rol was never found, nor any trace of him. Where he had perished was never known; how he had perished was known only by an awful guess—a wild beast had devoured him.

Christian heard the conjecture "a wolf"; and a horrible certainty flashed upon him that he knew what wolf it was. He tried to declare what he knew, but Sweyn saw him start at the words with white face and struggling lips; and, guessing his purpose, pulled him back, and kept him silent, hardly, by his imperious grip and wrathful eyes, and one low whisper.

That Christian should retain his most irrational suspicion against beautiful White Fell was, to Sweyn, evidence of a weak obstinacy of mind that would but thrive upon expostulation and argument. But this evident intention to direct the passions of grief and anguish to a hatred and fear of the fair stranger, such as his own, was intolerable, and Sweyn set his will against it. Again Christian yielded to his brother's stronger words and will, and against his own judgment consented to silence.

Repentance came before the new moon, the first of the year, was old. White Fell came again, smiling as she entered, as though assured of a glad and kindly welcome; and, in truth, there was only one who saw again her fair face and strange white garb without pleasure. Sweyn's face glowed with delight, while Christian's grew pale and rigid as death. He had given his word to keep silence; but he had not thought that she would dare to come again. Silence was impossible, face to face with that Thing, impossible. Irrepressibly he cried out:

"Where is Rol?"

Not a quiver disturbed White Fell's face. She heard, yet remained bright and tranquil. Sweyn's eyes flashed round at his brother dangerously. Among the women some tears fell at the poor child's name; but none caught alarm from its sudden utterance, for the thought of Rol rose naturally. Where was little Rol, who had nestled in the stranger's arms, kissing her; and watched for her since; and prattled of her daily?

Christian went out silently. One only thing there was that he could do, and he must not delay. His horror overmastered any curiosity to hear White Fell's smooth excuses and smiling apologies for her strange and uncourteous departure; or her easy tale of the circumstances of her return; or to watch her bearing as she heard the sad tale of little Rol.

The swiftest runner of the country-side had started on his hardest race: little less than three leagues and back, which he reckoned to accomplish in two hours, though the night was moonless and the way rugged. He rushed against the still cold air till it felt like a wind upon his face. The dim homestead sank below the ridges at his back, and fresh ridges of snowlands rose out of the obscure horizon-level to drive past him as the stirless air drove, and sink away behind into obscure level again. He took no conscious heed of landmarks, not even when all sign of a path was gone under depths of snow. His will was set to reach his goal with unexampled speed; and thither by instinct his physical forces bore him, without one definite thought to guide.

And the idle brain lay passive, inert, receiving into its vacancy restless siftings of past sights and sounds: Rol, weeping, laughing, playing, coiled in the arms of that dreadful Thing: Tyr—O Tyr!—white fangs in the black jowl: the women who wept on the foolish puppy, precious for the child's last touch: footprints from pine wood to door: the smiling face among furs, of such womanly beauty—smiling—smiling: and Sweyn's face.

"Sweyn, Sweyn, O Sweyn, my brother!"

Sweyn's angry laugh possessed his ear within the sound of the wind of his speed; Sweyn's scorn assailed more quick and keen than the biting cold at his throat. And yet he was unimpressed by any thought of how Sweyn's anger and scorn would rise, if this errand were known.

Sweyn was a sceptic. His utter disbelief in Christian's testimony regarding the footprints was based upon positive scepticism. His reason refused to bend in accepting the possibility of the supernatural materialised. That a living beast could ever be other than palpably bestial—pawed, toothed, shagged, and eared as such, was to him incredible; far more that a human presence could be transformed from its god-like aspect, upright, free-handed, with brows, and speech, and laughter. The wild and fearful legends that he had known from childhood and then believed, he regarded now as built upon facts distorted, overlaid by imagination, and quickened by superstition. Even the strange summons at the threshold, that he himself had vainly answered, was, after the first shock of surprise, rationally explained by him as malicious foolery on the part of some clever trickster, who withheld the key to the enigma.

To the younger brother all life was a spiritual mystery, veiled from his clear knowledge by the density of flesh. Since he knew his own body to be linked to the complex and antagonistic forces that constitute one soul, it seemed to him not impossibly strange that one spiritual force should possess divers forms for widely various manifestation. Nor, to him, was it great effort to believe that as pure water washes away all natural foulness, so water, holy by consecration, must needs cleanse God's world from that supernatural evil Thing. Therefore, faster than ever man's foot had covered those leagues, he sped under the dark, still night, over the waste, trackless snow-ridges to the far-away church, where salvation lay in the holy-water stoup at the door. His faith was as firm as any that wrought miracles in days past, simple as a child's wish, strong as a man's will.

He was hardly missed during these hours, every second of which was by him fulfilled to its utmost extent by extremest effort that sinews and nerves could attain. Within the homestead the while, the easy moments went bright with words and looks of unwonted animation, for the kindly, hospitable instincts of the inmates were roused into cordial expression of welcome and interest by the grace and beauty of the returned stranger.

But Sweyn was eager and earnest, with more than a host's courteous warmth. The impression that at her first coming had charmed him, that had lived since through memory, deepened now in her actual presence. Sweyn, the matchless among men, acknowledged in this fair White Fell a spirit high and bold as his own, and a frame so firm and capable that only bulk was lacking for equal strength. Yet the white skin was moulded most smoothly, without such muscular swelling as made his might evident. Such love as his frank self-love could concede was called forth by an ardent admiration for this supreme stranger. More admiration than love was in his passion, and therefore he was free from a lover's hesitancy and delicate reserve and doubts. Frankly and boldly he courted her favour by looks and tones, and an address that came of natural ease, needless of skill by practice.

Nor was she a woman to be wooed otherwise. Tender whispers and sighs would never gain her ear; but her eyes would brighten and shine if she heard of a brave feat, and her prompt hand in sympathy fall swiftly on the axe-haft and clasp it hard. That movement ever fired Sweyn's admiration anew; he watched for it, strove to elicit it, and glowed when it came. Wonderful and beautiful was that wrist, slender and steel-strong; also the smooth shapely hand, that curved so fast and firm, ready to deal instant death.

Desiring to feel the pressure of these hands, this bold lover schemed with palpable directness, proposing that she should hear how their hunting songs were sung, with a chorus that signalled hands to be clasped. So his splendid voice gave the verses, and, as the chorus was taken up, he claimed her hands, and, even through the easy grip, felt, as he desired, the strength that was latent, and the vigour that quickened the very finger-tips, as the song fired her, and her voice was caught out of her by the rhythmic swell, and rang clear on the top of the closing surge.

Afterwards she sang alone. For contrast, or in the pride of swaying moods by her voice, she chose a mournful song that drifted along in a minor chant, sad as a wind that dirges:

> "Oh, let me go!
> Around spin wreaths of snow;
> The dark earth sleeps below.
>
> Far up the plain
> Moans on a voice of pain:
> 'Where shall my babe be lain?'
>
> In my white breast
> Lay the sweet life to rest!
> Lay, where it can lie best!

'Hush! hush its cries!
Dense night is on the skies:
Two stars are in thine eyes.'

Come, babe, away!
But lie thou till dawn be grey,
Who must be dead by day.

This cannot last;
But, ere the sickening blast,
All sorrow shall be past;

And kings shall be
Low bending at thy knee,
Worshipping life from thee.

For men long sore
To hope of what's before,—
To leave the things of yore.

Mine, and not thine,
How deep their jewels shine!
Peace laps thy head, not mine."

Old Trella came tottering from her corner, shaken to additional palsy by an aroused memory. She strained her dim eyes towards the singer, and then bent her head, that the one ear yet sensible to sound might avail of every note. At the close, groping forward, she murmured with the high-pitched quaver of old age:

"So she sang, my Thora; my last and brightest. What is she like, she whose voice is like my dead Thora's? Are her eyes blue?"

"Blue as the sky."

"So were my Thora's! Is her hair fair, and in plaits to the waist?"

"Even so," answered White Fell herself, and met the advancing hands with her own, and guided them to corroborate her words by touch.

"Like my dead Thora's," repeated the old woman; and then her trembling hands rested on the fur-clad shoulders, and she bent forward and kissed the smooth fair face that White Fell upturned, nothing loth, to receive and return the caress.

So Christian saw them as he entered.

He stood a moment. After the starless darkness and the icy night air, and the fierce silent two hours' race, his senses reeled on sudden entrance into warmth, and light, and the cheery hum of voices. A sudden unforeseen anguish assailed him, as now first he entertained the possibility of being overmatched by her wiles and her daring, if at the approach of pure death she should start up at bay transformed to a terrible beast, and achieve a savage glut at the last. He looked with horror and pity on the harmless, helpless folk, so unwitting of outrage to their comfort and security. The dreadful Thing in their midst, that was veiled from their knowledge by womanly beauty, was a centre of pleasant interest. There, before him, signally impressive, was poor old Trella, weakest and feeblest of all, in fond nearness. And a moment might bring about the revelation of a monstrous horror—a ghastly, deadly danger, set loose and at bay, in a circle of girls and women and careless defenceless men: so hideous and terrible a thing as might crack the brain, or curdle the heart stone dead.

And he alone of the throng prepared!

For one breathing space he faltered, no longer than that, while over him swept the agony of compunction that yet could not make him surrender his purpose.

He alone? Nay, but Tyr also; and he crossed to the dumb sole sharer of his knowledge.

So timeless is thought that a few seconds only lay between his lifting of the latch and his loosening of Tyr's collar; but in those few seconds succeeding his first glance, as lightning-swift had been the impulses of others, their motion as quick and sure. Sweyn's vigilant eye had darted upon him, and instantly his every fibre was alert with hostile instinct; and, half divining, half incredulous, of Christian's object in stooping to Tyr, he came hastily, wary, wrathful, resolute to oppose the malice of his wild-eyed brother.

But beyond Sweyn rose White Fell, blanching white as her furs, and with eyes grown fierce and wild. She leapt down the room to the door, whirling her long robe closely to her. "Hark!" she panted. "The signal horn! Hark, I must go!" as she snatched at the latch to be out and away.

White Fell's Escape

For one precious moment Christian had hesitated on the half-loosened collar; for, except the womanly form were exchanged for the bestial, Tyr's jaws would gnash to rags his honour of manhood. Then he heard her voice, and turned—too late.

As she tugged at the door, he sprang across grasping his flask, but Sweyn dashed between, and caught him back irresistibly, so that a most frantic effort only availed to wrench one arm free. With that, on the impulse of sheer despair, he cast at her with all his force. The door swung behind her, and the flask flew into fragments against it. Then, as Sweyn's grasp slackened, and he met the questioning astonishment of surrounding faces, with a hoarse inarticulate cry: "God help us all!" he said. "She is a Were-Wolf."

Sweyn turned upon him, "Liar, coward!" and his hands gripped his brother's throat with deadly force, as though the spoken word could be killed so; and as Christian struggled, lifted him clear off his feet and flung him crashing backward. So furious was he, that, as his brother lay motionless, he stirred him roughly with his foot, till their mother came between, crying shame; and yet then he stood by, his teeth set, his brows knit, his hands clenched, ready to enforce silence again violently, as Christian rose staggering and bewildered.

But utter silence and submission were more than he expected, and turned his anger into contempt for one so easily cowed and held in subjection by mere force. "He is mad!" he said, turning on his heel as he spoke, so that he lost his mother's look of pained reproach at this sudden free utterance of what was a lurking dread within her.

Christian was too spent for the effort of speech. His hard-drawn breath laboured in great sobs; his limbs were powerless and unstrung in utter relax after hard service. Failure in his endeavour induced a stupor of misery and despair. In addition was the wretched humiliation of open violence and strife with his brother, and the distress of hearing misjudging contempt expressed without reserve; for he was aware that Sweyn had turned to allay the scared excitement half by imperious mastery, half by explanation and argument, that showed painful disregard of brotherly consideration. All this unkindness of his twin he charged upon the fell Thing who had wrought this their first dissension, and, ah! most terrible thought, interposed between them so effectually, that Sweyn was wilfully blind and deaf on her account, resentful of interference, arbitrary beyond reason.

Dread and perplexity unfathomable darkened upon him; unshared, the burden was overwhelming: a foreboding of unspeakable calamity, based upon his ghastly discovery, bore down upon him, crushing out hope of power to withstand impending fate.

Sweyn the while was observant of his brother, despite the continual check of finding, turn and glance when he would, Christian's eyes always upon him, with a strange look of helpless distress, discomposing enough to the angry aggressor. "Like a beaten dog!" he said to himself, rallying contempt to withstand compunction. Observation set him wondering on Christian's exhausted condition. The heavy labouring breath and the slack inert fall of the limbs told surely of unusual and prolonged exertion. And then why had close upon two hours' absence been followed by open hostility against White Fell?

Suddenly, the fragments of the flask giving a clue, he guessed all, and faced about to stare at his brother in amaze. He forgot that the motive scheme was against White Fell, demanding derision and resentment from him; that was swept out of remembrance by astonishment and admiration for the feat of speed and endurance. In eagerness to question he inclined to attempt a generous part and frankly offer to heal the breach; but Christian's depression and sad following gaze provoked him to self-justification by recalling the offence of that outrageous utterance against White Fell; and the impulse passed. Then other considerations counselled silence; and afterwards a humour possessed him to wait and see how Christian would find opportunity to proclaim his performance and establish the fact, without exciting ridicule on account of the absurdity of the errand.

This expectation remained unfulfilled. Christian never attempted the proud avowal that would have placed his feat on record to be told to the next generation.

That night Sweyn and his mother talked long and late together, shaping into certainty the suspicion that Christian's mind had lost its balance, and discussing the evident cause. For Sweyn, declaring his own love for White Fell, suggested that his unfortunate brother, with a like passion, they being twins in loves as in birth, had through jealousy and despair turned from love to hate, until reason failed at the strain, and a craze developed, which the malice and treachery of madness made a serious and dangerous force.

So Sweyn theorised, convincing himself as he spoke; convincing afterwards others who advanced doubts against White Fell; fettering his judgment by his advocacy, and by his staunch defence of her hurried flight silencing his own inner consciousness of the unaccountability of her action.

But a little time and Sweyn lost his vantage in the shock of a fresh horror at the homestead. Trella was no more, and her end a mystery. The poor old woman crawled out in a bright gleam to visit a bed-ridden gossip living beyond the fir-grove. Under the trees she was last seen, halting for her companion, sent back for a forgotten present. Quick alarm sprang, calling every man to the search. Her stick was found among the brushwood only a few paces from the path, but no track or stain, for a gusty wind was sifting the snow from the branches, and hid all sign of how she came by her death.

So panic-stricken were the farm folk that none dared go singly on the search. Known danger could be braced, but not this stealthy Death that walked by day invisible, that cut off alike the child in his play and the aged woman so near to her quiet grave.

"Rol she kissed; Trella she kissed!" So rang Christian's frantic cry again and again, till Sweyn dragged him away and strove to keep him apart, albeit in his agony of grief and remorse he accused himself wildly as answerable for the tragedy, and gave clear proof that the charge of madness was well founded, if strange looks and desperate, incoherent words were evidence enough.

But thenceforward all Sweyn's reasoning and mastery could not uphold White Fell above suspicion. He was not called upon to defend her from accusation when Christian had been brought to silence again; but he well knew the significance of this fact, that her name, formerly uttered freely and often, he never heard now: it was huddled away into whispers that he could not catch.

The passing of time did not sweep away the superstitious fears that Sweyn despised. He was angry and anxious; eager that White Fell should return, and, merely by her bright gracious presence, reinstate herself in favour; but doubtful if all his authority and example could keep from her notice an altered aspect of welcome; and he foresaw clearly that Christian would prove unmanageable, and might be capable of some dangerous outbreak.

For a time the twins' variance was marked, on Sweyn's part by an air of rigid indifference, on Christian's by heavy downcast silence, and a nervous apprehensive observation of his brother. Superadded to his remorse and foreboding, Sweyn's displeasure weighed upon him intolerably, and the remembrance of their violent rupture was a ceaseless misery. The elder brother, self-sufficient and insensitive, could little know how deeply his unkindness stabbed. A depth and force of affection such as Christian's was unknown to him. The loyal subservience that he could not appreciate had encouraged him to domineer; this strenuous opposition to his reason and will was accounted as furious malice, if not sheer insanity.

Christian's surveillance galled him incessantly, and embarrassment and danger he foresaw as the outcome. Therefore, that suspicion might be lulled, he judged it wise to make overtures for peace. Most easily done. A little kindliness, a few evidences of consideration, a slight return of the old brotherly imperiousness, and Christian replied by a gratefulness and relief that might have touched him had he understood all, but instead, increased his secret contempt.

So successful was this finesse, that when, late on a day, a message summoning Christian to a distance was transmitted by Sweyn, no doubt of its genuineness occurred. When, his errand proved useless, he set out to return, mistake or misapprehension was all that he surmised. Not till he sighted the homestead, lying low between the night-grey snow ridges, did vivid recollection of the time when he had tracked that horror to the door rouse an intense dread, and with it a hardly-defined suspicion.

His grasp tightened on the bear-spear that he carried as a staff; every sense was alert, every muscle strung; excitement urged him on, caution checked him, and the two governed his long stride, swiftly, noiselessly, to the climax he felt was at hand.

As he drew near to the outer gates, a light shadow stirred and went, as though the grey of the snow had taken detached motion. A darker shadow stayed and faced Christian, striking his life-blood chill with utmost despair.

Sweyn stood before him, and surely, the shadow that went was White Fell.

They had been together—close. Had she not been in his arms, near enough for lips to meet?

There was no moon, but the stars gave light enough to show that Sweyn's face was flushed and elate. The flush remained, though the expression changed quickly at sight of his brother. How, if Christian had seen all, should one of his frenzied outbursts be met and managed: by resolution? by indifference? He halted between the two, and as a result, he swaggered.

"White Fell?" questioned Christian, hoarse and breathless.

"Yes?"

Sweyn's answer was a query, with an intonation that implied he was clearing the ground for action.

From Christian came: "Have you kissed her?" like a bolt direct, staggering Sweyn by its sheer prompt temerity.

He flushed yet darker, and yet half-smiled over this earnest of success he had won. Had there been really between himself and Christian the rivalry that he imagined, his face had enough of the insolence of triumph to exasperate jealous rage.

"You dare ask this!"

"Sweyn, O Sweyn, I must know! You have!"

The ring of despair and anguish in his tone angered Sweyn, misconstruing it. Jealousy urging to such presumption was intolerable.

"Mad fool!" he said, constraining himself no longer. "Win for yourself a woman to kiss. Leave mine without question. Such an one as I should desire to kiss is such an one as shall never allow a kiss to you."

Then Christian fully understood his supposition.

"I—I!" he cried. "White Fell—that deadly Thing! Sweyn, are you blind, mad? I would save you from her: a Were-Wolf!"

Sweyn maddened again at the accusation—a dastardly way of revenge, as he conceived; and instantly, for the second time, the brothers were at strife violently.

But Christian was now too desperate to be scrupulous; for a dim glimpse had shot a possibility into his mind, and to be free to follow it the striking of his brother was a necessity. Thank God! he was armed, and so Sweyn's equal.

Facing his assailant with the bear-spear, he struck up his arms, and with the butt end hit hard so that he fell. The matchless runner leapt away on the instant, to follow a forlorn hope.

Sweyn, on regaining his feet, was as amazed as angry at this unaccountable flight. He knew in his heart that his brother was no coward, and that it was unlike him to shrink from an encounter because defeat was certain, and cruel humiliation from a vindictive victor probable. Of the uselessness of pursuit he was well aware: he must abide his chagrin, content to know that his time for advantage would come. Since White Fell had parted to the right, Christian to the left, the event of a sequent encounter did not occur to him.

And now Christian, acting on the dim glimpse he had had, just as Sweyn turned upon him, of something that moved against the sky along the ridge behind the homestead, was staking his only hope on a chance, and his own superlative speed. If what he saw was really White Fell, he guessed she was bending her steps towards the open wastes; and there was just a possibility that, by a straight dash, and a desperate perilous leap over a sheer bluff, he might yet meet her or head her. And then: he had no further thought.

It was past, the quick, fierce race, and the chance of death at the leap; and he halted in a hollow to fetch his breath and to look: did she come? had she gone?

She came.

She came with a smooth, gliding, noiseless speed, that was neither walking nor running; her arms were folded in her furs that were drawn tight about her body; the white lappets from her head were wrapped and knotted closely beneath her face; her eyes were set on a far distance. So she went till the even sway of her going was startled to a pause by Christian.

"Fell!"

She drew a quick, sharp breath at the sound of her name thus mutilated, and faced Sweyn's brother. Her eyes glittered; her upper lip was lifted, and shewed the teeth. The half of her name, impressed with an ominous sense as uttered by him, warned her of the aspect of a deadly foe. Yet she cast loose her robes till they trailed ample, and spoke as a mild woman.

The Race

"What would you?"

Then Christian answered with his solemn dreadful accusation:

"You kissed Rol—and Rol is dead! You kissed Trella: she is dead! You have kissed Sweyn, my brother; but he shall not die!"

He added: "You may live till midnight."

The edge of the teeth and the glitter of the eyes stayed a moment, and her right hand also slid down to the axe haft. Then, without a word, she swerved from him, and sprang out and away swiftly over the snow.

And Christian sprang out and away, and followed her swiftly over the snow, keeping behind, but half-a-stride's length from her side.

So they went running together, silent, towards the vast wastes of snow, where no living thing but they two moved under the stars of night.

Never before had Christian so rejoiced in his powers. The gift of speed, and the training of use and endurance were priceless to him now. Though midnight was hours away, he was confident that, go where that Fell Thing would, hasten as she would, she could not outstrip him nor escape from him. Then, when came the time for transformation, when the woman's form made no longer a shield against a man's hand, he could slay or be slain to save Sweyn. He had struck his dear brother in dire extremity, but he could not, though reason urged, strike a woman.

For one mile, for two miles they ran: White Fell ever foremost, Christian ever at equal distance from her side, so near that, now and again, her out-flying furs touched him. She spoke no word; nor he. She never turned her head to look at him, nor swerved to evade him; but, with set face looking forward, sped straight on, over rough, over smooth, aware of his nearness by the regular beat of his feet, and the sound of his breath behind.

In a while she quickened her pace. From the first, Christian had judged of her speed as admirable, yet with exulting security in his own excelling and enduring whatever her efforts. But, when the pace increased, he found himself put to the test as never had he been before in any race. Her feet, indeed, flew faster than his; it was only by his length of stride that he kept his place at her side. But his heart was high and resolute, and he did not fear failure yet.

So the desperate race flew on. Their feet struck up the powdery snow, their breath smoked into the sharp clear air, and they were gone before the air was cleared of snow and vapour. Now and then Christian glanced up to judge, by the rising of the stars, of the coming of midnight. So long—so long!

White Fell held on without slack. She, it was evident, with confidence in her speed proving matchless, as resolute to outrun her pursuer as he to endure till midnight and fulfil his purpose. And Christian held on, still self-assured. He could not fail; he would not fail. To avenge Rol and Trella was motive enough for him to do what man could do; but for Sweyn more. She had kissed Sweyn, but he should not die too: with Sweyn to save he could not fail.

Never before was such a race as this; no, not when in old Greece man and maid raced together with two fates at stake; for the hard running was sustained unabated, while star after star rose and went wheeling up towards midnight, for one hour, for two hours.

Then Christian saw and heard what shot him through with fear. Where a fringe of trees hung round a slope he saw something dark moving, and heard a yelp, followed by a full horrid cry, and the dark spread out upon the snow, a pack of wolves in pursuit.

Of the beasts alone he had little cause for fear; at the pace he held he could distance them, four-footed though they were. But of White Fell's wiles he had infinite apprehension, for how might she not avail herself of the savage jaws of these wolves, akin as they were to half her nature. She vouchsafed to them nor look nor sign; but Christian, on an impulse to assure himself that she should not escape him, caught and held the back-flung edge of her furs, running still.

She turned like a flash with a beastly snarl, teeth and eyes gleaming again. Her axe shone, on the upstroke, on the downstroke, as she hacked at his hand. She had lopped it off at the wrist, but that he parried with the bear-spear. Even then, she shore through the shaft and shattered the bones of the hand at the same blow, so that he loosed perforce.

Then again they raced on as before, Christian not losing a pace, though his left hand swung useless, bleeding and broken.

The snarl, indubitable, though modified from a woman's organs, the vicious fury revealed in teeth and eyes, the sharp arrogant pain of her maiming blow, caught away Christian's heed of the beasts behind, by striking into him close vivid realisation of the infinitely greater danger that ran before him in that deadly Thing.

When he bethought him to look behind, lo! the pack had but reached their tracks, and instantly slunk aside, cowed; the yell of pursuit changing to yelps and whines. So abhorrent was that fell creature to beast as to man.

She had drawn her furs more closely to her, disposing them so that, instead of flying loose to her heels, no drapery hung lower than her knees, and this without a check to her wonderful speed, nor embarrassment by the cumbering of the folds. She held her head as before; her lips were firmly set, only the tense nostrils gave her breath; not a sign of distress witnessed to the long sustaining of that terrible speed.

But on Christian by now the strain was telling palpably. His head weighed heavy, and his breath came labouring in great sobs; the bear-spear would have been a burden now. His heart was beating like a hammer, but such a dulness oppressed his brain, that it was only by degrees he could realise his helpless state; wounded and weaponless, chasing that terrible Thing, that was a fierce, desperate, axe-armed woman, except she should assume the beast with fangs yet more formidable.

And still the far slow stars went lingering nearly an hour from midnight.

So far was his brain astray that an impression took him that she was fleeing from the midnight stars, whose gain was by such slow degrees that a time equalling days and days had gone in the race round the northern circle of the world, and days and days as long might last before the end—except she slackened, or except he failed.

But he would not fail yet.

How long had he been praying so? He had started with a self-confidence and reliance that had felt no need for that aid; and now it seemed the only means by which to restrain his heart from swelling beyond the compass of his body, by which to cherish his brain from dwindling and shrivelling quite away. Some sharp-toothed creature kept tearing and dragging on his maimed left hand; he never could see it, he could not shake it off; but he prayed it off at times.

The clear stars before him took to shuddering, and he knew why: they shuddered at sight of what was behind him. He had never divined before that strange things hid themselves from men under pretence of being snow-clad mounds or swaying trees; but now they came slipping out from their harmless covers to follow him, and mock at his impotence to make a kindred Thing resolve to truer form. He knew the air behind him was thronged; he heard the hum of innumerable murmurings together; but his eyes could never catch them, they were too swift and nimble. Yet he knew they were there, because, on a backward glance, he saw the snow mounds surge as they grovelled flatlings out of sight; he saw the trees reel as they screwed themselves rigid past recognition among the boughs.

And after such glance the stars for awhile returned to steadfastness, and an infinite stretch of silence froze upon the chill grey world, only deranged by the swift even beat of the flying feet, and his own—slower from the longer stride, and the sound of his breath. And for some clear moments he knew that his only concern was, to sustain his speed regardless of pain and distress, to deny with every nerve he had her power to outstrip him or to widen the space between them, till the stars crept up to midnight. Then out again would come that crowd invisible, humming and hustling behind, dense and dark enough, he knew, to blot out the stars at his back, yet ever skipping and jerking from his sight.

A hideous check came to the race. White Fell swirled about and leapt to the right, and Christian, unprepared for so prompt a lurch, found close at his feet a deep pit yawning, and his own impetus past control. But he snatched at her as he bore past, clasping her right arm with his one whole hand, and the two swung together upon the brink.

And her straining away in self preservation was vigorous enough to counter-balance his headlong impulse, and brought them reeling together to safety.

Then, before he was verily sure that they were not to perish so, crashing down, he saw her gnashing in wild pale fury as she wrenched to be free; and since her right hand was in his grasp, used her axe left-handed, striking back at him.

The blow was effectual enough even so; his right arm dropped powerless, gashed, and with the lesser bone broken, that jarred with horrid pain when he let it swing as he leaped out again, and ran to recover the few feet she had gained from his pause at the shock.

The near escape and this new quick pain made again every faculty alive and intense. He knew that what he followed was most surely Death animate: wounded and helpless, he was utterly at her mercy if so she should realise and take action. Hopeless to avenge, hopeless to save, his very despair for Sweyn swept him on to follow, and follow, and precede the kiss-doomed to death. Could he yet fail to hunt that Thing past midnight, out of the womanly form alluring and treacherous, into lasting restraint of the bestial, which was the last shred of hope left from the confident purpose of the outset?

"Sweyn, Sweyn, O Sweyn!" He thought he was praying, though his heart wrung out nothing but this: "Sweyn, Sweyn, O Sweyn!"

The last hour from midnight had lost half its quarters, and the stars went lifting up the great minutes; and again his greatening heart, and his shrinking brain, and the sickening agony that swung at either side, conspired to appal the will that had only seeming empire over his feet.

Now White Fell's body was so closely enveloped that not a lap nor an edge flew free. She stretched forward strangely aslant, leaning from the upright poise of a runner. She cleared the ground at times by long bounds, gaining an increase of speed that Christian agonised to equal.

Because the stars pointed that the end was nearing, the black brood came behind again, and followed, noising. Ah! if they could but be kept quiet and still, nor slip their usual harmless masks to encourage with their interest the last speed of their most deadly congener. What shape had they? Should he ever know? If it were not that he was bound to compel the fell Thing that ran before him into her truer form, he might face about and follow them. No—no—not so; if he might do anything but what he did—race, race, and racing bear this agony, he would just stand still and die, to be quit of the pain of breathing.

He grew bewildered, uncertain of his own identity, doubting of his own true form. He could not be really a man, no more than that running Thing was really a woman; his real form was only hidden under embodiment of a man, but what it was he did not know. And Sweyn's real form he did not know. Sweyn lay fallen at his feet, where he had struck him down—his own brother—he: he stumbled over him, and had to overleap him and race harder because she who had kissed Sweyn leapt so fast. "Sweyn, Sweyn, O Sweyn!"

Why did the stars stop to shudder? Midnight else had surely come!

The leaning, leaping Thing looked back at him with a wild, fierce look, and laughed in savage scorn and triumph. He saw in a flash why, for within a time measurable by seconds she would have escaped him utterly. As the land lay, a slope of ice sunk on the one hand; on the other hand a steep rose, shouldering forwards; between the two was space for a foot to be planted, but none for a body to stand; yet a juniper bough, thrusting out, gave a handhold secure enough for one with a resolute grasp to swing past the perilous place, and pass on safe.

Though the first seconds of the last moment were going, she dared to flash back a wicked look, and laugh at the pursuer who was impotent to grasp.

The crisis struck convulsive life into his last supreme effort; his will surged up indomitable, his speed proved matchless yet. He leapt with a rush, passed her before her laugh had time to go out, and turned short, barring the way, and braced to withstand her.

She came hurling desperate, with a feint to the right hand, and then launched herself upon him with a spring like a wild beast when it leaps to kill. And he, with one strong arm and a hand that could not hold, with one strong hand and an arm that could not guide and sustain, he caught and held her even so. And they fell together. And because he felt his whole arm slipping, and his whole hand loosing, to slack the dreadful agony of the wrenched bone above, he caught and held with his teeth the tunic at her knee, as she struggled up and wrung off his hands to overleap him victorious.

Like lightning she snatched her axe, and struck him on the neck, deep—once, twice—his life-blood gushed out, staining her feet.

The stars touched midnight.

The death scream he heard was not his, for his set teeth had hardly yet relaxed when it rang out; and the dreadful cry began with a woman's shriek, and changed and ended as the yell of a beast. And before the final blank overtook his dying eyes, he saw that She gave place to It; he saw more, that Life gave place to Death—causelessly, incomprehensibly.

The Finish

For he did not presume that no holy water could be more holy, more potent to destroy an evil thing than the life-blood of a pure heart poured out for another in free willing devotion.

His own true hidden reality that he had desired to know grew palpable, recognisable. It seemed to him just this: a great glad abounding hope that he had saved his brother; too expansive to be contained by the limited form of a sole man, it yearned for a new embodiment infinite as the stars.

What did it matter to that true reality that the man's brain shrank, shrank, till it was nothing; that the man's body could not retain the huge pain of his heart, and heaved it out through the red exit riven at the neck; that the black noise came again hurtling from behind, reinforced by that dissolved shape, and blotted out for ever the man's sight, hearing, sense.

———

In the early grey of day Sweyn chanced upon the footprints of a man—of a runner, as he saw by the shifted snow; and the direction they had taken aroused curiosity, since a little farther their line must be crossed by the edge of a sheer height. He turned to trace them. And so doing, the length of the stride struck his attention—a stride long as his own if he ran. He knew he was following Christian.

In his anger he had hardened himself to be indifferent to the night-long absence of his brother; but now, seeing where the footsteps went, he was seized with compunction and dread. He had failed to give thought and care to his poor frantic twin, who might—was it possible?—have rushed to a frantic death.

His heart stood still when he came to the place where the leap had been taken. A piled edge of snow had fallen too, and nothing but snow lay below when he peered. Along the upper edge he ran for a furlong, till he came to a dip where he could slip and climb down, and then back again on the lower level to the pile of fallen snow. There he saw that the vigorous running had started afresh.

He stood pondering; vexed that any man should have taken that leap where he had not ventured to follow; vexed that he had been beguiled to such painful emotions; guessing vainly at Christian's object in this mad freak. He began sauntering along, half unconsciously following his brother's track; and so in a while he came to the place where the footprints were doubled.

Small prints were these others, small as a woman's, though the pace from one to another was longer than that which the skirts of women allow.

Did not White Fell tread so?

A dreadful guess appalled him, so dreadful that he recoiled from belief. Yet his face grew ashy white, and he gasped to fetch back motion to his checked heart. Unbelievable? Closer attention showed how the smaller footfall had altered for greater speed, striking into the snow with a deeper onset and a lighter pressure on the heels. Unbelievable? Could any woman but White Fell run so? Could any man but Christian run so? The guess became a certainty. He was following where alone in the dark night White Fell had fled from Christian pursuing.

Such villainy set heart and brain on fire with rage and indignation: such villainy in his own brother, till lately love-worthy, praiseworthy, though a fool for meekness. He would kill Christian; had he lives many as the footprints he had trodden, vengeance should demand them all. In a tempest of murderous hate he followed on in haste, for the track was plain enough, starting with such a burst of speed as could not be maintained, but brought him back soon to a plod for the spent, sobbing breath to be regulated. He cursed Christian aloud and called White Fell's name on high in a frenzied expense of passion. His grief itself was a rage, being such an intolerable anguish of pity and shame at the thought of his love, White Fell, who had parted from his kiss free and radiant, to be hounded straightway by his brother mad with jealousy, fleeing for more than life while her lover was housed at his ease. If he had but known, he raved, in impotent rebellion at the cruelty of events, if he had but known that his strength and love might have availed in her defence; now the only service to her that he could render was to kill Christian.

As a woman he knew she was matchless in speed, matchless in strength; but Christian was matchless in speed among men, nor easily to be matched in strength. Brave and swift and strong though she were, what chance had she against a man of his strength and inches, frantic, too, and intent on horrid revenge against his brother, his successful rival?

Mile after mile he followed with a bursting heart; more piteous, more tragic, seemed the case at this evidence of White Fell's splendid supremacy, holding her own so long against Christian's famous speed. So long, so long that his love and admiration grew more and more boundless, and his grief and indignation therewith also. Whenever the track lay clear he ran, with such reckless prodigality of strength, that it soon was spent, and he dragged on heavily, till, sometimes on the ice of a mere, sometimes on a wind-swept place, all signs were lost; but, so undeviating had been their line that a course straight on, and then short questing to either hand, recovered them again.

Hour after hour had gone by through more than half that winter day, before ever he came to the place where the trampled snow showed that a scurry of feet had come—and gone! Wolves' feet—and gone most amazingly! Only a little beyond he came to the lopped point of Christian's bear-spear; farther on he would see where the remnant of the useless shaft had been dropped. The snow here was dashed with blood, and the footsteps of the two had fallen closer together. Some hoarse sound of exultation came from him that might have been a laugh had breath sufficed. "O White Fell, my poor, brave love! Well struck!" he groaned, torn by his pity and great admiration, as he guessed surely how she had turned and dealt a blow.

The sight of the blood inflamed him as it might a beast that ravens. He grew mad with a desire to have Christian by the throat once again, not to loose this time till he had crushed out his life, or beat out his life, or stabbed out his life; or all these, and torn him piecemeal likewise: and ah! then, not till then, bleed his heart with weeping, like a child, like a girl, over the piteous fate of his poor lost love.

On—on—on—through the aching time, toiling and straining in the track of those two superb runners, aware of the marvel of their endurance, but unaware of the marvel of their speed, that, in the three hours before midnight had overpassed all that vast distance that he could only traverse from twilight to twilight. For clear daylight was passing when he came to the edge of an old marl-pit, and saw how the two who had gone before had stamped and trampled together in desperate peril on the verge. And here fresh blood stains spoke to him of a valiant defence against his infamous brother; and he followed where the blood had dripped till the cold had staunched its flow, taking a savage gratification from this evidence that Christian had been gashed deeply, maddening afresh with desire to do likewise more excellently, and so slake his murderous hate. And he began to know that through all his despair he had entertained a germ of hope, that grew apace, rained upon by his brother's blood.

He strove on as best he might, wrung now by an access of hope, now of despair, in agony to reach the end, however terrible, sick with the aching of the toiled miles that deferred it.

And the light went lingering out of the sky, giving place to uncertain stars.

He came to the finish.

Two bodies lay in a narrow place. Christian's was one, but the other beyond not White Fell's. There where the footsteps ended lay a great white wolf.

At the sight Sweyn's strength was blasted; body and soul he was struck down grovelling.

The stars had grown sure and intense before he stirred from where he had dropped prone. Very feebly he crawled to his dead brother, and laid his hands upon him, and crouched so, afraid to look or stir farther.

Cold, stiff, hours dead. Yet the dead body was his only shelter and stay in that most dreadful hour. His soul, stripped bare of all sceptic comfort, cowered, shivering, naked, abject; and the living clung to the dead out of piteous need for grace from the soul that had passed away.

He rose to his knees, lifting the body. Christian had fallen face forward in the snow, with his arms flung up and wide, and so had the frost made him rigid: strange, ghastly, unyielding to Sweyn's lifting, so that he laid him down again and crouched above, with his arms fast round him, and a low heart-wrung groan.

When at last he found force to raise his brother's body and gather it in his arms, tight clasped to his breast, he tried to face the Thing that lay beyond. The sight set his limbs in a palsy with horror and dread. His senses had failed and fainted in utter cowardice, but for the strength that came from holding dead Christian in his arms, enabling him to compel his eyes to endure the sight, and take into the brain the complete aspect of the Thing. No wound, only blood stains on the feet. The great grim jaws had a savage grin, though dead-stiff. And his kiss: he could bear it no longer, and turned away, nor ever looked again.

Sweyn's Finding

And the dead man in his arms, knowing the full horror, had followed and faced it for his sake; had suffered agony and death for his sake; in the neck was the deep death gash, one arm and both hands were dark with frozen blood, for his sake! Dead he knew him, as in life he had not known him, to give the right meed of love and worship. Because the outward man lacked perfection and strength equal to his, he had taken the love and worship of that great pure heart as his due; he, so unworthy in the inner reality, so mean, so despicable, callous, and contemptuous towards the brother who had laid down his life to save him. He longed for utter annihilation, that so he might lose the agony of knowing himself so unworthy such perfect love. The frozen calm of death on the face appalled him. He dared not touch it with lips that had cursed so lately, with lips fouled by kiss of the horror that had been death. He struggled to his feet, still clasping Christian. The dead man stood upright within his arm, frozen rigid. The eyes were not quite closed; the head had stiffened, bowed slightly to one side; the arms stayed straight and wide. It was the figure of one crucified, the blood-stained hands also conforming.

So living and dead went back along the track that one had passed in the deepest passion of love, and one in the deepest passion of hate. All that night Sweyn toiled through the snow, bearing the weight of dead Christian, treading back along the steps he before had trodden, when he was wronging with vilest thoughts, and cursing with murderous hatred, the brother who all the while lay dead for his sake.

Cold, silence, darkness encompassed the strong man bowed with the dolorous burden; and yet he knew surely that that night he entered hell, and trod hell-fire along the homeward road, and endured through it only because Christian was with him. And he knew surely that to him Christian had been as Christ, and had suffered and died to save him from his sins.

The Unknown Sea

CHAPTER I

A solitary fisher ploughed the lively blue of a southern sea. Strength of limb, fair hair, and clear grey eyes told of a northern race, though his skin had been tanned to a red-brown, dark as the tint of the slender, dark-eyed, olive-skinned fishers born under these warm skies. In stature and might a man, he was scarcely more than a boy in years; beardless yet, and of an open, boyish countenance. As his boat raced eagerly forward he laughed for pride of heart, and praised her aloud after a fashion native to the south: she was his beloved, his bird, his blossom, his queen; and for his warrant well built she was, promising strength and speed in due degrees, and beautiful obedience to him. Her paint was bright, her ruddy canvas unstained, in contrast to a pile of tackle, black from age and use: the nets and the weighted cross-beams of coral fishing.

White wings against the sky, and white crests upon the sea, broke the entire blue. Far away to eastward, faint and hazy, suave lines extended; but a coast that the boy neared lifted gaunt and desolate cliffs, overlooking a waste of roaring breakers. Midmost of these, sheer and black as the crags beyond, a dark mass rose dominant, like a sullen outcast from the land holding rule, whose mere aspect fitted well the name, Isle Sinister, without an evil implication that went therewith. The young fisher's memory was stored with dark tales, born long ago to night and fear, cherished by generations into fine growth, not by such as he to be utterly scouted. The sound of buoy-bells reached his ears for warning, but he eyed the intricate lines of breakers, he recalled ominous reports, only to estimate the nerve of body and mind needful to any mortal bent there upon a perilous trespass.

For a tale went that kept every fisher well aloof, to shun a danger worse than shipwreck. Little gain was it held for any once driven within the buoy-bells to work clear again to open sea, since sorrow and disaster would dog thenceforward, nor cease till due forfeit were paid: the boat broken up and burnt, her very ashes delivered to the sea. Woe even to the man who dare take any least splinter to burn on his hearth, for sickness and death would desolate his home. Nay, if a shifting wind but carried the ashes landwards, blight or murrain would follow surely. So went tradition, and conviction attended it well, since not within memory had any hardy or unfortunate supplied a living test. Now truly this boy, who came coasting perilously, needed to have in his veins the blood of an alien race, over and above youth and great strength, to be traversing a superstition of such dark credit, in others bred deep and strong.

Years ago he had been fascinated by the terrors and mystery of the place, and with a human desire after the unattainable, most strong and unregulated in youth, he had fearfully longed for a strength to do and a heart to dare more than all his world: to get footing where never man had stood: to face black luck and its befitters with a higher faith, defying a supremacy of evil. Very early, out of the extravagant vagaries of a child's brain, an audacious word had escaped, sped by a temper aflame, for which he had suffered—from youngsters a day's derision, from a strict elder a look that was worse disgrace. He deemed that might come to be recalled to his credit. Now that he was grown to a strength unmatched, with a heart proud and eager, impatient of any mastery not of love and reverence, a notion pleased him that like enough these tales had been magnified to recover the self-esteem of balked adventurers: a presumption not extreme in one whose superb strength had lowered old records, who found that none could withstand him to his full satisfaction. Here in the bright sunshine of high day, the year's eager spring quick in every vein, young virile audacity belittling all hazards, the lad's heart rode so high and sure that he could laugh outright in answer to the expostulation of the Sinister buoys. Yet he crossed himself more than once.

"We will do it, Beloved, you and I."

To and fro he hovered awhile to consider the lie of the reefs and select his way. Then the sail clapped and swelled again, and the boat heeled, as boldly he turned her, and steered within the buoy-bells away for the breakers. Again he crossed himself as now were he and his boat committed on a challenge to fortune.

Gracious to bold and dexterous handling the boat glided into the maze. The disposition of the outer channels was so favourable as to have gone far in beguiling the boy to his rash undertaking; but there were hedges of wicked breakers that thwarted him and turned him aside disappointed. Creeping along warily with only a corner of sail, steering with fine sleight through the narrows, and avoiding eddies, he carried his boat unscathed where never another man he knew could dare to follow. But ah! how meagre was that satisfaction, since far, yet too far from him the Isle Sinister held reserve. But at least he was able to scan the rocky mass to advantage. It towered up with straight, repellent walls towards the land; it sloped down steeply where he desired to win; but there to balk him, minatory in aspect, stood the Warders—five detached rocks—so lofty that the highest columns of surf spouting there fell short of their crowns. The ugliest threat he recognised bided there, close against success.

"No fault is yours, Beloved, if we cannot do it: nor hardly mine either, I think. Were but one other with us we might be well-nigh confident. With Philip at the oars! None we wanted to share with us—and yet! Ah! no. Not he nor any would."

He was deeply involved. At least a mile of grim discouragement stretched on every hand. Then he came upon the sunken hulk of an old wreck. Fiercer eddies and narrower channels constrained him to drop sail and take to the oars. A hard, dangerous, disheartening struggle set him nearer by a poor measure, but lost him in hope on the way.

"Fools and cowards all! Pleased would they be were I foiled, they knowing. How they would jeer; ay, with worse, too. It might go hard with me. But you, Beloved, never fear that I should fail you, if they tried—no, they would not,—not if they care for whole bones.

"To think that if we win, not for months may I praise you by the tale, not till we both have disproved and outlived the following of bad luck. Defend us from one spying us here."

The boy glanced about with anxiety, giving special scrutiny to one high cliff opposite. There, scarcely distinguishable from the crags, stood up a grey tower, the bell-tower of an ancient devout institution, the House Monitory. His face grew rigid under a sudden apprehension. If he were sighted from above, what should stay those bells from knelling for him. He held his breath, and listened for them to break silence on the instant, realising one peril which he had not before considered. "Hark!" would go the word, "why does the House Monitory ring? in daylight, in fair weather? Who can be in peril off the Isle Sinister?" From cliffs to coves the word would drop, and start the swiftest sails out to investigate, for his exposure to ridicule or worse.

In a past century three bells had been towered there: consecrated and named after three Saints, to knell for souls that passed, unconfessed, unhouseled, in that place of wrecks; to be potent against the dominion of powers darker than death, too regnant there. The best, the only, succour was this that human fellowship could accomplish for doomed lives. Now, though cultured intelligence smiled at the larger superstition, the simple held it at its old worth; and still, to the comfort of their souls, a pious community kept the custom, serving the bells; and for their more tangible welfare tended a beacon light.

A little chill ran in the boy's veins as he anticipated the outbreak of those ominous bells; never yet had they rung for any, far involved as he, who had known escape. He betook himself more desperately to his endeavour. Necessity pressed him hard, for the tide ran, and suddenly declared that retreat to the open sea was cut off: where he had sailed free channels rocks grinned; reason withstood a fancy that they had lain in ambush, and risen actually to hem him in. Twice he risked with the narrowest of chances, and slid safe on the heave of a wave; on the third challenge a treacherous, swirling eddy caught the boat, swung it aslant, crashed it upon a lurking rock. A plank gave way splintered, and water spirted within.

The boy rowed desperate, straining by quick strokes and few, after deliverance from the narrows. Yet when he dared to lay aside the oars for an instant to check the leak, the boat was pitching with threats close in on every side. He could spare only a moment to catch up his coat, plug with it hastily, and drag atop the heavy cross-beams of his tackle; quick upon the oars again he needed to be, desperate of baling. Still the water oozed and trickled in, to lie up to his ankles and slowly to rise. There was no making out to sea; from the Isle Sinister he owned himself cut off by thick-set barriers; only the shore remained not absolutely unattainable though furthest it was.

Patiently and cautiously the boy felt his way. From stroke to stroke he held on safely, steady, quick-eyed, but told by the gradual water against his shins that his boat must shortly founder. Conscience smote him hard; the near sure prospect of swimming for bare life among the breakers opened his eyes. He had held as his very own to risk at will his boat and his life; now, with pangs of remorse, he recognised the superior claim of a grey-haired couple, who had been parents to him, who bereft of him would go down to the grave in grief and poverty. Of life, and the means of living, but little right had he to dispose, considering their due and their need.

The gunwale sank low, lower, till a lurch might displace the cross-beams, for they lost in weight as the water within the boat deepened. Yet point by point success attended, and released the foolhardy lad and his boat from dire extremity. They have chance of clean deliverance; they are past the last girdle of breakers, hardly a furlong from the shore; they are upon sleek water, with the tide against them but lazily.

The boy rowed on with long, smooth strokes; the mere sway of his body was as much as the boat could carry, so little above the water was the gunwale. He had halved the distance, when down she went beneath him; and he swam, waded, stood ashore, the first man who had ever won there living by way of the sea.

But little elate could he be. He could glean drifting oars and stretchers, his boat might be recovered from the out tide, but the Isle Sinister lay remote as ever. And his heart had fallen.

Ugly necessity gave no choice but to face the breakers again in retrace of his perilous way; for an alternative he could not entertain that would entail certain evils more to be dreaded than any risk.

Straying aimlessly along the desolate shore, the boy pondered, nervous now of many risks he had braved hardily. He stopped once at sight of a grey patch of calcined rock. There it must have been that, not so long ago, wreckage had been gathered and burned scrupulously, and with it the bodies of two drowned men, according to the custom of the coast. Instinctively he crossed himself, with a brief prayer for the souls of those two, cut off from life in that evil place, where no help had reached but the heavy knell, pitiful.

Greatly desiring the silence of the bells, if he were to escape with life, the boy turned his eyes aloft, inclining to bespeak it. A lively suspicion of hunger impelled decision; and up the cliff he went, his abashed vigour fain of any new output. An uncertain path promised fairly till half way, where a recent lapse turned him aside on to untried slopes and ledges: a perilous ascent to any not bold and sure and practised. The spice of danger kindled the boy's blood; he won to the top with some loss of breath, but his head was high, and his heart was high, and ultimate failure envisaged him no longer.

He stood among graves.

CHAPTER II

The lonely community had laid its bones to rest in a barren acre. No flower could bloom there ever, only close, dun turf grew. Below, the broken, unquiet sea dirged ceaselessly. The spot was in perfect keeping with the sovereign peace of the grave; that blank, unadorned environment of nature had the very beauty that can touch human sense with the concord of death. The young fisher stood motionless, as if his presence were outrage to the spirit of the silent dwellers below, so eager was he for life, so brim with passion and play and hearty thirst for strong years of sunshine and rain. "Yet how so," said his heart, "for I too shall come to die?"

Softly and soberly he took his way past the ranks of low mounds, and considered his approach to the House Monitory, whose living dwellers might be less tolerant of his trespass. For he realised that he had come within their outer precincts unallowed. On the one hand lay a low wall to indicate reserve; on the other he approached the base of the bell-tower itself, and the flanks of the House Monitory. He looked up at the walls, fully expecting to be spied and brought to rebuke; but all was blank and quiet as among the dead outside. The tower rose sheer into the air; for the rest, a tier of the cliff had been fashioned for habitation by the help of masonry and some shaping and hollowing of the crude rock. The window lights were high and rare. Except from the tower, hardly could a glimpse below the sky-line be offered to any within.

He came upon a door, low and narrow as the entrance of a tomb. It looked so obdurate he never thought to knock there. Then the sound of low, monotonous chanting, by women's voices, poor and few, told him that he stood without their chapel; and he understood that the low door giving upon the place of graves had not been fashioned for the living. Truly he was alien and incongruous, although that day he had surely been many degrees nearer death than any dweller there.

He made for the boundary wall, overleaped it, and then by legitimate pathways came before the entrance door. There he stood long, not finally determined what he had come to say. It was repugnant to him to ask of any mortal cover for his doings, the more when they were somewhat amiss.

While he stood, casting about for decision, he was a-stare heedlessly on a rocky spur near by that bore the moulding of three figures. High upon its face they stood, where a natural suggestion had been abetted by man, a rough pediment shaped above, a rough base below, and the names hewn large: St. Mary, St. Margaret, St. Faith. Of life size they were, and looked towards the sea.

Ashamed of his own indecision, the boy lifted his hand and knocked at the wicket, so to force a resolution within the limit of seconds left. The stone figures clapped back an echo. His heart sprang an invocation in response, and straightway he relinquished thought of asking an irksome favour of lower agents. So when the wicket opened, this was all he had to say: "Of your charity give food to a hungry body."

To the pale, spare Monitress, half shrouded in the gloom, the ruddy young giant, glowing in the sunshine, said this: "Of your charity give food to a hungry body." She paused and looked at the boy, for his great stature, his fair hair, and grey eyes made him very singular.

The questioning he half feared and expected did not come. The Monitress withdrew silently, and presently returning handed a portion of bread. She said, "Not food for the body, but prayer for the soul is chiefly asked of our charity."

The boy's face flamed, understanding how he was rebuked. Thanks stumbled on his tongue, and no word to excuse could come; so the wicket closed upon his silence.

Not so closely but that the Monitress could look again, to sigh over that creature of gross wants with angel-bright hair. Surprised, she saw that he was instantly away, and mounted high by the three stone saints. She saw that he touched their feet reverently, that he knelt down, crossed himself and prayed, in a very seemly fashion. She went away, of her charity in prayer for his soul.

He stood there still, after his prayer was finished, and his bread, and looked over the sea long and earnestly; for from that high ledge he saw away to the Isle Sinister, encompassed with its network of reefs; the tide running low showed them in black lines, outspread like a map below.

An audacious design he revolved, no less than to achieve the Isle Sinister yet. The long lines of reefs forbade his boat, but him they fairly invited, if strong swimming and deft footing could pass him on, from rock to wave, and from wave to rock, out to the far front of the great mass where the Warders stood.

He argued with his conscience, that it was no such risk as that he was bound to encounter for regaining the open sea, since this attempt need never commit him past retreat.

Sighting his boat uncovered, without delay he went down. He got it emptied, the leak plugged quite sufficiently for the time, the anchor set out against the return of the tide; then he raced, plunged, and swam for the Isle Sinister.

The first stretch went fairly; he met the rough handling of the waves as a sturdy game, and opposed with an even heart. Before long he had to recognise grim earnest, and do battle with all his might, so hard were the elements against him and so cruel. The waves hustled and buffeted and hurled; and though he prevailed by slow degrees, the rocks connived for his detriment. Again and again he won to a resting-place, so battered, breathless, and spent, that to nourish fortitude, he needed to consider the steady ascent of the vast rock up from the horizon against his nearing. A moment of elation it was, when, looking back to compare, he noted that the shore cliffs were dwarfed by the nearer proportions of the Isle.

But his stout heart made too little allowance for the strain upon loyal members, so that at last he bungled, fell short at a leap disastrously, and was swept away, hardly escaping, gashed and stunned. His memory afterwards could but indistinctly record how he fared thenceforward with rock and wave. A nightmare remained of swirling waters mad for his life, and of dark crags swinging down upon him; coming nearer, swinging lower; with a great shock they smote him. So he came to the Isle Sinister.

He clung precariously, lashed by the waves into an effort after a higher ledge. As he drew himself up to safety, his brain was clearing and his breath extending, nor was it long before his faculties were in order for wonder, gratulation, exultation. Then he shouted aloud. Against the roar of the surf his voice struck out wild and weak. The ledge was so narrow, that while his back rested against the rock his feet dangled; he was nearly naked; he was bleeding; soon for return he must face peril again. Looking down at the waters below, leaping and snarling, and over the wild expanse he had passed, to the shore half a league away, counting the cost in wounds and bruises, still his young heart mounted above pain and doubt, to glory in indomitable strength. He flung back his wet head to laugh and shout again and again, startling sea-birds to flight and bringing out echoes hearty enough to his ears.

Surely that rock answering so was the first Warder.

Spite of weariness and unsteadiness of head, he got on his feet, and passed from that difficult ledge of rock round to the front, where by steep grades the Isle showed some slight condescension to the sea. As he advanced he tried for ascent, unsatisfied still.

The five Warders stood in full parade; their rank hemmed him round; against his level the shadow of the Isle rested above their knees, between each and each a narrow vertical strip of sea and heaven struck blindingly sweet and blue. Sea-birds wheeled and clamoured, misliking this invasion of their precincts. To his conceit the tremendous noise of the breakers below sounded an unavailing protest against his escape.

He came upon a sight that displaced his immediate desire to scale the heights above: from the base below the tide had withdrawn, and there lay a stretch of boulders and quiet rock pools within a fringe of magnificent surf. Down he sped straightway to hold footing debatable with the jealous sea. Close against the line of surf, at a half-way point between the solid wall of the Isle and the broken wall of the Warders, he looked up at either height north and south. Equal towards the zenith they rose, here based upon sombre quiet, there upon fierce white tumult, that sent up splendid high columns, whose spray swept over the interspace of tumbling sea and touched the shine of the pools with frore grey. He sighed towards those unattainable Warders.

The air was charged with brine; its damp stayed on his skin, its salt on his lips. Thirsting, he went about with an eye for a water-spring, and made straight for a likely cleft. Darkest among the many scars of the rock it showed; deep it went, and wound deeper at his nearing. He entered the gape over boulders, and a way still there was wide before him; he took nine paces with gloom confronting, a tenth—aslant came a dazzling gleam of white. Amazed he faced to it, held stone-still an instant, sped on and out; he stood in full sunlight, and winked bewildered at the incredible open of fair sands before him.

The wonder dawned into comprehension. Though far eyes were deluded by a perfect semblance of solidity, the half of the Isle was hollow as a shell. Over against him rose the remaining moiety; high walls of rock swept round on either side, hindered from complete enclosure by the cleft of his entrance. He turned and looked back through the gorge, and again over the sunlit open; it was hard to believe he was out of dreamland, so Eden-bright and perfect was this contrast to the grand sombre chasm he had left. White and smooth, the sands extended up to the base of the dark rocks. There rich drapery of weed indicated the tide-mark; strips of captured water gleamed; great boulders lay strewn; coves and alcoves deeply indented the lines of the enclosing walls. To the boy's eyes it looked the fairest spot of earth the sea could ever find to visit. Its aspect of lovely austere virginity, candid, serene, strictly girt, touched very finely on the fibres of sense and soul.

He stepped out on firm blanch sand ribbed slightly by the reluctant ebb. Trails of exquisite weed, with their perfect display of every slender line and leaf, betokened a gracious and gentle outgoing of the sea. In creamy pink, ivory, citron, and ranges of tender colour that evade the fact of a name, these delicate cullings lay strewn, and fragile shells of manifold beauty and design. There, among weed and shell, he spied a branch of coral, and habit and calling drew him to it instantly. He had never fetched up its like, for the colour was rare, and for its thickness and quality he wondered. Suddenly the coral drops from his hand; he utters an inarticulate cry and stands amazed. His eye has fallen on a mark in the sand; it is of a human footstep.

Blank disappointment at this sign of forestalling struck him first, but startled wonder followed hard, and took due prominence as he looked around on his solitude encompassed by steep black heights, and heard the muffled thunder outside that would not be shut off by them. He stooped to examine the naked footprint, and was staggered by the evidence it gave; for this impression, firm and light, had an outward trend, a size, a slightness, most like a woman's. It was set seaward towards the gorge. He looked right and left for footprints of return—none were there! A lone track he saw that led hardly further, growing faint and indistinct, for the feet had trodden there when the wash of the ebb was recent.

He turned, and following reversely at a run, came to the far wall, where every sign failed among pools and weedy boulders; circled with all speed, snatching a sight of every cove and cleft, and then sprang back through the gorge.

The gloom and the fierce tumult of that outside ravine smote with a shock upon masculine wits that now had conceived of the presence of a woman there. Compassion cried, Poor soul! poor soul! without reservation, and aloud he called hearty reassurance, full-lunged, high-pitched. Though but a feeble addition to the great noises there, the sea-birds grew restless: only the sea-birds, no other living thing moved in response.

He made sure of a soon discovery, but he leapt along from boulder to boulder, hunting into every shadow, and never a one developed a cave; but he called in vain. The sea limited him to a spare face of the Isle; when that was explicit, he was left to reckon with his senses, because they went so against reason.

The irreconcilable void sent him back to the first tangible proof, and again he stood beside the footprints pondering uneasily. Had he scared a woman unclothed, who now in the shame and fear of sex crouched perdue? But no, his search outside had been too thorough, and the firm, light, even pace was a contradiction.

Up and down he went in close search, but no other sign of human presence could he find, not a shred of clothing, not a fragment of food. That single line of naked footprints, crossing the level sands from inscrutable rock to obliterate sea, gave a positive indication circumstantially denied on every hand. The bewildered boy reckoned he would have been better satisfied to have lighted on some uncanny slot of finned heels and splay web-toes, imperfectly human; the shapely print excited a contrast image of delicate, stately, perfect womanhood, quite intolerable to intellect and emotion of manly composition.

The steeps all round denied the possibility of ascent by tender feminine feet; for they thwarted his stout endeavour to scale up to the main rock above, that from the high wall receded and ascended in not extreme grades to the topmost pitch, where the sun was hanging well on the ponent slope.

His strict investigation took him round each wide scallop of the enclosure, a course that was long to conclude by reason of exquisite distractions that beset every hollow of the way. For the clear rock pools he found in these reserves held splendours of the sea's living blossoms: glowing beds of anemones full blown, with purples of iris and orchis, clover red, rose red, sorrel red, hues of primrose and saffron, broad spread like great chrysanthemums' bosses. And above the wavy fringes, never quite motionless, dark wet buds hung waiting for the tide; and the crystal integrity mirroring these was stirred by flashes of silver-green light, the to-and-fro play of lovely minute rock-fish.

He had circled two-thirds and more when to his vigilant perceptions a hint came. Some ribbons of glossy weed hanging from shoulder height stirred a trifle overmuch in their shelter to the touch of wind. Instantly the wary boy thrust a hand through and encountered, not rock, but a void behind; he parted the thick fall of weed, and a narrow cleft was uncurtained, with blackness beyond, that to his peering dissolved into a cool, dim sea-cave, floored with water semilucent, roofed with darkness. Eagerly he pressed through, and dropped knee-deep into the still, dark water. Involuntarily his motions were subdued; silently, gently, he advanced into the midst of encompassing water and rock and darkness.

Such slight intrusion of daylight as the heavy kelp drapery allowed slanted into the glooms in slender, steady threads; from his wading hosts of wan lights broke and ran for the walls, casting up against them paler repeats; when he halted, faint sound from them wapped and sobbed, dominant items in a silence hardly discomposed by the note of far-off surf, so modulated by deflecting angles as to reach the ear faint and low as the murmur that haunts the curves of a shell.

For a long minute he stood in the midst motionless, while the chill of the water told on his blood, and the quiet darkness on his spirit. Mystery stepped here with an intimate touch, absent when under the open sky the sands presented their enigma. His heart did not fail; only resolution ordered it now, not impulse.

He spoke again to presumable ears. Only his own words he heard multiply in fading whispers through the hovering darkness. Silence came brooding back as he stood to hearken.

As his eyes dilated to better discernment, he suspected that an aisle withdrew, from a faint pallor, narrowing as it tended towards his height, explicable if water receded there, gathering vague translucence from some unseen source of light. To verify, he was advancing when a considerate notion turned him about. He left the dim cavern, returned in the blinding sunshine to the footprints, knelt by the last, and set his fingers in the sand for inscription. For a long moment he considered, for no words seemed effectual to deliver his complexed mind. When he wrote it was a sentence of singular construction, truly indicative of how vague awe and dread had uprisen to take large standing beside simple humane solicitude. He traced three large crosses, and then three words. Simple construing would read thus: "In the name of the Father, the Son, and the Holy Ghost at your service." Moderately content with that rendering, he transcribed it thrice on the rocks, graving with the branch of coral. At either end of the entrance gorge he set it, and again large and fair above the hidden mouth of the cave.

Back into darkness he dived to take up research, and wading towards the tremor of light, entered a long recess that led under low arches of rock, till light grew more definite, and the water-way ended, closed in by a breastwork of rock. But, this surmounted, the boy saw water again, of absolute green, dark as any stone of royal malachite. The level was lower by several feet, perhaps the true tide-level, perhaps yet another limited reservoir that the sea replenished daily. He slid down the scarp and went on, heartened by the increase of light.

The depth of the water varied, and the boy swam more often than he waded. The colour of the water varied; now it strengthened into a lucent green, now darkness threatened it, and he swam warily till it altered again, unaccountably. As his passing troubled the placid water, and ripples of colourless light, circling away from him, sent wavering lines of dim light rippling in response upon the sides of the passage, he caught vague, uncertain glimpses of dark rich colour mantling the rocks.

Suddenly, when light and colour were strongest, his way was barred, a wall of rock closing it abruptly. Baffled and perplexed, the boy swam to and fro in vain quest of an outlet, till his wits leapt on a fair surmise that inlets for light there must be submerged. Down he dived, groped, found justification in the arching rock, emerald flooded, struck boldly through it, and rose to the surface beyond.

A glory of light and colour dazzled him, momentarily repulsing his faculties from possession of a grand cavern, spacious, lofty, wonderful, worthy to be the temple of a sea-god.

He found recovery, he found footing, then straightway lost himself in wonder, for such splendours he had never dreamed could be.

Fathoms overhead the great vault hung unpropped. Sunlight shot in high up in rays and bars through piercings and lancet clefts, and one large rent that yet afforded no glimpse of the blue. The boy's eyes wavered and sank for solace to the liquid paving below, flawless and perfect as the jasper sea of heaven. There pure emerald melted and changed in subtle gradations to jade green and beryl green; from pale chrysoprase to dark malachite no stone of price could deny its name to colourings else matchless. And there reflection struck down a rich inlay that sard could not excel: not sard, agate, essonite, chalcedony, in master work of lapidaries; for the sombre rocks were dressed with the deep crimson of sea-moss, velvet fine. Amid the sober richness of weeds hung the amber of sponge-growths, blonds to enhance intense tertiaries. He saw that nature's structure showed certain gracious resemblances to human architecture: sheer rocks rose up from the water like the shattered plinths of columns; there were apses; there were aisles receding into far gloom; rayed lights overhead made a portion raftered, and slanting down a way hinted gothic sheaves and clerestory ruins. Temple and palace both it was to the eyes of the intruder. He could not conceive of any mortal, though noble and exalted among men, entering, possessing, presiding adequately in this wonderful sea sanctuary that nature had fashioned so gloriously, and hidden away so cunningly, with a covering of frowning crag, and fencing of reef and wave. He amended the thought to except the noblest dead. Supreme in dignity, excellent even here, high death crowning high life might be worshipped duly by such sepulture. A slab of rock like an altar tomb in the midst touched his perceptions to this issue.

CHAPTER III

Importunate above measure grew the question, barely displaced in the full flood of discovery: Was the unseen habitant familiar here? present here by some secret, easier ingress? He drew himself up from the water on the first rock, and, quiet as a watching otter, leant prone, till his faculties, abroad with wonder and awe, returned to level service. Not a sound, not a ripple came to disprove his utter solitude.

He slipped back into the water to examine further; a sense of profanation, not to be shaken off, subdued his spirit, and constrained him to diffident movement through the exceeding beauty of those jewelled aisles. Wherever he went play of light and colour encircled him: luminous weavings that strayed into shadowy angles, investing and adorning with delicate favours. Slender isles crept away into gloom, extending into mystery the actual dimensions of the great cavern: these he must enter, every one, for his thorough satisfaction. More than once the marbling and stains of the rocks deluded him, so like were they to frescoes—of battle array in confusion under a fierce winged sunset, of sea-beasts crouched and huddled, prone and supine, and again of sea-beasts locked together in strife. He came upon the likeness of a skull, an ill omen that dealt him a sudden thrill of superstitious fear. It needed close scrutiny in the vague light to decide that no hand of man had shaped all these. Once light broke in from above, and he saw overhead a narrow strip of intense blue, and a white flash from the wing of a passing sea-mew. He tried to scale the cleft, so to reach the heights of the main island; but the steep rocks gave no sufficient foothold, and he dropped back into the water bruised and discomfited. Tunnels and archways there were, too low and strait to let him pass. Attempting an arch, submerged like the way of his entrance, his broad shoulders got wedged, and he struggled back, strangling, spent, and warned against needless hazards.

He never noticed that in the great cavern one after another the rays of sunlight overhead shifted and withdrew, till twilight, advancing below, surprised him. His reckoning of time had been lost utterly, charmed out of him in the vast of beauty and mystery. In a moment he also realised that the lowest tiers of rocks had vanished below the water. The tide was rising. Hurriedly he shot away for return, and groped along the dim passage. The water had risen half-way towards the upper level, so that he mounted there with no difficulty, and made his way on, through the entrance cave, through the kelp-curtained cleft, and out again upon the smooth white sands.

Too late! That he knew by the sound of heavy waves booming from the outer ravine before his eyes could certify how the tide had made hours' advance, and was coming in with a strong, resistless swell that would make short work with the best swimmer alive. He scrambled up to a shoulder to get a sight of the reefs that had helped him on his way; the nearest was already gone, and a tumbling whirlpool marked its place. Except in the slack of the ebb it were madness to make the attempt. Sunlight still touched the heights, but the quick southern twilight makes short stand against night. Without question, till daybreak came with another ebb, on the Isle Sinister must he abide.

To make the best of his case, he sought while daylight lasted after shell-fish to stay his growing hunger. Then in the dusk he gathered dry weed and spread it for his couch on a ledge as high above the tide-mark as he could reach. It was a lateral cleft, as good for his purpose as any there. But he selected it not wholly with regard to comfort of body; its high remove above the mysterious footprints lent it best recommendation. For with growing darkness came a dread upon him; in an access of arrant superstition he conceived of some unimaginable thing stealing near upon woman's feet. Reason stood up for a mild human presence if any, but on ground no better than a quicksand, very lacking in substantial elements. Whence had those feet come? whither had they gone? He could not imagine a hiding too fine for his best vigilance, not in the open at least, in directions that the footprints positively indicated.

As darkness fell, all the tales that had made the place sinister in name and reputation came thronging his mind, assuming an aspect more grim than they ever before had worn. The resolution, the firm reason he had relied on for defence, began to quail before dread odds. What wonder? That day such an assault against reason had been made, such a breach lay wide and unrepaired, as left self-possession hard bestead. Then was he faithful to right worship; he prayed, and mortal terror invested him no longer.

Though faulty, ignorant, superstitious, the young fisher was, a rare sincerity ruled his spirit, an essential quality if prayer be to any purpose, even great in efficacy by its own intrinsic value.

As, crossing himself, he lay down and turned to sleep, plainly above the surf the Warders returned him the sound of a far-off bell—of three bells tolling together. He knew the voice of the House Monitory. Most comfortable was it, an expression of human commiseration extended to him, of special virtue also, he believed, to succour souls against leaguers of darkness. All night he knew, aloft on the cliff in the desolate bell tower, a monitress would serve each bell, and two would wait on a beacon-light, and the prayers of the five would not cease for souls of the living and souls of the dead, victims to fell powers of the sea. Ah, blessed bells! And ah, dear saints whose names they bear!—St. Mary, St. Margaret, St. Faith! The House Monitory prays to the dear saints; but the simple, the ignorant, who go most in peril of that dangerous coast, when they bless three names—St. Mary's, St. Margaret's, St. Faith's—do not discriminate consciously between the saints whose influence lives in heaven, and the bells that ring in evidence of how that influence lives on earth. He fell asleep.

The tide came in, crept up the sand, blotted out footprints and weeds, covered anemone pools and boulders, reached the full, turned and ebbed back again. The moon rose, and as she mounted the dark clear-cut shadows of the rocks shrank. The lad slept the dreamless sleep of healthful weariness, till midnight was long past, and a wide stretch of sand lay bare again. Then in her course the moon put back the shadows that had covered his face; his breathing grew shorter; he stirred uneasily, and woke.

Looking down, he saw the sand bared of the sea, white and glistening in the moonlight. Quite distinct came the even stroke of the bells. The night wind had chilled him, half naked as he was, so he crept from his niche and dropped to the sands below, to pace away numbness. Only a few steps he took; then he stood, and not from cold he trembled. A line of footprints crossed the sand, clear and firm, and so light, that the dainty sand-wrinkles were scarcely crushed out beneath them. And now the mark of the heel is nearest the sea.

He knelt down to peer closer, stretched a hand, and touched one footprint. Very fact it was, unless he dreamed. Kneeling still, he scanned the broken lights and shadows that clung round the margin of rock-girt sand. Ha! there in the shadow moves something white; it is gliding half hidden by boulders. A human figure goes there at ease, rising, stooping, bending to a pool. Long it bends, then with a natural gesture of arms flung up, and hands locked upon the nape, steps out into the full moon-light, clear to view.

The kneeling boy thrills to the heart at the beautiful terror. Whiter than the sands are the bare, smooth limbs, and the dark, massed hair is black as are the night-shadows. Oh! she comes. Does she see? does she care? The light, swift feet bring her nearer, straight on, without a falter. Her shadow falls upon him, and she stays and stands before him, beau-tiful, naked, and unabashed as a goddess.

Could she be one of God's creatures? No! Yet because she was shaped like a woman, youthful pudicity, strong in the boy, bent his head, lowered his eyes to the ground. He felt a shame she could not know, for her shadow moved, her white feet came within the range of his lowly vision. Perfect ankles, perfect feet, foam-white, wonderfully set! When the Evil One wrought in human shapes, surely his work was ever flawed as to feet!

Still kneeling, he lifted his head, encountered her gaze, and made the sign of the cross. She met his eyes with a merciless smile, but before the sign stepped back uneasily; yet her beauty remained unblighted. Then must it be that a sea-witch could be young and fair, of loveliness innate, not spell-wrought to ensnare him. He dreaded her none the less, afraid as never he had been in his life before.

And yet, because his eyes were steady to meet hers, she read such defiance as she would not suffer. She clapped her hands together, and laughed in cruel triumph till echoes sprang.

"You are a dead man. Do you know?"

He stood and fronted her boldly now, recovering faith, most need-ful for the encounter. By what he could see of her face it was cruel and cold as death itself, and the gleam of her eyes was like the keen, sharp glitter of a treacherous sea. For he had not seen, when his eyes had been on the ground, on her feet, a flash of wonder and pity, for one in-stant softening. Wonder at his large-limbed youth remained covert; but his defiant eyes, his gesture, had routed pity.

"Your bones shall lie apart," she cried. "I will choose a fair nook for you in the great sea sepulchre. All the bones of other wretches who have perished among these rocks lie piled in a common heap—piled high! But you alone of many a score having set foot alive in this my garden—by strength, or courage, or cunning—no matter how, your momentary success shall receive some recognition. Maybe, if I remember, when your skull is white and bare, I will crown it with sea-blossom now and then; and whenever I pass by, cast you a tribute of coral, till the hollows of your ribs are overfilled."

He felt that she had the power to make good her taunting words.

"I have faced death before now," he answered simply.

She was angered, and hated him, because he stood upright before her, with eyes that did not waver, and words like proud disdain. She longed to abase him before she compassed his death.

"How shall I take the forfeit? Shall I bid sea-serpents crawl from the ooze of the deep to crush out your life in scaly folds; or set a watch of sharks about my garden to tear your live limbs piecemeal when you venture hence; or make the waves my agents to toss you and wrestle with you, to batter out all comeliness of form, and break your bones as reeds beneath the gale?"

Look, tone, gesture, drove home the full horror of her words. Brave as the boy was, the blood forsook his cheek, a momentary tremor passed, and involuntarily his eyes turned to the eastern sky, whereunder lay a well-known shore, and his home, and the grey-haired couple, who, bereft of him, would go to the grave sorrowing. They faced each other in silence, as two wrestlers mark each the other's strength. A strangely unequal pair! The tall lad, long-limbed, muscular, broad-chested, the weight of whose finger was stronger than her full-handed might, knew he was powerless, knew at least that no physical strength could prevail against the young witch; she, slender, smooth-limbed, threatened him with torture and death, strong in witch-might and witch-malice.

Keen-eyed, she had seen that he quailed, softening, was half minded to forgive his trespass.

"Kneel again and pray for your life; perchance I yet may grant it you."

Should his christened body grovel to her, a witch? A ring of scorn was in his answer.

"Not to you," he said; "I kneel and pray only when I love and fear."

She hated him again: he meant that her he hated and despised.

"Fool!" she cried, raging, "you defy me? Do you not know that you are wholly in my power?"

"Not wholly—no. Though, because I have done amiss, my life be given into your hands, my soul is in God's."

She put her hands to her brow suddenly, as though she had received a blow. She stood quite silent. Then she looked about her as though she sought vaguely for something she could not find. Anger had passed away.

"Your soul!" she said, on a note of wonder. "Your soul!" she repeated, and broke into a scornful laugh. "Ay, I remember something: I had a soul once; but it is gone—dead. I gave it in exchange for sea-life, sea-power, sea-beauty. I drank of the nepenthe cup, and in it my past was washed out and my soul was drowned."

"Wretched creature!" he cried, "better for you had it been your death-draught."

She read in his face horror, pity, loathing, and longed with her whole being to abase him lower than she was in his eyes. Better than to slay outright would it be to break down the self-respect that would not stoop before her even to escape death. Oh, but she would try for very perfect revenge; not by quick death, cheap and insufficient; not by captivity and slow death—no, not yet. He should live, yes—and go free, and then she would conquer him body and soul; biding her time, plotting, waiting in patience, she would so make her triumph full, complete, absolute, at last.

Involuntarily she had drawn away into the shadow of the rocks, leaving the lad standing alone in the moonlight. She saw that his lips moved. He was praying silently, unmindful of her. With her dark brows drawn together and a smile of scorn she wove cunning plans for his ruin. Swiftly she chose her line: for a witch confident, audacious, subtle, it was a game easy and pleasant to play.

Again the boy saw her stand before him. Her face was mild, her voice low and gentle.

"Tell me your name."

"Christian."

She threw back her head with an uneasy movement, but recovering instantly, resumed her part.

"How came you here? and why?" Though not to be lightly reassured, he told her frankly. Her dark eyes were intent upon his face; then they dropped, and then she sighed, again and again. Her breast was heaving with a storm of sighs.

"Oh!" she broke out, with a voice of passionate grief. "Oh, shame! you, who have the wide world whereon you may range, you will not leave me this one poor shred of land. A greedy breed it is dwelling ashore, that must daily be rifling the sea of its silver lives, of its ruddy thickets, and will yield no inch in return. And you have outpassed your fellows in greed—you have owned it—you have boasted. Ah! I grant your courage and strength excellent, taken by the measure of the land; but, oh, the monstrous rapacity!"

Her voice broke with indignation. She turned aside and surveyed the moon-white level. Soon she resumed in a quick, low whisper.

"How can I let him go? How can I? Oh dear, fair garden-close, mine, mine, all mine alone till now—if your shining pools never mirror me again, if your sands take the print of my foot never again—oh no—I cannot—no—no—"

Swift pity responded as her lament sank away to a moan.

"Never think so! One brief trespass made in ignorance is all you have to resent—is all you shall have: not a soul shall have word by me of your favoured haunt. Moreover," he added and smiled, "I know no man who could win here, were he minded to more strongly than I."

She smiled back. "Then go in peace." She passed him by to follow the sea.

This sudden grace struck him dumb. All too briefly glanced and worded was it for his satisfaction. So fair at heart she was too. A first young flicker of male worship kindled in the boy's eyes as he turned to look after her going.

She halted, facing, and lifting her hand to him.

"Your boat was broken, you say," she said as he came. "I tell you, your peril will be more extreme when you try the reefs again for an outlet, except you have a pilot of me."

"You!" he said.

"Not I," she laughed. "The guide that I shall send will be a gull pure white, whose flight you shall follow. I have trusted you; do you trust me?"

"I will, I will."

"A strict promise! Though you seem to be going upon certain death, you will trust and follow?"

"I will trust and follow, on my word, strictly kept as the oaths of the many."

"Your pilot you will know by his call. Listen: 'Diadyomene! Diadyomene!'" she shrilled like a sea-bird. "It is my name—Diadyomene— of a good signification for you. I hold your promise; when you hear 'Diadyomene' you are pledged to follow."

She waited for no answer; with a gesture of farewell was away for the sea, from the moon-white sand springing into the shadows over the harsh interval of boulders. The vista let a vague moving shape show, lessening as she sped across the desolate chasm without. One strip of moonlight lay half-way, at the edge of the retreating sea. There a swift silver-white figure leapt clear, with dark hair flying an ineffectual veil, with arms rising wide in responsive balance to the quick free footing. It was gone—gone utterly—a plunge beyond restored her to her sea.

Christian stood motionless long after she had disappeared, so long that the moon paled, that dawn quickened in the east, that day spread wide. Responding to the daylight, broad awake rose reason to rebuke his senses for accepting fair words and a fair shape as warranty for fair dealing. And till midday reason domineered; while he abode the slack, while he battled for shore, while he mended and launched, while the cry "Diadyomene! Diadyomene!" swept down on white wings, went before, shifted, wheeled; while, so guided, reefs and breakers threatened close on every hand, fell behind and left him scatheless.

Oh, safe upon the waveless blue reason fell prostrate, abashed; and the heart of Christian, enfranchised, leapt high in exultation, so that with laughter, and glad praise, and proud and happy calls of farewell, he set sail for home and was carried away from the Isle Sinister.

CHAPTER IV

Though day was high, Lois, the mother adoptive of Christian the Alien, sat in shadow, for her small lattice was nearly blinded by the spread of vivid fig-leaves jealous for the sun. Flawless order reigned in the simple habitation. No sign of want was there, but comforts were few, and of touch or tint for mere pleasure there was none. Over an opened Bible bent a face worn more by care than time. Never a page was turned; the hands held the edges, quiet, but a little tense. For an hour deliberate calm held.

Then the soft, quick pat of bare feet running caused a slight grip and quiver. The door swung wide, not ungently, before Christian flushed and breathless, and a flash of broad day framed with him. He peered within with eager, anxious eyes, yet a diffident conscience made him falter.

"What have I done? Oh, mother!"

So frail she seemed to his large embrace. In his hand hers he felt ever so slightly tremble. He knelt beside her, love and reverence big in his heart.

"Why should you trouble so?" he said.

She laid her hands on his head for pardon. "Christian," she said, "were you in peril last night?"

"Yes."

She waited for more to follow, vainly.

"What was it? Where have you been? What have you done?"

"Mother, you were praying for me!"

"Answer, Christian."

"I gave a promise. I thought I owed it—yes, I think so," he said, perturbed, and looked in her eyes for exoneration. There he read intelligence on a wrong tack that his honesty would not suffer.

"No, mother, it was not on a venture—I have come back empty-handed. I mean not such a venture as you think," he corrected, for among the fishers the word had a special significance, as will show hereafter.

"Say at least," said Lois, "you have done nothing amiss—nothing you would be ashamed to tell me."

"But I have," he confessed, reddening, "done amiss—without being greatly ashamed—before."

His heart sank through a pause, and still lower at his mother's question, spoken very low.

"Then I am to know that though I should question, you would refuse an answer to me?"

He could not bear to utter the word till she insisted.

Her face twitched painfully; she put him back, rose, and went pacing to and fro. Helplessly he stood and watched her strange distress, till she turned to him again.

"My boy—no—you can be a boy no more; this day I must see you are a man. Listen, Christian: I knew this day must come—though it seems oversoon to me—and I was resolved that so soon as you should refuse any confession to me, I—I—must make confession to you."

She silenced his pained protest, and went on.

"When my child was born, eighteen years ago come Christmas Eve, our priest was no worthy man as now; little good was known of him, and there was bad guessed at. But there was this that none here guessed—I only. And you must know—it is part of my confession."

She spoke painfully, sentence by sentence. After eighteen years her voice yet vibrated with hot, live passion.

"My sister—my young sister—came to make her home with us; she would, and then she would not, for no cause—and went away. She died— she died on the night my child was born—and hers. Then I vowed that neither I nor my child should receive sacrament of God from that man's hands. He dared no word when I passed by with my unbaptized child in my arms; he met my eyes once—never after. We were two living rebukes, that he but no other could read plain enough. 'Twas in those days that my man Giles went seafaring, so the blame was the more all mine. He indeed, knowing all from me, would have had the child away to be baptized of other hands. But in those days the nearest were far, and I put him off with this plea and that; and come a day, and gone in a day, and months away, was the way with him then. For this thwart course, begun out of fierce resentment, so long as that did not abate, I found I had no will to leave. Yet all along I never meant to hold it over a week more, or a week more, or at most a month more. So two years went, and a third drew on, and that wolf of the fold was dead.

"On the day he was laid underground God took my child from me.

"I knew—the first word of missing—I knew what I had done. Conscience struck away all hope. From the print of children's feet we traced how the smallest went straying, how little hands shell filled went grasping for more. I gleaned and keep. They said it was hours before, at the ebb. Then the tide stopped us, and that was all.

"In my bitter grief I said at the first that God was just but not merciful; since He took the dear body from me and hid it in the sea that I, who had not wrapped it for christening, should never wrap it meetly for the grave. Most just, most merciful! afterwards He sent you to me by the very sea. I knew and claimed you as you lay on the shore, a living child, among twoscore dead men, and none withstood me.

"In ignorant haste, eager to atone, I was loath to believe what the cross at your neck told, with its three crosses inscribed, and your sole name 'Christian,' and on the reverse a date. Like a rebuff to me then it was, not realising that I was to work out an atonement more full and complete. I have tried. O Christian, it will not be in vain!

"All these years your conscience has been in my keeping; you have freely rendered to me account of thoughts and deeds, good and ill; you have shared no secret, no promise apart from me. To-day you tell me that your conduct, your conscience, you will have in your own sole charge.

"My boy, you do no wrong; this is no reproach, though I cannot but grieve and fear. But know you must now, that in you I present to God my great contrition; in you I dare look for His favourable grace made manifest; a human soul seeks in you to see on earth salvation."

Christian shrank before the passionate claim. His sense of raw, faulty youth was a painful shame, confronted by the bared remorse of this austere woman, whom his heart held as mother and saint. "O God, help us," he said, and his eyes were full of tears.

"Ay, Christian," she said, "so I prayed last night."

"Mother," he said, awed, "what did you know? how did you know?"

"Nothing, nothing, only great fear for you, and that sprung of a dream. Often the wind and the waves have crept into my sleep and stolen you from me. Last night I dreamed you lay dead, and not alone; by you lay my little one, a small, white, naked shape crouched dead at your side. I woke in great fear for you; it would not pass, though the night was still; it grew rather, for it was a fear of worse than death for you. Yes, I prayed."

Through his brain swept a vision, moonlighted, of the fair witch's haunt, and her nude shape dominant as she condemned him. The omniscience of God had been faint sustenance then compared with this feeble finite shadow of the same that shot thrilling through the spirit of the boy. So are we made.

Outside a heavy step sounded, and a voice hailed Christian. "Here, boy, lend a hand."

He swung out into the clear world. There Giles, empty-handed, made for the rear linhay, and faced round with a puckered brow.

"What the devil have you been up to?"

"Trying her paces," said Christian.

"Who's to blame then—you or she?"

"Oh, not she!" said Christian hastily, jealous for the credit of his new possession.

"Well, well, that ever such a duffer should be bred up by me," grumbled Giles. "Out with it all, boy. How came it?"

Christian shut his mouth and shook his head.

"What's this? Don't play the fool. As it is, you've set the quay buzzing more than enough."

"Who cares?"

"And you've broken Philip's head within two minutes of touching, I believe."

"'Twas done out of no ill-will," protested Christian. "A dozen swarmed over, for all the world as if she were just carrion for them to rummage like crabs. So I hitched one out again—the biggest by preference,—and he slipped as you called to speed me off here. If he took it ill, 'tis no great matter to square."

"I would for this once he or any were big enough to break your head for you as well as you deserve," said Giles savagely.

"We're of a mind there," said Christian, meekly and soberly.

Giles perversely took this as a scoff, and fumed.

"Here has the wife been in a taking along of you; never saying a word, going about like a stiff statue, with a face to turn a body against his victuals; and I saying where was the sense? had you never before been gone over a four-and-twenty hours? And now to fix her, clean without a cause, you bring back a hole to have let in Judgment-day. Now will come moils to drive a man daft.

"And to round off, by what I hear down yonder, never a civil answer but a broken head is all you'll give. 'Look you there now,' says Philip, and I heard him, and he has a hand clapped to his crown, and he points at your other piece of work, and he says, says Philip: 'Look you there now, *he* was never born to drown,' and he laughs in his way. Well, I thought he was not far out, take it either way, when I see how you have brought the poor thing in mishandled. It passes me how you kept her afloat and brought her through. Let's hear."

Though Giles might rate, there was never a rub. Years before the old man and the boy had come to a footing strangely fraternal, set there by a common despair of satisfying the strict code of Lois.

Again Christian shook his head. Giles reached up a kindly hand to his shoulder.

"What's amiss, boy? It's new for you to show a cross grain. A poor spirit it is that can't take blame that is due."

Christian laughed, angry and sore.

"O Dad!" he said, "I must blame myself most of all. Have your say. Give me a taste of the sort of stuff I may have to swallow. But ask nothing."

Giles rubbed his grey locks in perplexity, and stared at the perverse boy.

"It can't be a venture—no," he thought aloud. "Nor none hinted that.

"Well, then; you've been and taken her between the Tortoises, and bungled in the narrows."

Christian opened his mouth to shout derision at the charge, gasped, and kept silence.

"There's one pretty guess to go abroad. Here's another: You've gone for the Land's End, sheared within the Sinister buoys, and got right payment. That you can't let pass."

"Why not that?" Christian said, hoping his countenance showed no guilt.

"Trouble will come if you don't turn that off."

"Trouble! Let them prate at will."

"Well," complained Giles, "I won't say I am past work, but I will own that for a while gone I had counted on the near days when I might lie by for a bit."

"But, Dad, that's so, all agreed, so soon as I should have earned a boat of my own, you should have earned holiday for good."

"Then, you fool, speak clear, and fend off word of the Sinister buoys, or not a soul but me will you get aboard for love or money."

Eager pride wanted to speak. Giles would not let it.

"You think a mere breath would drive none so far. Ay, but you are not one of us, and that can't be forgot with your outlandish hair and eyes. Then your strength outdoes every man's; then you came by the sea, whence none know, speaking an unknown tongue; and then—" Giles paused.

The heart of the alien swelled and shrank. He said very low: "So I have no friends!"

"Well," Giles admitted, "you would be better liked but for a way you have sometimes of holding your head and shutting your mouth."

He mimicked till Christian went red.

"Do I so? Well," he said, with a vexed laugh, "here's a penance ready against conceit. The Tortoises! I indeed! and I must go humble and dumb."

"Such tomfoolery!" cried Giles, exasperated. "And why? why? There's something behind; you've let out as much. I don't ask—there, keep your mystery if you will; but set yourself right on one point—you will—for my sake you will."

Christian looked at the old man, bent, shrunken, halt, and smiled out of bland confidence.

"The burden shall not light on you, Dad. And has no one told you what I have done single-handed? just for display of her excellent parts, worked the boat and the nets too, and hauled abreast of any. Not a boat that watched but cheered the pair of us."

"I heard, I heard," said Giles ungraciously. "A show off for an hour or two. What's that to work week in, week out?"

Christian was looking aside. He saw the head of Lois leaning out, attentive to all.

He took a heavy heart out of her sight. "She does not trust me," he said of her face.

CHAPTER V

Scattered far and wide over the fishing-grounds lay the coral fleet. There, a solitary, went Christian to a far station. Yet not as an outcast. He had tried his strength against his world, and the victory inclined to him. For a week he had been baited hard and cut off, as Giles had forewarned; and through it all he had kept his own counsel, and his temper, and his place with the fleet, defiant, confident, independent. And luck attended his nets. Therefore another week saw unsubstantial suspicion waning; scoffs had their day and died of inanition; and the boy's high-hearted flouting of a hard imposition annulled its rigour. Not a few now would be fain to take their chance with him. For Giles's consolation he had not rejected all advances, yet as often as not he still went alone, declining another hand. Thrift and honest glorying in his strength so inclined him, though a perverse parade may not be disclaimed. Yet none of these accounted for a distinct gladness for solitude that grew unawares.

What colour were her eyes? The moonlight had withheld certainty, and he had not given his mind to it then. Dark, he knew, to match her hair: rare eyes, like pansies dewy in shade?

Down swung with their swags of netting the leaded cross-beams from his hands into the shadowed water, and its dark, lucid green was faced with eddies. Down, deeper than the fathoming of his eyes, plunged his spirit, and walked the sea's mysteries in vain imaginings. Mechanically he set the boat crawling while he handled the guys. A trail of weed swam dim below; it entangled. His wits said weed, nothing but weed, but his pulse leapt. Day after day, not to be schooled, it had quickened so to half-expectancy of a glimpse at some unguessed secret of the deeps. He was glad to be alone.

Body and mind he bent to the draught, till the cross-beams rose, came out dripping up to the gunwale, and neatly to rest. A ruddy tangle hung among the meshes. He paused before outsorting to resolve an importunate doubt: was this more than mere luck to his nets? It was not the first time he had had occasion to debate an unanswerable question. The blank westward seas, near or far, returned no intelligence to his eager survey, nothing to signify he was not quit of obligation.

A witch she was, of an evil breed, one to be avoided, pitied, and abhorred. No conscious impulse moved Christian to seek her again, though her beauty was a wonder not to be forgotten, and she had dealt with him so kindly. Yet of the contrary elements of that strange encounter the foul stood unchanged, but the fair had suffered blight, because from the small return demanded of him his mother's heart had taken hurt. A full confession would indeed but change the current of distrust. He sighed, yet smiled a little; he would have to own that a wish persisted to know the colour of those eyes.

From the sweat and ache of toil he paused a moment to see where he lay. Under a faint breath from the south he had been drifting; the fleet also had drifted to leeward.

Within a grand enclosure, satisfying coolness and peace, and splendid shade reigned, for no man's solace and reward.

The sun rode high, and the west breathed in turn, bringing a film of haze. A delicate blue veil, that no eye could distinguish from the melting blue of sea and heaven, an evanescent illusion of distance, hung, displacing the real.

Above the boy's head a seagull dipped and sailed. It swooped low with a wild note, "Diadyomene, Diadyomene," and flew west.

Christian upturned a startled face. The drifting fleet had vanished; he was alone with the gracious elements.

Too loyal of heart to dream of excuse, he rendered instant obedience to the unwelcome summons, headed round, hoisted every stitch, and slanted away after the white wings. Yet he chafed, angry and indignant against so unwarrantable an imposition on his good faith. Go he must, but for a fair understanding, but to end an intolerable assumption that to a witch creature he owed payment indefinitely deferred at her pleasure.

He owed her his life; no less than that she might exact.

He found he was smiling despite a loath mind and anxious. Now he would see of what colour were her eyes.

The young witch Diadyomene leaned forward from a rock, and smiled at the white body's beauty lying in the pool below. She was happy, quivering to the finger-tips with live malice; and the image at her feet, of all things under heaven, gave her dearest encouragement. Her boulder shelved into a hollow good for enthronement, draped and cushioned with a shag of weed. There she leant sunning in the ardent rays; there she drew coolness about her, with the yet wet dark ribbons of seaweed from throat to ankle tempering her flesh anew. No man could have spied her then.

By a flight of startled sea-birds, he nears. She casts off that drapery. Through the gorge comes Christian, dripping, and stands at gaze.

With half-shut eyes, with mirth at heart, she lay motionless for him to discern and approach. She noted afresh, well pleased, his stature and comely proportions; and as he neared, his ruddy tan, his singular fair hair and eyes, she marked with no distaste. The finer the make of this creature, the finer her triumph in its ruin.

He came straight opposite, till only the breadth of water at her feet was between.

"Why has 'Diadyomene, Diadyomene' summoned me?" he said.

Against the dark setting of olive weed her moist skin glistened marvellously white in the sun. A gaze grave and direct meeting his could not reconcile him to the sight of such beauty bare and unshrinking. He dropped self-conscious eyes; they fell upon the same nude limbs mirrored in the water below. There he saw her lips making answer.

"I sent you no summons."

Christian looked up astonished, and an "Oh" of unmistakable satisfaction escaped him that surprised and stung the young witch. He stood at fault and stammered, discountenanced, an intruder requiring excuse.

"A seagull cried your name, and winged me through the reefs to shore, and led me here."

"I sent you no summons," she repeated.

A black surmise flashed that the white bird was her familiar, doing her bidding once, this time compassing independent mischief. Then his face burned as the sense of the reiteration reached his wits: she meant to tell him that he lied. Confounded, he knew not how to justify himself to her. There, below his downcast eyes, her reflected face waited, quite emotionless. Suddenly her eyes met his: she had looked by way of his reflection to encounter them. Down to the mirror she dipped one foot, and sent ripples to blot out her image from his inspection. It was a mordant touch of rebuke.

"Because I pardoned one trespass, you presume on another."

"I presume nothing. I came, unhappily, only as I believed at your expressed desire."

"How? I desire you?" She added: "You would say now you were loath to come."

"I was," he admitted, ashamed for his lack of gratitude.

"Go—go!" she said, with a show of proud indifference, "and see if the gull that guided you here without my consent will guide you hence *without my consent.*"

Insult and threat he recognised, and answered to the former first.

"Whatever you lay to my charge, I may hardly say a word in defence without earning further disgrace for bare truth."

"You did not of yourself return here? For far from you was any desire ever to set eyes on me again?"

So well did she mask her mortal resentment, that the faint vibration in her voice conveyed to him suspicion of laughter.

"On you—I think I had none—but for one thing," he said, with honest exactitude.

"And that?"

Reluctantly he gave the truth in naked simplicity.

"I did desire to see the colour of your eyes."

She hid them, and broke into charming, genuine laughter.

"Do you know yet?" she said.

"No, for they are set overdeep for a woman, and the lashes shadow so."

"Come nearer, then, and look."

He stepped straight into the pool knee-deep and deeper, and with three strides stood below. She bent her head towards him with her arms upon her knee, propping it that a hand might cover irrepressible smiles. Her beautiful eyes she opened wide for the frank grey eyes to consider. Many a breath rose and fell, and neither offered to relinquish the intimate close.

Beautiful eyes indeed! with that dark, indescribable vert iris that has the transparent depth of shadowed sea-water. They were bright with happy mirth; they were sweetly serious; they were intent on a deep inquiry into his; they were brimming wells not to be fathomed; oh, what more? what haunted their vague, sad, gracious mystery?

"Are you satisfied yet of their colour?" she asked quietly, bringing him to a sense of the licence he indulged.

"Of their colour—yes."

"How, then, are you not satisfied?"

"I do not know."

"Bare truth!"

"What thoughts, then, lay behind while you looked down so?"

She kept her mouth concealed, and after a pause said low as a whisper: "Looking at your eyes, I wondered if they would alter greatly when your time came—to die."

"Ah, no, no," he said, startled; "how could you!" His mind only caught the suggestion to reflect upon her transparent eyes stricken with the tragedy of death. From so gentle a tone he could not gather a sinister hint; moreover, she smiled to effect a blind.

"Now that your quest is over, I in turn desire certain knowledge. Gratify me, and so shall your rash footing here to-day stand redeemed."

She signed for him to follow, and led the way by rock and pool to the entrance of the cave. There upon a boulder she leaned, and pointed him up to the rock above, where the rough inscription he had set there remained unimpaired.

"That is your handiwork?"

"Yes."

"What does it mean?"

His heart thumped. To her he had addressed that legend, not knowing what she was.

"I do not know that you are fit to hear."

Her just indignation refrained from him, and his heart smote him.

"Ah! I should not judge. Hear then!" and he read.

For an instant her face fell, troubled, and she moved restlessly.

"And who are They? Who is the Father?"

"God the Father Almighty, Maker of heaven and earth."

"He did not make me."

"But He did."

"Say that He made you if so you please: I speak for myself. Pass on now. Who is the Son?"

"Jesus Christ His Son, our Lord, who suffered and died to save us from our sins."

"Suffered and died!" she exclaimed, and then added, "I have no sins."

"Ah, you have!" said Christian, aghast.

"You may have, may be, but not I. Pass on. Who is the other one?"

"The Holy Ghost the Comforter."

"Whose comforter? Theirs? yours? not mine—I need no comfort."

When he said, "O poor, lost soul, God have mercy!" she rose to passion.

"You shall not say so; I will not endure it. And why should you look at me so? and why should you speak it low? Am I to be pitied—and pitied of you, who but for my pity would by now be a shredded and decayed patch sunk deep?"

"My body."

Diadyomene recovered herself instantly, recalled to the larger conquest she designed.

"Yet pass on again: there is more—'At your service!' Whose?"

"Yours."

"Mine! That is not possible," she said coldly; "nor of the whole can I make sense."

"It means that I offered to serve her whose footprints I had seen—yours,—and pledged myself by the sacred names that she should have no fears."

"Fears!"

Christian flushed painfully. It was not possible to intimate to her how he had considered that a woman unclothed would surely shrink from a man's presence.

"You make for a simple end by strange means!"

"How is it," she resumed, "that since quite freely you pledged yourself so sacredly to my service, you came most unwillingly when you thought I had need of you?"

Before her penetrating gaze shame entered.

"For your need I would have come gladly; yes—I think so—in spite of incurring worse; but for your pleasure—"

"Not, for instance, had I wished to see the colour of your eyes?"

It was but poor sport to put him out of countenance. Quite kindly she asked, "What now have you incurred that worse should be to dread?"

He began of the name "Sinister," and of all it implied. She laughed, asking him why he should expound that. He went on to the definite ills that had beset him, because the injury to his boat betrayed him to inquisition.

"But how?" she asked; "you admitted nothing, else you failed in your promise to me."

"No, but challenged, I could not deny I had dared here."

"Why not?"

"It would not have been true," he said, puzzled.

Diadyomene opened her eyes wide and laughed.

"And do you use your powers of speech only to say what is true?"

"Yes," he said, indignant.   "How else?"

"Now I," she said, "use speech to disguise truth, with foul or with fair, or sometimes to slay and bury it out of sight."

"Then, when you declared you had not summoned me, was that untrue?"

"If I now answered 'Yes' or 'No,' you could be no nearer satisfaction; for you have not the wit to weigh my word with mood, disposition, circumstance, to strike a balance for truth."

Christian pondered, perplexed and amazed at that perverse argument.

"I would another were here to unreeve this tangle you are in. There is one, wise, tender, a saint."

Diadyomene levelled her brows.

"A woman! And you love her!" she said, and astonished the inexperienced boy.

"Above all! She is mother to me."

He said timidly: "Of all evils incurred by my presumption here, the worst is that between her and me your secret stands a bar to perfect confidence. I did not guess it would gall her so. I may not tell you how."

"Yes, tell me."

"I cannot."

"A secret."

"Not strictly; some day I might, but not now."

She shot a keen glance, suspicious by that heedless reservation that, after all, he was shrewdly playing his own game. He went on.

"With her your secret would be absolutely safe; and if her you would but include—"

"But I will not," she said peremptorily, "nor shall you take counsel with her, nor come back well charged for convincing me of what you may be pleased to call sin; for presently we part for ever—for ever, alive or dead."

That struck silence for a minute. Then Christian straightened and said:

"I have then much to say first. I have a message to you."

"To me—a message!"

"The message of the Gospel. In the name of the Father, and of the Son, and of the Holy Ghost."

"Ah yes," she said; "we were to return to that. 'Suffered and died,' you said of one—the Son."

The young gospeller took up his task void of all vain conceit; but humility, simplicity, and honesty alone could not prevail over the quick-witted witch when she was bent on entangling him. A long hour he laboured with the story of the Redemption, she questioning to his bewilderment, involving him in contradiction, worsting him again and again, though he would not know it; till, weary of harassing, she heard him in silence, with an unmoved attention that was worse discouragement.

His own incompetence he had known, but he had not thought himself so unstable that the pressure of patient eyes could weigh down his clear sense; that the lifting of night-black hair in the light wind, the curve of a neck, the slow play of idle hands, could distract him. He knew he had failed utterly, that he did not deserve to succeed before ever her comment began.

"O the folly of it!" she said with wonder and scorn. "Truly I am well quit of a soul if it bring intelligent creatures of flesh and blood to worship, as highest excellence conceivable, a joyless life, a degraded death.

For others? The more foolish. And you would have me repent and be converted to that? I—I repent, who have gained this?"

She rose to her feet, flung up head and arms; her bosom heaved with a breath of ecstasy, her lips parted, her eyes shone; the glory, power, magic, of the deep flashed into visible embodiment in her. The perfect woman, possessed by the spirit of the sea, unawares took worship of the boy's heart. To seal her supremacy, a wave leaping in the gorge broke to him the unnoted advance of the tide. He thrilled as though the sea had actually responded to her passion.

To a new, wonderful note of power and sweetness she began, with a face and gesture that alone were eloquent:

"O poor mortal! the deeps to you are abysses of death, while the storm-winds, ravening, hunt you. Oh, 'tis pitiful! Deep, deep in the heart of the sea dwells eternal peace, and fear is dead to all who dwell there. Starry sea-blossoms grow stilly, by the winnowing of broad fins stirred only. When stormy terrors fall with black night on you above, with me below is a brooding blank of light and sound, and a darkness that can be felt lulls every sense. From that deep calm I float, I rise, to feel the upper pulses of the sea; to meet strong currents that in the very hair wake vigour; to leave silence far underfoot; to taste of the glorious battle of wind and wave. Strong, foam-headed bearers take me, whirl me as I will. There is madness, rout, and drunken frenzy of the elements for honour of my presence. O the roar! O the rains! O the lightning!

"Deep, deep in the heart of the sea the broad glare of this full sunlight is softened into a mystery of amber twilight, clear and cool; and quivering cloud-shadows dim it to pearl, and sunset throbs into it a flush. There the light of the white moon is a just perceptible presence of grey silver to tell me a night is cloudless. She draws me—she draws me—to her I yearn. My heart, my love, my life, rise large and buoyant in worship of her. To her fair face you have never looked up as I, at poise, with earth far below and the air fathoms above. Ah, so large and near and gracious she lies! In the faint swell of a calm she shrinks and expands, as though she breathed with me—with the sea; a ripple of wind will comb her into quivering lines of silver; and the heave of a wave shatter her to fragments that vainly slide and dance to close back into the perfect disk. Involuntarily your hands would snatch at the near splinters of living silver. I rise through them to rarer air, and lo! my moon has fled up immeasurably, and shines remote, concentrated, placid.

"Deep, deep in the heart of the sea, within unhewn walls, are splendid courts, where marbles discover their shy translucence, and drink mellow life from widespread floors of sand, golden, perfect, unwrinkled and unstained from age to age; and drink milky fire that hangs where nebulous sea-stars cluster that night may never prevail. Inmost wait vacant shrines to gratify worship of sleep and dreams—pure amber one, great crystals one, and rainbow spars. One there is of moony mother-of-pearl, meetest covert of rest, when life grows a little weary of conquest and play, and greatly enamoured of dreams. Ah, dreams! You with a soul—can you dream? Nay—but I will not know.

"Deep, deep in the heart of the sea hide brine-bred monsters; living there, dying there; never touching the thin, vacant air, never facing the broad eye of heaven. Quick death by the grip of huge jaws meets the drowning there. Your might—yours—is puny: you never could cope with the fierce sea-wolves. And your limbs are heavy and slow: you could not play with the dolphin and mock at the shark. To me come all by love or fear. The frailest shape afloat, that fears a shadow, into my palms drops from the waves; and uncouth herds leave browsing to hustle their finned heads under my hands. And the terrible breeds, the restive, I catch by the mane and school, against their resistance driving sharp ivory hard between the joints of their mail. How they wrestle and course, as pride of their strength is mine, and joy of their speed is mine—ah! most supremely when they most dispute it. Your eyes declare wonder, since your broad limbs could match the banded strength of a score of my slight mould. I grant it here, where the touch of the earth and the touch of the air are dull, faint, weak, to flesh and blood nourished of the deeps; but life and vigour and strength transcendent evolve from the embrace of the salt, cold sea, from deep indraughts of keen brine.

"Down in the deepest lies sleeping the oldest of living creatures, placid in a valley of the sea. His vast green coil spreads out for leagues; where his great heart beats slow the waters boil; he lifts an eyelid, and the waves far, far above are lit with phosphor light. Runs a tremor because of his dreams, I sink to the weedy ears and chant peace, unaffrighted, sure that no fret can withstand my song. Shall he once roar and lash with all his spines, your coasts will crumble and be not.

"What, you—you with a soul, get quickened breath and eager eyes from a few empty words, as though even in you woke the sting of a splendid desire for entering the reserves of the sea, with intimacy and dominion like mine. No—no—stand off! content you with the earth and air. Never—never shall you lay your hand upon my breast, nor set your lips to mine, nor gain the essential word, for you count your soul as priceless, and never will let it go."

She ceased. Christian suddenly crossed himself, turned his back, and went from her and her magic. The forward tide checked his feet; its crisp murmur and great undertones uttered a voluble, soft chorus on that strange monologue. He came to himself to know that he offered outrageous offence to virgin pride, unwarrantable, and far from his mind. Her free, bold words were too coldly proud for any thought of disrespect. He turned again hastily. She was gone.

He sprang to the brimming cave. "Diadyomene," he called; "Diadyomene," and followed up the moving water; but he had no definite sight of her, and got no answer till he came to the great cavern. No witch she looked beside the jasper mirror, but just a slender, solitary maiden. She did not lift her pensive head, nor move nor look at him as he drew to her.

"Diadyomene," he supplicated, "have out on me all that is in your mind. Call me dumb-squint, beetle-head in mind and manners."

With a quite impassive countenance she answered gently:

"It is in my mind that the sun is low and the tide high. It is in my mind to put you in a way where both may yet serve for your safe homing."

Out came a sovereign smile of humour, sweet raillery, and condonation blended, instant on her investigation of his eyes. Humbled and exalted at one fine touch, Christian's judgment surrendered to her. She hindered a word of it.

"I can show you an outlet that will take you to a sheltered reach behind the landward walls of this Isle. So will you evade the worst races of the tide. Furthermore, from the mainland to the open you will need aid."

He answered unsuspiciously that of her grace he had learned the reefs fairly.

"Ah yes, and conned through but once," she said smoothly, and eyed him.

"Conned twice—once either way."

"I sent you no summons," she expostulated quietly.

"Do you think that I have lied to you?"

She did not answer.

With indignant emphasis he repeated, "Do you think I have lied?"

"Do you think *I* have?"

Not a quiver crossed her front with the mendacious alternative; not even for laughter, when the face of Christian lent ample occasion; for, as a fish with a barb in the gullet not to be spewed out, was he impotent and spun.

While still he gasped, Diadyomene slid forward into the deep and bade haste for daylight. Fine swimmer he was, but his strokes compared ill with an effortless ease like a wing-wide bird's. Refraction gave her limbs a lovely distortion, and pearly soft they were through the beryl wash. Behind her merged head the level just rocked and quivered; cleft by his chin it rebelled in broad ripples. She turned her head, curious of his clumsy method; she could not forbear a smile; she reverted hastily beyond the blind of her floating hair.

But he could not follow where she offered to lead, for she dropped her feet, and sank, and walked the under-floor of rock, entering a deep gallery. He dived, entered after, then breath gave out, and he shot back to gasp.

She presented a face of grieved surprise. "There is another way to the same end," was all she said on his deficiency.

He mounted after her then, by shelf and ridge, an intricate, retiring way, till she showed him a dark gulf at their feet.

"Leap!" she said, "no hurt lies there."

Utter blackness lay below, repugnant to his nerves; yet not therefore he stayed.

"Diadyomene," he said, with desperate temerity, "you do not forbid me ever to see you again."

Daylight struggled feebly in there. Her answer was not direct, and it laboured.

"I have no—desire—ever to see you again."

Quick for once: "Have you a desire never to see me again?" he said, and held his breath.

He saw her step to the verge, lift her arms, and poise. She delivered an ingenious master-stroke to wound.

"Be under no such apprehension. I will convince you: for your assurance I will go first."

"Hold back!" with a savage sob cried Christian; leapt, and dropped with straightened feet perpendicular in the gulf.

With a thin sigh and a vigorous kiss two elements received his descent. Diadyomene leaned over the dark, and called "Farewell." The word was echoed back by him hoarsely; and again from further distance it came, ringing sound.

Beneath her breath she said, "Some day I will have grey eyes weeping before my face." Then laughter possessed her, and away she sprang, to revel in the release of peals of wicked delight.

Very cold-hearted the sea-bred are, and their malice is very keen.

CHAPTER VI

Lois drew forward a young creature, whose dark head did not fully uplift.

"Christian," she said, "this is your cousin Rhoda."

He blurted out "Cousin!" in astonishment. Two faces stiffened; the girl's eyes declined.

"My niece," said Lois briefly, "and so cousin by adoption."

Giles kicked his heel, so he guarded his tongue duly.

Considerate of embarrassing the girl with open observation, he took note discreetly how kin was just legible on the two faces. The eyes of both were set overdeep for womankind; they were alike in the moulding of the bones; but the face of Rhoda gave promise of a richer beauty than could ever have been the portion of Lois. For a minute it bloomed in a vivid blush, for their eyes met as she, too, by stealth was observing him for his great height and breadth and alien complexion.

When afterwards his mother said, "You know whose child she is?" he answered, "Yes."

"Christian, I thank God for my good man."

Her sense he could not adjust till long afterwards, when a fuller account of Rhoda's past was given to him. Now Giles told but little.

"No, she had never set eyes on her before. I? Oh yes, I had—the pretty little piece! But when I bring her in, and have said no more than one cough, the wife goes clean past me, and has the girl in her arms, and calls her by her sister's name, and sobs hard and dry like a man. It turned me silly and rotten, it did. I knew for a minute she didn't fairly know it was not somehow her sister; no older than Rhoda she was, poor thing, when she last stood under our roof; and their last parting had not been over tender. Well, I had messed the business—I knew I should,— for there was the wife going on, saying things, and there was Rhoda getting scared and white, and putting out a hand to me. And then I go one worse, for I get hold of her, and say, 'She takes you for your mother, child,' that the wife may get the hang of it; and at that down she sits sudden, all of a shake. But the poor wench says, 'My *mother!*' for—well, I suppose I had lied sometime—she thought she was the truly begotten orphan of an estranged brother. Nothing would come handy but the

104

truth—the wife being there; so I even told it all. Yes, I did, though it did seem cruel hard for a young wench to have that story from a beard. But it worked well; for when the poor child knew not how to bestow her eyes, nor to bear the red of shame, up stands the wife to her, just woman by woman, and looks fierce at me, and to her Rhoda closes all a-quiver, and in a moment the wife has kissed her, blight and all, and Rhoda is crying enough for both. That was over an hour before you came in on us, when out jumped 'cousin' and 'niece' to clinch the business. I knew she would never go back on them. To think that all these years—well—well."

"Well, Dad—all these years?" said Christian, incited by Lois's words to be curious of Giles's conduct; for he was a comrade of easy imperfection, not insistent of the highest rectitudes, nor often a consistent exemplar of Lois's strict precepts. Giles drew in.

"A grape has grown from a thorn, that's all," he said.

"But how came you—"

"And a pumpkin has overgrown too. Here—clear out, you've left a moderate body no room to turn."

So Christian understood he was to be excluded from full confidence. Loyal every inch of him, he respected Giles's reserve and never questioned Rhoda herself. He did but listen.

Clear, colourless years, regulated under convent control, was all the past she knew; serene, not unhappy, till the lot of a portionless orphan lay provided for her in a sordid marriage, that her young instinct knew to be prostitution, though the Church and the world sanctioned it as a holy estate. To her this blessed transplantation into a very home gave a new, warm atmosphere that kindled fresh life. The blanch bud expanded and glowed, fresh, dewy, excellent as the bloom of her name. And very sweet incense her shy gratitude distilled.

It was to Giles she gave her best affection, to Lois most reverence and devotion. But to Christian went a subtle tribute, spontaneous even in an innocent convent-girl, to an admirable make of manhood; some quick shivers of relief that a certain widower with yellow teeth did not possess her. And in Christian thrilled an equivalent response; though he knew not how Rhoda's maiden charm, her winning grace, her shadow even, her passing breath, evoked unaware; with a keen, blissful sting at heart, vivid remembrance of the sea-witch Diadyomene.

"She likes the old hunks best of the lot," said Giles with complaisance. "My bright little bird! There's never a one of you young fellows stands to cut me out."

He cocked an eye at Christian.

"Now Philip comes along, and will have her for seeing the caught frigate-bird. And off she is flying, when back she skims and will have me too. Oh! but he looked less than sweet, and he's a fine figure too for a maid's eye, and a lad of taste—he is."

"He! May be, for his fancies are ever on the brew, hot or cold," said Christian in scorn.

"She's a rare pretty wench, and a good," said Giles, with a meditative eye.

"She is: too rare and good for any of Philip's make; an even blend of conceit and laziness is he."

"That's so, that's so," returned Giles coolly to this heat, "but I don't say he would make a bad pair for just so much as the boundary walk."

"How!" said Christian, "but she will walk with me—she's my cousin."

"Have you asked her?"

"No."

"Well, I think she's worth an asking. She's shy, and she's nice, and she's got a spirit too, and more than one, I wager, won't be backward. Rhoda! Rhoda! why, what's this grave face you are bringing us, my pretty?"

The girl's eyes addressed Christian's with childlike candour and wonder. "Why is it," she said, "that the mother of that tall Philip doubles her thumb when you pass by?"

He flushed with knit brows, but laughed and jested: "I guess because she does not like the colour of my hair." But Rhoda had noted a pause, and a quick turn of the eye upon Giles.

"When the boundary is walked, Rhoda, will you pair with me?"

"Oh!" she said, "Philip wanted to bespeak me, and I said him no, till my uncle should have had the refusal of me first."

She curtsied before the old man in bright solicitation.

"Ah! my maid, here's a lame leg that can't manage the steep. You must take my proxy, Christian here."

"But that's another matter," she said; "I doubt if I be free."

Christian's face clouded, but he had no notion of pressing her to exchange obligation for inclination. When he was away, Rhoda asked, troubled and timid:

"I have vexed him. Is it for this? or that I was curious—"

"About that doubled thumb? Not that. He'll clear that to you himself if I know him. Well, then, I will, to spare it him."

He set forth Christian's position and the ordeal not yet quite suspended.

Rhoda went straight after Christian. She presented both hands to him. With a glowing cheek and brave eyes, "I will walk with you!" she said.

"I am proud, cousin! But so? What of Philip?"

With a saucy sparkle she said, "Do not flounces become a girl's wear, then? You shall see. Or do you expect a broken head of him?"

There was more of childish mischief than of coquetry in her face.

"Stay, Rhoda, I have to tell you something."

"No need—no need. Can you think I have not heard?" and she left him to slow enlightenment.

Thereafter brotherly solicitude and responsibility developed in Christian, and his liking for the bright young creature grew warm, in natural degree to match the shy preference and grateful glow that answered for her appreciation.

Soon, so soon, his jealousy, his honest, blameless jealousy, came to be piercingly sweet to the girl's heart. How else, when day by day Giles instructed her of his worth with tales of his champion feats, and of all his boyhood, its pranks and temerities, its promise by tender honour and fortitude of the finest quality of man; when her own observation told her that in the ranks of youth he was peerless, in strength, in outward fashion, in character, in conduct; generous, gentle, upright; of a sensitive conscience that urged extremes of pride and humility; and brave. And to her this worshipful youth condescended; nay, but it was even with deference that he honoured her and attended. One touch of saintliness that had rarefied him was dispelled to her naughty content.

"Rhoda, my child," said Lois, "where is the Book? Bring it." And away the girl went.

Lois had found that the Bible, formerly left mostly to her sole use, had, since Rhoda's coming, made unseen departures and returns. Well pleased with the girl's recluse piety, she was awhile patient of its want.

"Do you leave the Book outside, child? When it is out of hand, you should lay it back here."

"It was in the linhay," said Rhoda, "and not out of hand. And do you think 'tis I who take it? 'Tis Christian."

"Christian!" said Lois, in a voice of such surprise that Rhoda was disillusioned. "Then do you never study the Book alone?"

"No," confessed Rhoda, "I but listen to your reading and the Church's."

Lois was disquieted. She had ever secretly deplored the infirm masculine constitution of Giles and Christian, who accepted from her a spiritual ration with never a sign of genuine, eager hunger of soul. Yet this departure was little to her liking. Though fain would she have recognised the working of the Spirit, she dreaded rather that this was no healthy symptom in Christian's raw development. A cruel stroke to her was this second reserve of independence, invading the fastest hold of a mother's influence. Back came the earlier conviction that her boy's withdrawal from her must be for wrong-going, and the strain of watchful scrutiny and prayer returned. It had slackened when her God had shown such favour as to take out of her soul that iron that for years had corroded there, that she had vainly striven to expel.

She approached Christian with a diffidence that was painful to him to perceive; she recommended counsel in any difficulty—not her own, she said sincerely, though with a touch of bitterness. He was embarrassed by her close, tender surveillance.

"I have already taken counsel," he admitted, "and I think I have got understanding—at least I have got certain information by heart."

"Of his Reverence?"

"Yes."

"Christian, you are not of the doubters?"

"No, mother, of the ignorant."

Her piercing eyes examined his.

"Who has told you so? You did not know it of yourself. What evil communication corrupts you?"

There was no answer but the sufficient one of the boy's conscious face. There was that in the fire of it that inspired Lois to groan in her heart: "My boy has met a daughter of perdition."

She did not miss her Bible again.

Lois's divination of the truth preceded Christian's, though again into the presence of Diadyomene had he made his way. There he went high-hearted on a service that sanctioned all risks—the recovery to the fair witch of her lost soul, fair too he was sure.

When he summoned her to baptism with the first breath, she laughed him off. No, no, she would have none of it. Let him tell her first that of the nature of a secret, as he said he would some day. And Christian, seeing it was indeed germane, delivered the story of the child cut off unbaptized, to the mother's undying remorse. She rewarded him.

"And she would have cared for the little dead body to kiss! Ah, poor mother!" she said softly and regretfully, so that his eyes grew moist.

"Diadyomene, if I die of the sea, would you be so far pitiful as to render to her my body again?"

"No," she mocked; "I myself would keep it. Did I not promise as much at the first?" Then she derided the poor limitation that would die of the sea through foolish preference of a soul.

He took up his mission with all his best powers well ordered; but to no purpose he persisted—she fenced too well for him. She began by denying any value to her soul; before they ended she challenged him to prove his own existence; and, to his amazement, he found that he could not against her, and rude demonstration he did not dare.

He brought off with unsuccess, great joy by her least favour, sharp stings by her least resentment, yet no suspicion that the sea-witch had him in the toils.

Giles mending Rhoda's shoes clacked fondly: "A pretty little foot she has. Such a pit-a-pat little pair I never did see."

Away to sacred white sands flew Christian's thoughts: he wondered if slender footmarks lay there, and which way set. A little folly came into his mind: to plant his bare feet over those dints pace by pace—delicate near paces; for the soles of his feet to walk intimate with the mould of hers. The little folly in his mind extended, set also his palm to the sand, his cheek, his brow. He came to himself from foot to face tingling, and amazed.

"A sweet, pretty wench!" was Giles's refrain. "Eh?"

Christian assented.

"One more to my taste does not tread shoe-leather. Eh?"

With a singular expression Christian gave a "No" of sufficient emphasis. He looked at Rhoda and grew red.

Rhoda and Christian went amidst the fig-tree and trained it up to the eaves. Lois and Giles looked on from the porch; when they spoke, it was low as the rustle of the boughs. "Young Adam and Eve" slid to Christian's ears. He looked at Giles; saw the fond, complacent smile and the shrewd eye; saw his mother's face, grave, concerned, tender; glanced down at Rhoda, and met her shy, happy eyes. He understood, and like lightning shot the revelation that with body and soul he loved Diadyomene.

CHAPTER VII

He found her curved in a nest of sleep full in the sun. Her breath was gentle as childhood's, and as guileless her face. Her head was regal, for the hair dried crowned it in a dark coil wound and bound with wisps of splendid pearls.

The young lover's passion resolved itself into prayer. As never before in his life, with concentration and fervour he importuned his God for the redemption of her lost soul. The shadow of his crest edged her shoulder; a movement brought to the line of her cheek the shadow of his. At that, prayer failed for an amorous instant; eclipse dipped across her brow; sleep parted; she was looking at him.

"Ah, Grey Eyes!" she said, and smiled.

"Be gracious by one little word, Diadyomene. Why never yet will you call me by my name?"

"Your name? No, 'tis an ill-made name. Put it away and bear another that I will choose."

"I could not. Yet what would you choose?"

"Diadyomenos, may be!" she said softly, smiling.

The honour of the consort name caught his breath.

"But I could not; not even for that could I lay aside the name I had in baptism."

"Baptism ever!" she frowned. "Inadvertently did I utter Diadyomenos. Asleep, I had dreamed—of you—enfranchised."

From scorn to regret she modulated, and his blood sang to the dominant close.

She strained to dislocate sleep, on her back-thrown head planting both hands. Her fingers, with careless grip, encountered the pearls; they sprang scattering, and her dark hair drifted down. With languid indifference she loosened and fingered the length of soft splendours; another lustrous morsel flew and skipped to the boy's feet. Covetous longing fastened upon it, not for its rare beauty, its immense value. A thing that had passed through her hands and lain in her hair was to him beyond price; and yet he forbore sternly to seek after possession, because an honest scruple would not allow that an orient pearl could come to his hands but by magic purveyance.

"If a name were to seek for me?" she was pleased to inquire, on the watch for colour which sprang when her words were gracious.

"I know," he said, "what most fitly would express you—oh! too well, for it is over a defect that secretions of the sea have constructed a shape of perfect beauty; the name of a pearl only—Margaret. If you—when you shall come to be baptized—"

"You dare!" she said, and froze him with her look.

"It has come into my mind that you may be a traitor."

"No!"

"Hear now! Look me in the eyes and deny it if you can. It is for the sake of another that you seek after me; that persuading, beguiling, if you can coercing me—me—who spared you, tolerated you, inclined to you, you would extract from the sea an equivalent for her loss, and proclaim that her reproach is taken away."

There was such venom in look and tone, that his face grew strained and lost colour.

"For your sake first and foremost."

"By no means for your own?"

"Diadyomene, I would lay down my life for you!" he breathed passionately.

"But not give up your soul—for me?"

Ever so gently she said this. The boy quivered and panted against suspecting the words of their full worth. She directed her eyes away, to leave him to his own interpretation. The sunlight turned them to gems of emerald; the wind swept her hair about her clear throat; one hand clasped the curve of her knee. Never yet had he touched her, never felt so much as a thread of blown hair against his skin. One hand lay so near, straitly down-pressed on the rough rock, fragile, perfect; shell-pink were the finger-tips. He said "No" painfully, while forth went his hand, broad, sunburnt, massive, and in silent entreaty gently he laid it over hers.

Cold, cold, cold, vivid, not numbing, thrills every nerve with intense vitality, possesses the brain like the fumes of wine. The magic of the sea is upon him.

Rocks, level sands, sky, sun, fade away; a misty whirl of the sea embraces him, shot with the jewelled lightnings of swift living creatures, with trains of resplendent shapes imperfectly glimpsed, with rampant bulks veiled in the foam of their strength. A roar is in his ears, in all his veins; acclaim and a great welcome of his presence swells from the deep, all life there promising to him dominion. Intangible and inarticulate the vision spins; and through it all he knows, he feels, that beneath his palm lies the cold white hand of the fairest of the sea-brood; he perceives dimly a motionless figure seated, and the hand not in his clasps her knee, and the eyes look away, and the hair drifts wide. Then to his ears through the great murmurs comes her voice, soft and low and very clear, but as though it has come from a great way off: "Lay your hand upon my breast—set your lips to mine—give up your soul."

"Christ! Christ! ah, Lord Christ!"

Diadyomene's hand lay free. Christian stared at his palm to find that it had not come away bleeding. His lips were grey as ashes; he shook like a reed. With haggard eyes he regarded the serene visage where a smile dreamed, where absent eyes did not acknowledge that she had verily spoken. Virtue was so gone from him that he was afraid, of her, of the sun. He dropped to his knees for escape.

When he lifted his head, it was to solitude and long shadows. Her feet bruised his heart as he tracked the signs of her going; for they had approached him, and then retired; they had gone toward the sea, and half-way altered back by two paces; they had finished their course to the gorge and again turned; there they had worked the sand. A little folly! Enacted it was a large frenzy.

Yet he took not a single pearl away.

Heavily drove the night, heavily drove the day over Christian, comfortless, downcast, blank. Was her going with anger and scorn divided by pity? or with stately diffidence? adorable, rendering him most condemnable.

The dredge rose and swung in to great sighs of labour. Black coral!

In choice branches hard from the core, all rarity was there; delicate pink and cream, scarce green, and the incomparable black. Precious—oh! too precious for the mart—this draught was no luck, he knew, but a gift direct from Diadyomene; a goodwill token of her generous excuse sent for his solace. Fair shone love in the sky, and the taste of the day grew sweet. No scruple could hold out against this happy fortune.

When the black coral was sighted by Giles from the quay, he raised such a shout as gathered an eager knot. In a moment one flung up a hand, palm outwards, to display the doubled thumb. Every hand copied. Christian saw and went hot with anger, too plainly expressed in his dangerous eyes. Yet would he have little liked to see his treasures go from hand to hand.

"Not for present trade, I reckon?" asked Giles.

"No," said Christian, "my price can bide," and he carried his prize away with him home.

Not even Rhoda could admire and handle that coral void of offence; Lois and Giles only. One little branch, shell-pink, took the girl's fancy; she turned it over, frankly covetous. Christian saw by her shy eyes and pretty, conscious smile she made sure he would presently say, "Keep it, cousin." He could not. A gift, fresh from the cold white hands of the sea-maid he loved, he could not give straightway into the ardent hold of one who offered, he feared, to him her young love.

So sweet and dear had Rhoda grown as cousin, as sister, he hated the suspicion that she could care for him more than he desired or deserved; he hated himself when, loving her most, for her sake he was cold and ungracious. Rhoda, wounded, resented the change with a touch of malice; she allowed the advance of the handsome idler Philip, no friend of Christian's liking, she knew, though to her his faults were not patent. That gift withheld, on the morrow began Philip's benefit. Giles and Lois looked on, and neither wholly condemned the girl's feminine practice. Then what could Christian do, harassed and miserable, but return to brotherly guardianship to keep a dear heart safe from the tampering of an arrant trifler.

Too fatally easy was it to win her away, to keep her away. She came like a bird to the lure, with her quick, warm response, making Christian wretched; he gladdened a little only when he encountered Philip's scowl.

Compared with this sore trouble, but a little evil to him seemed the sharp return of the public ban for comment on Diadyomene's gift. He was ready to flout it as before, not heeding more ominous warnings plain in bent thumbs, in black looks, in silences that greeted him, and in mutterings that followed. A day came when hootings startled him out of his obstinate indifference, when from ambush stones flew, one with bloody effect; a later day, when a second time he had brought in too invidious a taking.

"I sent no gift!" had declared Diadyomene, with wide, steady eyes, but that time Christian did not believe her, though hardly with blame of the untruth. On the morrow her second gift rose. When the boy sought her again she disclaimed once more; and curious of his perplexity and of his gashed face, drew from him something of his plight. Her eyes were threatening when she said, "Fling away, then, what you fear to take." To her face then he laughed for pride and joy that she should prove him. When that same hour came round, he drew up her third gift.

He cared too little that in the interim a mischance had fallen against him; he had at last been descried fairly within the Sinister buoys, and chased by an unknown sail far west, escaping only under dark to circle for home beneath midnight stars.

"O damnation!" was Giles's exclamation on the third prize. "This won't do—'tis too like devil's luck. Ah, lad!" He faltered, caught at Christian, and peered in his face: "You have not—you have not—got fee-penny of them below!"

Christian reeled. "Dad, O dad!" he gasped.

"Steady, lad, steady! Here come spies as usual. There's no stowing a scrap unseen. Ah, they gape! Here, clear off home with this confounded stuff. I'll see to the nets."

Rhoda's eyes shone like stars, her cheeks were like angry dawn. She hovered about Christian with open devotion, at once tender and fierce, playing the child for some cover to that bold demonstration. Christian's heart shrank, for he could not understand her nor appreciate her. But Giles had a tale to unfold that brought light. Rhoda had come in flaming from a stormy passage with Philip. He had gained her ear to hint a warning against Christian, justifying it against her passion with a definite charge and instance that he had the evil eye. She, loyal in defence, carried away into attack, had rashly invaded with exasperating strokes.

"She's made bad blood, I doubt—the little hawk!" said Giles. "He's mortal savage now, and there's mischief enough brewing without."

"What do you know?"

"A sight more than I like, now I've gone to pry it out. It looks as if not a beast has gone and died by nature or mischance, not a bone gets out or broken, but there's a try to fix it on you with your evil eye. We've been in the dark overlong—though an inkling I must own to."

"I too, by token of doubled thumbs."

"Christian," said the old man with authority, "never again bring in the black or the green or any rarity; you can't afford it again."

Christian's head rose defiantly.

"Drop your airs, you young fool! Why, your inches are enough against you as it is. If you weren't so uppish at times, there would now be less of a set against you."

"On my word," protested Christian, "I have borne much and been silent. I know the young cur I owe for this scar, and have I laid a finger on him? To turn the other cheek is beyond me, I own," he added, with some honest regret.

It so fell out that on the very morrow that same toleration witnessed against him fatally. From the snap of a rabid dog a child died, under circumstances of horror that excited a frenzy against Christian, who had been seen handling the beast after the night of stoning, when the victim's brother it was who had marked him for life. So his iniquities crowned the brim, to seethe over with a final ingredient when mooting came along the coast of a trespasser off the Isle Sinister, by timing, incontestably, the alien.

When the fleet lay spread dredging, Christian, obedient to direction from Giles, stationed his boat in the midst; but one by one his neighbours edged away, till he lay isolated deliberately. This manifestation of mislike was not unexpected, but it galled that weary day when the burdens of his life were weighing heavy.

Exceeding the gross of more solid apprehensions, Rhoda's face haunted him to disquiet. By an unjust transfer, shame possessed him, even as when Diadyomene had advanced naked and unabashed before his diffident eyes. Indefinite reproach clamoured all day at his conscience, What have I done? what have I done? And a further unanswerable question, What can I do? beset him to no purpose.

Before his mind hung a vision of prompt, delicious escape, which he did not banish, only because he did not think it could seriously attempt his will. But the hours told so on the aching boy, that for once he abandoned his own strict standard of fortitude, and his distress cried aloud to solitude, "Diadyomene! O my love, Diadyomene, Diadyomene!"

First, a silver shoal close beneath his eye leapt into air and slid again; then his stare discerned a trail of weed upfloating tranquilly: no weed, two dim hands part it to the showing of a moony countenance graciously inquisitive, and pearly shoulders brightening as they rose, till glistening white to the air Diadyomene lay afloat cradled by happy waves.

"Diadyomenos!" she said softly, and her eyes invented dreams.

For an instant, so mad was Christian rendered by this consummate favour, that he clutched the gunwale on an impulse to overleap it finally. Like hounds straining on the leash, natural passions tried the control of the human soul. He dared not speak.

Diadyomene drifted gently lower with never a word more, and lower yet imperceptibly, till her upturned face began to dim. She poised. Ah, beautiful reluctance! Unaffronted? O heart that aches, that breaks to give worthy response! He saw her lips moving; he knew what speech they framed as certainly as though he could hear: your hand upon my breast—your lips to mine—demanded of him.

Christian fell back, and crouched, and lay sobbing dry-eyed until twilight drew.

Home he came. By the way none greeted him of all he met, and a many they were for the hour; and none hooted after him, but shrilling whistles at his back made him turn to wonder what was afoot. Quick figures dodged past him and sped.

Apprehension dawned when he crossed the threshold to find two scared women, and Giles ghastly and bandaged.

"Who did this?"

"An accident, an accident," muttered the old man, seeing the boy ablaze with wrath and pity before ever he heard a word.

Out came a tale of outrage: while the house was empty, Lois and Rhoda away bleaching, the linhay had been forced, and the coral laid there, Christian's store of precious, sacred coral, looted entire. Giles, coming on the scene, had been tripped up and left for stunned by one unaware how an unhappy blade had gashed his fall.

"And who did it?" said Christian, hoarse with his passion.

"Don't say!" ordered Giles, and the women were mute.

"I will know," he cried, stamped out ungovernable, and beat away.

The three looked at each other, pale and fearful. Then Giles staggered to his feet. "Help me after him, wife."

"Rhoda," said Lois, "go quick for his Reverence—if he be abroad, follow him quick."

Seething with just indignation, Christian sped reckless after vengeance. Alarm of his coming sprang up and flew before him along the shore. Thence struck the ring of axes, thence shone the flare of torches, showing a black, busy swarm. Like a wounded beast he yelled out once: the Beloved, his boat, lay there under torture and dismemberment. Then he hurled upon the throng, raging to kill.

Two went down instantly, damaged for life under his bare hands, but the rest by sheer weight of numbers overbore him. Axes rose imminent, but there was no room for a sure stroke in the close, desperate wrestle. Thrice Christian gained his feet again; then had he no need to strike any man but once; those he gripped in the downfall had broken bones of him. Cries and curses thickened, he only fought mute. Foul strokes on him were fair enough: they struck him together, they struck from behind, they caught him by the knees and toppled him down, they fell on him prostrate, they trampled and kicked. He was on his feet again, breathed and fain, when one from behind got in a stroke at his head with a spar; then he flung up his hands and dropped among them.

When Christian came to himself he was made fast hand and foot. Torches and dark figures flashed and swayed before his giddy sight; all round they hemmed him in. He wanted sense, remembrance, and settled vision. What meant this savage, cruel hate looking out of every face? these yells, curses, and accusations dinning at his ears? He was bound upright in the midst—where? no, where! One came and wrenched off remnants of his shirt; another stood by making ready. The wretched boy understood, and strained and struggled desperately for freedom.

Such a scene was not unprecedented among the fishers. According to a rough, unwritten law, the punishment of thieves they took into their own hands, and enforced confession and restitution. Scrupulous to a fault, honourable, proud, Christian maddened at the intolerable degradation threatening. A thief's portion dealt out to him! the shame of it he could not bear.

The circle of pitiless, excited eyes watched the swell of splendid strength expended to exhaustion against stock and cord. He could not escape from bonds; he could not escape from life; with bleeding wrists, panting, trembling, sane, impotence confronted him with his inevitable award.

The shame of it he had to bear. And he could not even effectually hide his face.

He heard the common formula when confession was demanded concerning unlawful takings. Truly his eyes looked wicked then, and his teeth showed in a vicious grin. He heard more, charges so monstrous, that he deemed them sprung of mere insolent mockery, or else of delirium. Dead silence fell, that he might answer. He would not. Oh, frenzy was returning, revolting him against meet despair.

The pain that he had to bear broke upon his body.

Of all the watching throng, none pitied him, none questioned the just rigour of any penal extreme upon him. To the long distrust and the later developed abhorrence, the day had brought forth a new fierce lust after vengeance, exasperated now the might of his hands, super-human, had done such terrible work. None but with pulse of satisfaction must keep time to the stroke of the subjugated boy's long torture; none but would reckon long fortitude to his last discredit.

How long? How long? As, motionless and bleeding, he gave no sign of failing endurance, resentment kindled against his indomitable obstinacy, and silence for his benefit no longer held. A mutter ran: "The devil has cared for his own—he cannot feel." And to make sure that he had not passed from consciousness, a torch was shifted to show his face. It was pale as death, and beaded with great sweat; but his eyes were wide and steady, so they cursed and went on.

The long-suffering northern spirit, the hardy carcass that did not give out, excelling the make of the south, outstayed the patience of animosity. High upon a clamour swelling anew one cried, "Try fire!" snatched a torch, and tested the substance of an arm. It was Philip. When Christian's eyes struck at his he defied them with his thumb.

Yelled a confused chorus: "There, see there! proof enough. Make an end of the creature! Send him back to the devil by the way he came!" The note of death was recognised of the victim; he blessed it, for his agony was great.

But a little way on was the stretch of sand where, fourteen years before, the sea had cast up a bright alien child. Thither was drawn the half-killed boy; and there, made fast to a mooring-post, with his face set to the sea, knee-deep in the tide, he was left to die. Along the shore pickets were formed to preclude a miscarriage to justice; and there, while the sea trod forward, the flame of mob violence died down to its underglow of settled vengeance, and torches were douted and silence fell as the eyes of men began to shirk their fellows', and their ears to prickle at a word.

Christian lifted his head to comprehend immense clear spaces of sea and night, and a black triumph. Not death was before him now, but a new life. Hopeless patience departed before passions during long torture suppressed, and infernal laughter rolled in his heart at the prospect of a consummate vengeance when the powers of the sea should work with his will. He knew she would come. Undoubting the extent of her knowledge, her power, her gracious surveillance, he knew she would come, to offer a splendid exchange for death. O excellent compensation! The touch of her hand, the touch of her lips, the opening world of vast delight, and therewith power to satiate all his hates.

With every breath torment heaved over him still; raging thirst was there for fierce affliction, the cruel sting of brine touched his wrists, appalling in its promise of intolerable exasperation to raw wounds. Would she come as before, with sweet despatch if he could call "Diadyomene"? But he would not; because of other ears he would not utter her name; nor ever because of other eyes entreat her from the cover of the wave. Ah God, he prayed, give me heart to endure!

His sight was unsteady, so that the whirling of the stars and the exaggerated swell of the slow waves vexed his failing brain. But he dared not close his eyes, lest, ignoring her advent, he should lose her and die.

The disworship of an earlier hour, the comfortless void days, the bitter, hard reserves, drew form from delirium; they stood in rank, hateful presences, deriding the outcast: but to pass, he knew, as a sleeper can know of a dream—to pass when the magic of the sea should flow through his veins. My past washed out and my soul drowned.

Ah God, he prayed, grant that I remember! Ah God, he prayed, grant that I forget! Strong hate and strong affection rose dominant in turn. Stronger rose affection: through waves of delirium the dear home faces came and looked at him; the reproach of their eyes pierced deep. What have I done—what can I do? he challenged. God keep you all, dears! Oh, shut your eyes, there is no other way. And still they looked— Lois—Giles—Rhoda—sorrow of condemnation, sorrow of pity, sorrow of amazement; till before their regard he shrank and shuddered, for they delivered to his conscience a hard sentence—his God, their God, willed that he should die.

The tide was up to his belt before ever the human soul staggered up to wrestle. Too swiftly now it rose; too short was the span of life left. He was not fit to die: evil impulses, passions black as murder, were so live and strong in him. He could not die—he could not. To be enforced from mere life were bitter; to choose noble death were bitter; but to choose such a death as this, pitiful, obscure, infamous, to eschew such a life as that, glorious, superlative,—too hard, too cruel a trial was this for human endurance—he could not do it.

Yet he prayed voiceless: Diadyomene, Diadyomene, haste to deliver me; for the will of God roars against me, and will devour.

For pity, dear faces, keep off, or she may not come. She would quit me of this anguish—who could will to bear this gnawing fire? They, too, shall have torment, and die with horrors. The waves shall batter and break, and sharks shall tear their live limbs piece-meal, and down in the ooze coils of serpents shall crush them out. Ah God! ah God! I love her so. Would hell be undesirable if you were there, or heaven perfect if you were not? O poor soul, poor soul! who will have mercy? Kiss her, mother, dear; upon her breast lay your hand when she comes. O poor mother, who had not a little dead body to kiss! Go, go—I cannot bear your eyes. I want— Ah, ah, the power and the glory, for ever and ever. Amen.

He surrendered, and the tide was breast high.

Solitude drifted back, and cleared vision without and within. The despotism of torture succeeded on the exclusion of throes more virulent. He prayed for swift death, yet shrank humanly as promise swung hard at his face. He prayed against Diadyomene, and yet strove with wide eyes to prevent the darkness, quailing, pulsing at gleam of wave and sweep of weed. He would give up his soul if it were possible, not for carnal exchange, but that hers might revive.

Would she of the cold sea nature care greatly for his death? Would she remember where the outcast body lay, and fulfil her word uttered in scorn to lay sea-blossoms about the skull? Dead, void of pain, unresponsive to her touch could he be! O fair, calm life of the sea! O fair, calm sea-queen! No, no, not for him—death, only death, for him. God's merciful death.

The enfeebled brain fails again; sense and will flicker out into misty delirium; from helpless memory a reek distils, and the magic of the sea is upon him.

Through waves heaving gigantically to isolate him from the world, the flash and spin of eager life beckoned the blood left in him; great strengths loomed, his on the loosening of knots of anguish; a roar ran in his veins, noise and tremor beating through him, fluid to it but for his bones. Came trampling and singing and clapping, promising welcome to ineffable glories, ravishing the heart in its anguish to conceive of a regnant presence in the midst. Coming, coming, with ready hands and lips. Came a drench, bitter-sweet, enabling speech: like a moan it broke weak, though at his full expense, "Diadyomene." Came she.

Delirium flashes away. Face to face they hang, shattered life and lost soul. He shudders hard. "Deliver us from evil," he mutters, and bows his head for a fatal breath and escape.

CHAPTER VIII

"Too late. Wait till the tide go down. What was there?"

Hearts quailed at the sound that drove in, for it was not the last voice of a spent mortal, but shrill, but fierce, but like the first voice of his indignant ghost. Four only did not recoil; the rest, half-hearted brought to the rescue, urged again: "Wait till the tide go down," pulling back the two women from insane wading. But Giles was forward, staggering in the tide, floundering impotent against it; and his Reverence turned upon them as intolerable a countenance as when through his black flock he drove, threatening the curse of Heaven. Therefore two, though loath, swam out to fetch in the boy's body. They cut the ropes from him, and lifted him along with the waves to hard land.

Rhoda shrieked at sight of the deathly inertness and the rent flesh, and hopeless, fell to an anguish of weeping; but Giles and Lois, tearless, mute, with hand and ear over his heart, sought and sought for sign of life, finding none. Pitiless aid brought a torch, and held it to dispel all hope of a flicker of life. Could any look on the sad, serene face and still pronounce him worthy of death, worthy the burial of a dog? They did, even those whom kindness to the parents had constrained far, for among themselves they said: "Persuade them away, and his Reverence. Best to serve the body with its grave quick and meet, in the sea, lest they want it laid in holy ground." But Lois, who would not believe her son yet dead, and Giles, who could not believe him still alive, would have and hold him, living or dead, and none with heart of flesh could withstand them. So the limp, lifeless burden was taken up along the weary shore, past the doors of the street, close shut every one, and delivered to the weak shelter of home for the nonce.

Against life and decent burial had Christian's last desire been: these to impose was all the service great love for him could conceive, though the broken body, dreadful to see, dreadful to handle, made silent appeal against a common valuation of life. Through tireless effort to provoke breath despair hovered, hour-long, till response came in a faintest flutter of life at lips and heart; and chafed with cordials and wrapped about with warmth, the shadow of pain drew over his face and weak spasms flexed his hands as tyrannous vitality haled back the reluctant spirit into bondage. His eyes opened upon them with sense and recognition, a feeble effort to move fetched a groan, and again he relapsed deathlike. So and again all through the long night watches the desperate debate of life and death lasted.

Through close window and door the sigh of the night and the moan of the far sea spoke continually, and covered to dull and finite ears the sound of the sunrise coming over the distant hills.

Not dead, and not dead, and yet again not dead! With that recurrent stroke of sense was welded again the mortal unit half gone to dissolution. Day came filtering in on wan faces brightened to fearful hope, for Christian assuredly lived and would live: consciousness held, and his eyes waked and asked. The four knelt together, and thanked their God aloud for his life, tears running free; he turned his head away in great despair, knowing that he was condemned.

Whose prayers should prevail, theirs or his? He must die: he would die. But every hour brought firmer denial to his pitiful desire for death. What had he done, his anguish cried up to heaven, that his God should withhold an honest due? For death and its blessed ease and safety had he renounced the glorious sea-life, not for this intolerable infliction of a life miserable, degraded, branded for ever with memory of one disgraceful hour.

Fever declared that always still he stood within a circle of fire; his skin was hot with the heat of men's eyes; the stroke of his blood was pain and shame that he had to bear; always, always so it would be.

Healing came to close the wounds of his body, but the incurable wounds of a proud spirit gaped and bled hot and fresh, and even under the pitying eyes of love quivered and shrank. A sound from the outer world, of footstep or voice, crushed him intolerably under fresh weights of degradation.

The sound of footstep and voice would start hasty barring of shutter and door, hinting to him that his doom of life was yet remittant.

With infinite caution, and despite his great weakness and pain, he got his knife into his own secret keeping. Out of sight it lay bare for a fond hand to kiss its sweet keen line: life held some blisses it could promise him yet.

Indefinite revenge was not enough: the thought of actual elaborate murder grew so dear, he would not for any price forgo it. Himself would be satisfied, his hands, his eyes, his ears, with the circumstances of a bloody despatch from life of him, and him, and him, each witness of his torture and shame, beneath whose remembered eye his spirit now shrieked and writhed. Let him so doing perish body and soul. So low in the dust lay he, the dear hope of Lois, because the heart of his pride was broken.

Imperfectly he heard a young voice passionately urging for vengeance, retribution, redress, asking after the law of the land against a brutal custom carried to unaccustomed extreme.

Redress! His eyes he shut when his lips bade the girl believe that he had no desire to invoke any earthly powers to avenge his wrongs. On his hand her tears fell like rain; she bowed her head at his knees, with wonder within at the christian saint of so perfect a heart. Back to bare steel crept his hand, tear-wet.

But his fierce hate betrayed him. A gust of fever and madness lifted him up, enraged at the body unready, the burnt right arm unready; his left hand and the devil in him snatched out the knife, and drove it at the planks on his level in one instant of exuberant capacity. In and out again it went; he sobbed a great laugh for the cost and its sufficiency, and with spent force fell back a-sweat. Swift in trod Lois, and he was still, with the blade out of sight, not knowing that clean through the inches of wood the bright blade had looked in a line of sunlight straight to his mother's eye.

She was not gentle then, nor cared for his hurts; with quick mastery of him while he cowered and winced in nerveless collapse, she discovered and plucked away his naked paramour. Dumb-struck she stood in accomplished dismay. Into the impotent wretch defiance entered; with insolent assertion his eyes affronted hers; unmasked, from his face looked the very truth of hatred and lust of blood, shameless at exposure.

Mother and son drew breath for battle.

"What name shall I call you by?" she cried. "You have borne that name of Christ all your life, and now do renounce His cross."

"Diadyomenos" sang to him out of the past.

"Your face is the face of Cain already, not the face of my son, my dear son given me by the mercy of God. It is like the curse of God!"

She fell on her knees and grasped him hard. Her prayers came upon him like terrible strokes; heaviest to reach him were prayers to her God. He would not answer nor say amen; his own one passionate prayer had been unregarded, and he hardened his heart.

"I took you from the death of the sea, and loved you and cared for you as more to me than the child of my body. And when with manhood and freewill came trial by sorrow and pain—hard, oh! hard indeed—then I saw my blessing in you and touched reward. My son, my son, the son that never was, was brave and patient and long-suffering and meek, because he lay at the feet of the Lord Christ a faithful follower and servant; he never complained, nor cherished an evil hate; he forgave, and asked that none should avenge him. Who then, among mothers, could rejoice as I, and so glory in her son? Ah! ah! like a serpent tongue it flickered in the sunlight! Christian, the wretchedest of mothers asks you to have mercy upon her. Ah, you will—must. I will not rise from my knees, nor take my hands from you, except you promise to put vengeance out of your heart. Your hate blasts me, me first before all others. Your blade threatens my heart, will pierce it through if it strike for another's." She was moaning for woe of that hurt. He turned his face away, obdurate still, though the reproach of undeserved esteem had gone deep as any of undeserved shame.

The moaning fell into low prayer. The guilty soul heard that it was not for him she prayed; the old weary penitence for an unredeemed transgression was all her burden now: a sign she asked, one little sign that her poor effort at atonement was not rejected of Heaven. He would not give it; no, he could not. Yet he dreaded that her strenuous supplication must win response, in his great ignorance half believing that some power from above would, against his will, force him to concession.

He looked again at the dear grey head abased in his unworthy presence out of endless remorse for one error. Her God did not answer. Himself was weary of her importunity, weary of the pain of her hands: and he loved her so! And her God did not answer: and he loved her so!

Silently he laid his hand upon hers. His eyes were full of tears, as he said, "Kiss me, mother." She had conquered: he promised.

"Deliver me from blood-guiltiness, O God!" she said; and he repeated, "Deliver me from blood-guiltiness, O God."

"Mother, mother, pray that I may die!" and then he broke down utterly and wept like a child, and was not even ashamed.

Ah, poor mother! Soon she came to know that when her son gave up his will to her he shut up his heart the faster. His misery never spoke, but silent tears would flow unchecked and unconcealed, and she could give him no comfort.

Helpless need like his is a shadow of the Almighty by which men believe; but he could not with a right heart pray because, though he had renounced vengeance, forgiveness was a thing apart and impossible.

How to bear the world and its eyes was the prospect that filled his sky. All his waking hours his heart gazed and gazed thereat, and stayed unacquainted, still, and appalled.

Now that in sleep blood was out of his dreams a vision cruelly sweet came in place, and he was in the presence of Diadyomene, following her, reaching to her, close to her, yet never quite winning the perfect pressure of her lips, nor her gracious surrender to the worship of his hand; and waking was to unrighteous regret that he had turned from that splendid offer and lost it.

Too swift and few ran the suns, and the inevitable time was at hand for bearing the world and its eyes under the hard bond of his promise. The youth and vigour of his body set him on his feet oversoon, while all the soundness his spirit had gained was trembling for its weakness, fear for its cowardice, shame for its shame.

"Where shall he go?"

"Christian," said Lois, "where will you go?"

He wondered what she said. Open talk had passed over him unregarded; he had lost the knack of understanding except he tried hard.

Giles sighed. "Far, indeed, far; for where is our boy not known, the best fisher for his years, the best at sail and oar, the strongest proved in the pick of the coast. Far, indeed, for him not to be known."

That Christian understood, for he broke silence hoarsely.

"Say out: far indeed for him not to be known as beaten for a thief, drowned like a dog."

Rhoda's hand slipped to his, unseen; she drew it softly against her lips. He did not heed.

"My boy," said Lois, "what will you do?"

"Mother, do you bid me go?"

His hot brain knew of a grand enclosure where satisfying coolness and peace and splendid shade reigned, for no man's solace and award.

"You bid me go?"

"Dare you stay?" she said, "dare I bid you?"

His voice shook. "What sort—of killing?" he asked, daunted now.

Giles swore softly after the manner of his kind, under danger of tears.

"Where are your senses, lad? Great storms can't last. This is over, his Reverence will tell you that. Not twice in a lifetime, I guess, can the devil brew the like."

"You bid me go?"

"Not now, not yet," said Lois tremulously; "but sin and shame were to keep you to a trial beyond your strength."

He said quite brokenly: "You are looking for a broken promise."

"Not that. Only—only, we know that 'twould be easier for you to face stranger folk, and hard though it be to let you go, far harder were it for you to stay, and we cannot ask it."

Christian's head sank: they all knew that he had not strength nor courage to stand upright under a disgraced life; he need but acquiesce for the last spark of self-respect to be extinct.

It was long before he lifted his head; Rhoda only was there. He asked after Lois. She had gone with his Reverence up towards the church. He asked after Giles. He had gone down to the quay to his work of refitting the old boat.

Tears stung his brain for the wicked destruction of his own boat, that like a living creature he had loved, and had not saved, and could not avenge.

Rhoda left him but for a moment; passing out to the linhay, the door she left ajar.

Christian stood up, touched his brow once or twice with uncertain fingers, drew sharp breath, crossed himself, and stept out into the world.

He reeled in the sunlight. Its enmity struck at him, and he put up his hands against an unknown trouble, for in through his eyes into his brain flew strange little white birds and nested there and were not still.

He alone stood upright in the midst of a rocking world; under his feet walked the path, the road, the street, bringing up an ambush of eyes, and grey birds and fire.

In the street his coming started a scare. Only yesterday said he was long a-dying, so that now women fell back afraid of a ghost, for with every trace of sunburn gone his face was of a whiteness astonishing in the south. But some harder men cursed at the stubborn devil in the boy, that kept him alive out of all reckoning, and unsubdued. Face to face none met him till the corner where the street beached and the quay branched. There stood an idle group that suddenly gave before a reeling, haggard embodiment of hatred.

These very eyes he knew again, and the one memory within them legible; hot, red-hot, they burned him. Red birds and black flew in and sounded shrill, and beak and claw tore at a little nook where a promise lay shrunk and small. Again he crossed himself, and passed on, till none stood between him and the sea.

Hot, smooth sand stretched curving round the bay with the hard, grey quay lying callous upon it; tall masts peered, windows gleamed and glared, and behind him lay a lifetime of steep street. But strong salt gusts spoke to him from the blessed, lonely sea. The tide was leaping in fast and white; short waves crested and glittered over the expanse of moving blue.

Rhoda caught his sleeve and stood beside him panting and trembling, amazed at his strength and temerity.

Just set afloat by the tide, the old boat rocked against the quay; but Giles was pottering afar, and did not see, and could not hear. The weak pair made forward with one consent, till at the boat Christian halted and stept down.

Along the quay came lounging hateful curiosity; Philip was there, with half a score more. Rhoda faced round bravely; her fear was overborne by intense indignation; she was half a child still, loyal, reckless, and wild to parade before one and all her high regard for the victim of their brutal outrage: her esteem, her honour, her love. From the quay above she called to Christian, knelt, reached across, took him by the neck, and kissed him there for all the world to see. Afterwards she knew that all the child in her died on the kiss and left her full woman.

She kissed him first, and then she saw into his eyes: Christian was mad.

In terror she sprang up, looking for help vainly and too late. Giles was far off, slow of hearing, slow of foot; and the madman was casting off, and the boat began to rock away. In desperation she leapt across the widening interspace, and fell headlong and bruised beside him. The boat slanted off and went rollicking over the tumbled waves. All his mad mind and his gathered strength were given to hoist the sail.

Far back had the quay floated when the desperate girl rose. Giles was discernible making vehement gestures of recall. She stood up and answered with imploring hands, and with useless cries too. Christian never heeded. Then she even tried her strength against him, but at that the mad eyes turned so fierce and dangerous that she shrank away as though he had struck her.

None of the coral fleet was out on the rising wind and sea, and stray sails were standing in; yet Christian, frantically blind, was making for his old station on the fishing shoals. The old boat went eagerly over the waves under a large allowance of sail; the swift furrow of her keel vanished under charging crests. Low sank the shore, the dark verdure of it faded, the white houses of it dimmed. The strong, terrible sea was feeling his strength as a god when his pulses stir him to play.

Overhead a sea-gull dipped and sailed; it swooped low with a wild note. Christian looked up and laughed aloud. In an instant the boat lay for the west, and leaped and quivered with new speed.

Scudding for harbourage, under a corner of sail, two stout luggers passed; and the men, watching their mad course, waved to warn, and shouted unheard. Then Rhoda stood up and signalled and screamed for help. She thought that the wind carried her cry, for both boats put about and headed towards them. Hope rose: two well-manned boats were in pursuit. Terror rose: in an instant Christian, to a perilous measure of sail added more, and the boat, like a maddened, desperate thing, went hurling, bucking, smashing, over the waves, against the waves, through the waves.

Rhoda shut her eyes and tried to pray, that when the quivering, groaning planks should part or sink, and drop her out of life, her soul should stand at its seemliest in her Maker's sight. But the horrible lurches abating, again she looked. Pursuit was abandoned, soon proved vain to men who had lives of value and a cargo of weight: they had fallen back and were standing away.

The sun blazed on his downward stoop, with a muster of clouds rolling to overtake him before he could touch the edge of the world. In due time full storm would come as surely as would the night.

Christian over the gunwale stared down. He muttered to himself; whenever a white sea-bird swooped near he looked up and laughed again. Wild and eager, his glance turned ever to the westward sea, and never looked he to the sky above with its threat of storm, and naught cared he for the peril of death sweeping up with every wave.

A dark coast-line came forward, that Rhoda knew for the ominous place that had overshadowed Christian's life. The Isle Sinister rose up, a blot in the midst of lines of steady black and leaping white.

Over to the low sun the clouds reached, and half the sky grew splendid with ranges of burnished copper, and under it the waves leaped into furious gold. Rhoda's courage broke for the going down of her last sun; she wept and prayed in miserable despair for the life, fresh and young, and good to live, that Christian was wantonly casting away with his own. No hope dare live with night and storm joining hands, and madness driving on the cruelest coast known.

On they drove abreast of the Isle Sinister.

He clung swaying to the tiller, with groaning breath, gaping with a wide smile and ravenous looks fixed intently. A terror of worse than death swept upon Rhoda. She fell on her knees and prayed, shrieking: "Good Lord deliver us!"

Christian looked at her; for the only time with definite regard, he turned a strange dazed look to her.

A violent shock flung her forward; the dash of a wave took her breath; the boat lurched aslant, belaboured by wave on wave, too suddenly headed for the open sea. The tiller broke from his nerveless hands, and like a log he fell.

Rhoda's memory held after no record of what her body did then, till she had Christian's head on her knee. Had she mastered the great peril of the sail? had she fastened the rudder for drifting, and baled? she whose knowledge and strength were so scanty? Her hands assured her of what her mind could not: they were chafed by their frantic hurry over cordage.

She felt that Christian lived; yet nothing could she do for him, but hold him in her arms, giving her body for a pillow, till so they should presently go down together, and both be safely dead.

The buoy-bells jangled to windward, to leeward. Then spoke the blessed voices of the three Saints, and a light showed, a single murky star in a great cave of blackness, that leaned across the zenith to close round the pallid west. Ah, not here, not here in the evil place! She had rather they drown in the open.

The weak, desolate girl was yet clinging desperately to the barest chance of life. She laid her burden down; with awkward, aching hands she ventured to get out a corner of sail; and she tried to steer, but it was only by mercy of a flaw of wind that she held off and went blindly reeling away from the fatal surf. As night came on fully the light and the voice of the House Monitory passed away, and the buoy-bells, and the roar of breakers, and the heavy black of the coast. Past the Land's End in the free currents of open sea, she let the boat drive.

Crouching down again, she took up the dear weight to give what shelter she could, and to gain for herself some, for great blasts drove hard, and furious gusts of rain came scourging. Through the great loneliness of the dark they went, helpless, driving on to the heart of the night, the strength of the waves still mounting, and the fierceness of the wind; the long gathering storm, still half restrained, to outleap in full hurricane about the time of midnight.

CHAPTER IX

All night Lois and Giles were praying in anguish of grief for their children of adoption, even when hope was beaten out by the heavy-handed storm. For three days and nights the seas were sailless, though the hulks of two wrecks were spied drifting; and after, still they ran so high, that a fifth day dawned before a lugger beat in aside her course on a kindly errand. Then up the street leapt news to the desolate pair: how Rhoda and Christian lived; how their boat had been run down in the night, and themselves snatched gallantly from death; how they had been put ashore at the first port a mastless ship could win, and there received by the pity of strangers; and how all the while Christian lay raving and dying, and by now must be dead.

But to hope reborn this last was unbelievable. Lois said she should find him alive and to live, since Heaven had twice willed him to escape the jaws of death. And her heart of confidence she kept for more than two weary days of difficulty and delay. But when she reached his bed her hope wavered; she saw a shorn head, and a face blanched and bloodless like bone, fallen out of a shape she knew into strange hollows, with eyes showing but a glassy strip, and grey, breathless lips. "To-night," said Rhoda.

Breathless also through the night they watched till came the first shiver of dawn. Then his eyelids rose; he looked with recognition at Lois, and moved a hand towards hers; and with a quiet sigh his eyes closed, not for death, but for blessed, feverless, breathing sleep.

The one who wept then was Lois, and Rhoda clasped her in a passionate embrace of comfort, and herself shed no tear.

The child had deserted Rhoda for ever, as the boy Christian. She knew it: she had kissed her childhood dead on his lips, and now past any recall it had been buried, and lay deep under such a weight of sorrow as fate can hew only for a woman full. No tear she shed, no word she said, and she ordered her face to be serene.

She had a word for Lois not at first to be understood. "God has been good to heal," she would say; but the whole truth did not declare till Lois, regarding the future again, had sighed: "Where shall he go?" "Home," said Rhoda. Lois shook her head sadly: "He could not bear

133

it." The girl, with arms round her neck and a hid face, whispered again: "God has been good to heal—I think so—do you not know it yet?"

So a day came when a wasted shadow of the old Christian was borne along the quay and up the street, while men and women stept out to observe. Their eyes he met with placid recognition, clear of any disquiet.

The devil had gone out of the fellow at last, they said, when he could not lift a hand for injury, nor gloom a resentful look. And so hard doings were justified; and none intolerant could begrudge him the life he had brought away, even before a guess began that he had not brought away his full wits.

Out in the porch he would come to bask in the sun for hours with animal content. Out to the gate he would come, going weakly to and fro as he was bid. But Giles was surly to men, and to women Lois was iron cold, and Rhoda had deft ways of insult to repulse unwelcome intrusion; and so for a little while those three guarded him and kept close the secret of his ruin.

Then one at an unguarded moment won in, and spied, and carried her report of his mild, his brute-mild gaze, and his slow labour of speech: it was the mother of Philip. Rhoda found a token of her left beside Christian, a well-intended, small peace-offering, in a cheese of her sole make.

"Who brought this?" she asked; and he told.

"She offered it—to you?"

"To us," he returned quietly.

"And you took it—thanked her and took it?"

He looked up and studied her face for enlightenment.

"The mother was not here."

Rhoda's passion surged over. "How dared she, how dared she!" she stormed, and seized on the poor gift, cast it down, stamped it into the sandy path, and spurned it over the sweet herbs into the sluggy kail beyond.

Like a child, chidden for some uncomprehended fault, he looked at her, distressed at her condemnation, anxious to atone, wondering if his senses told him true. Her anger failing under an agony of pity and remorse, from the unendurable pain of his look she fled to hide her passionate weeping. When Lois came out to Christian he was deeply asleep.

Soon he carried into the street his brute-mild gaze, and his slow labour of speech. And no thumb turned against him. For all who chose to peer in on his blank mind found how shame and rancour could take no root in a void of memory. He met every face with an even countenance, showing no recall of a debt to any.

In a very literal sense it was now said that the devil had gone out of him. Willing belief held that he had been actually possessed, and delivered only when a right instinct of severity had spoiled him for habitation. Some compunction showed over the mooted point whether the pitiful lasting flaw had not rather come of the last spite of an evicted devil, than of the drastic measures of exasperated men.

In nowise did Christian's reason now work amiss, though it was slow and heavy; nor had his memory lost all its store, nor quite its power to store. Of earlier days his remembrance was clear and complete though a little unready, but of passing hours some only did not float clean out of mind to be forgotten. This was a deficiency that mended by degrees, and in time bid fair to pass. Where the break began, none who loved him ventured to discover. Once when, as shall be told, Giles incautiously touched, Christian turned a dazed, painful face, and grew white and whiter, and presently laid his head down on his arms and slept deeply. In those days frequent slumbers fell, and for the most part memory was blurred behind them.

Lois in her heart sometimes had a secret doubt that oblivion had not entirely satisfied him. His reason seemed too serviceable to lie down without an effort; and it was hard to imagine how it could account for certain scars that his body would carry to the grave; or account for the loss of two boats—the old drudge and his own murdered Beloved. Yet when in his presence they held anxious debate on the means to a new boat, he listened and made no comment.

The poor wronged household was hardly set. Restitution was unlooked for, and not to be enforced, for woe betide any who against the tyranny of the fishers' law invoked higher powers and another code. Though now the alien was tolerated under a milder estimate, an outcast he remained, and none were so hardy as to offer fellowship with him and his. The cost of a boat was more than Giles could contrive on his own poor securities, and none could he find to share for profit or risk in any concern that Christian would be handling. It was only on his Reverence offering surety for instalments that the dread of ruin and exile for one and all passed them by, and means to a livelihood were obtained.

Together, as in the long past days when Christian was yet a child, and Giles was still hale, the old man and the young returned to daily toil on the coral shoals. Giles was the better man of the two at the first, for necessity had admitted of no delay; but as the younger gained in strength the elder lost; by the month's end his feeble stock of strength, overdrawn, failed suddenly, not enough remaining for him to potter about the quay as before. In months succeeding, his goings came to be straitened, first to the garden, then to the house, then to one seat, one bed. Before the year's end it was to be to the straitest lodging of all—green turfed.

Alone, quite alone again, with sea and sky whispering together round him, and no sail near, well might those who loved Christian pray for him hourly.

His first return was so late that terrors beset all three. The two women were on the quay when his boat glided in under dusk, and up he stept with a load. The hearts of both were beating thick for dread of a rich load that would blast him afresh, for thus in old days had he glided in at dusk.

But what he bore was only his nets, which he dropped before them. He stood silent and downcast. They saw that one of the cross-beams was broken; they saw that the meshes were torn incredibly.

They saw that he was waiting in dumb distress to be told by them if he were to blame. Ah, dear aching hearts! not a word, not a look was there to weigh on him in his disappointment. Rhoda stripped off the netting and carried it home, with a gay boast of proving her proficiency, for she had learned net-making from Christian in his idle days of weakness. Half the next day she sat mending, and was proud of her finished task, expecting some reward of praise. But it never came. The fresh netting he had taken he brought back torn hideously, so that dismay fell.

Christian and Giles together had met only poor luck, but here came a stroke of so deliberate an aim that the word misfortune seemed indifferent to describe it.

And this was but the beginning of a long course; again and again Christian returned with spoiled nets; and, even on better days, few there were when his takings were not conspicuously poor in amount and quality. Such loss was the graver since an instalment was due at the season's close, and except the dawning autumn brought fair success, sore straits would come with the winter.

Rhoda proved good for bread-winning. Before, she had practised lace-making, taught her at the convent school, and now she turned to it with all her energy. Early and late found her bending over her pillow. No more net-mending for her: for the sake of unroughened hands she had to leave that to Christian and the elders. Yet her work was but poorly paid, and the sale uncertain.

As autumn came in, Christian still gained in physical strength up to near his old level; but Giles declined slowly, Lois grew thin and worn, and Rhoda was losing something of her bloom.

The heart of the old man yearned over the girl, and he knew that his time was but brief. For hours he would sit and watch, fondly and sadly, her dear bent head and her hands playing over her pillow in a patch of light under the pinned-back blind. At last he told Christian his heart, even Christian.

"Take care of my little maid, lad."

He answered "Ay," stupidly.

"For I reckon I may not be here long to care for her myself."

That was all he said at first, but that he would say often for some days, till he was sure that Christian had taken the sense in full, and had failed to quite disbelieve his foreboding.

"Before I lie down in the dark, I would like main to hear you take oath on it, lad."

"I take oaths never," said Christian mechanically.

"Right, right! save in this wise: before God's altar with ring and blessing."

Christian examined his face long to be sure of understanding; then he said, "No."

Giles was disappointed, but spite of the absolute tone he would not take a negative.

"When I am gone to lie yonder east and west, and when some day the wife shall come too to bed with me, how will you take care of my little maid? her and her good name?"

"Oh, God help us!"

"Look you to it, for I doubt she, dear heart, cares for you—now—more than for her mere good name."

"How can she!" he muttered.

Said Giles hazardously: "Once I knew of a girl such as Rhoda; as shy and proud and upright; and a lad she liked,—a lad, say, such as you, Christian, that she liked in her heart more than he guessed. Until he got shamefully mistook, miscalled, mishandled, when she up and kissed him at open noon in the face of all. And then, I mind, at need she followed him over seas, and nought did her good heart think on ill tongues. There is Rhoda all over."

He watched askance to see what the flawed wits could do, and repented of his venture; for it was then Christian so paled and presently so slept.

But Giles tried again.

"Do you mind you of the day of Rhoda's coming? Well, what think you had I at heart then? You never had a guess? You guess now."

Christian said, "I will not."

"Ah! lad, you do. And to me it looked so right and fit and just. That the wife might gainsay, I allowed; but not you. No; and you will not when I tell you all.

"Christian, I do not feel that I have left in me another spring, so while I have the voice I must speak out, and I may not let you be.

"You know of Rhoda's birth: born she was on the same night as our child. As for me, I could not look upon the one innocent but thought on the other would rise, and on the pitiful difference there was. Somehow, the wife regarded it as the child of its father only, I think always, till Rhoda stood before her, the very image of her mother. And with me 'twas just the other way about; and I was main fond of the poor young mother; a sweet, gentle creature she was—a quiet dove, not a brave hawk like little Rhoda. I wished the little thing could have shared with ours heart and home; but that the wife could not have abided, the man being amongst us too. But I went and managed so that none can cast up on Rhoda as a pauper foundling.

"Lad, as I would like you to think well of me when I am gone, God knows I can ill afford to have more than is due stand against me; so look you, lad, I was not such a wastrel as you had cause for thinking. I don't deny what may have been in old days before, but for a good seventeen year when I have gone off for a fling now and then, Rhoda has been the better for it, not I the worse. It has been hard on the wife, and I own I have done a deal of cheating by her and by you too, and have stinted you unfairly. There, there, hold your tongue, and let me start fair again.

"After our child was taken from us, and the poor wife took on so for our blame, it was borne in on me that the rightest amending was not far to seek; and I put it to her at last. But I spoke too soon, when her hurts were quick and raw, and she could not bear it. She was crazy-like then, and I put my notion by for a bit. You see, it was like this: I reckoned the fatal misdoing was unchristian rancour against the father, and care for his deserted child should best express contrition. But the wife couldn't look that way—and she got from the Book awful things to say against the wicked man and his children; and all she repented on was her wrong ways, in neglect of right worship to affront the man; and I think in her heart she cursed him more bitter than ever. A penance it would have been to her to do violence to her griefs and indignations by taking up the child; but it would have righted her as nothing else could, and that I knew, and I looked to bring her to it yet. For me, well, I was on other ground before then, and more than once Rhoda's baby hand had closed upon my finger, ay, upon my heart, though then she was not like my own. And that in a way made me slack to drive against the grain, when with me the point ran smooth and sweet.

"Now, Christian, what came next?"

The old man had been very slow with his tale, watching his listener intently all the while to be sure he heeded and understood. Christian shook his head, but there was very sensible apprehension on his face as he looked to Giles.

"You came, Christian.

"You took the place in heart and home that might have come to be little Rhoda's, as I hoped.

"You came from the sea that had taken our own, and so the wife said it was the hand of God. I thought the hand of God pointed otherwise. Christian, what say you?"

He could answer nothing: Giles waited, but he could not.

"You will take care of my little maid as I want?"

"I cannot! ah, I cannot!"

"All these years Rhoda has wanted a home as I think because of you; and because of you I could not hope for the wife's heart to open to her."

"She should hate me! you should!" said Christian. His face was scared.

"You can make ample amends—oh! ample; and Rhoda will count the wants of her youth blessed that shall lay the rest of her days to your keeping. She will—Christian, are you so blind?—she will.

"Ah, dear lad! I got so well contented that the wife had had her way and had taken you, when I saw what the just outcome should be; and saw her shaping in the dark towards the happy lot of the sweet little slip she ignored. Long back it began, when you were but a little chap. Years before you set eyes on her, Rhoda had heard of you.

"In the end I could fit out no plan for you to light on her; and a grubby suitor was bargaining for her, so I had to make a risky cast. She was to enter as a passing stranger I had asked to rest. The wife fell on her neck, before a word. Well, well, what poor fools we had both been!"

"Christian, why do you say No?"

"I wish her better."

"But she loves you! I swear she loves you! And I, O good Lord! I have done my best to set her affections on you. How shall I lie still in the grave while her dear heart is moaning for its hurt, and 'tis I that have wrought it."

To a scrupulous nature the words of Giles brought cruel distress. Christian's eyes took to following Rhoda, though never a word of wooing went to her. In the end he spoke.

"Dear Rhoda," he said, and stopped; but instantly she looked up startled. His eyes were on the ground.

"Rhoda, I love you dearly. Will you be my wife?"

She grew white as death, and stayed stone-still, breathless. Then he looked at her, stood up, and repeated resolutely: "Rhoda, dearest, will you be my wife?"

She rose to confront him, and brought out her answer:

"No."

He stared at her a moment in stupid bewilderment.

"You will not be my wife?" he said.

She put out all her strength to make the word clear and absolute, and repeated: "No."

His face grew radiant; he caught her in his arms suddenly and kissed her, once, twice.

"O my sister!" he cried, "my dear sister!"

She did not blush under his kisses: she shut her eyes and held her breath when his eager embrace caught her out of resistance. But when it slackened she thrust him back with all her might, broke free, and with a low cry fled away to find solitude, where she might sob and sob, and wrestle out her agony, and tear her heart with a name—that strange name, that woman's name, "Diadyomene."

She had his secret, she only, though it was nought but a name and some love titles and passionate entreaties that his ravings had given into her safe keeping.

On the morrow Christian's boat lay idle by the quay. Before dawn moved he had gone.

"I think—I think you need not fear for him," said Rhoda, when the day closed without him. "I think he may be back to-morrow."

"You know what he is about—where he has gone, child?"

First she said "Yes," and then she said "No."

In the dusk she crept up to Giles. Against his breast she broke into pitiful weeping.

"Forgive me! forgive me! I said 'No' to him."

CHAPTER X

With its splendour and peace unalterable, the great sanctuary enclosed them.

Face to face they stood, shattered life and lost soul. Diadyomene tried to smile, but her lips trembled; she tried to greet him with the old name Diadyomenos, but it fell imperfect. And his grey eyes addressed her too forcibly to be named. What was in them and his face to make her afraid? eyes and face of a lover foredoing speech.

The eager, happy trouble of the boy she had beguiled flushed out no more; nay, but he paled; earnest, sad, indomitable, the man demanded of her answering integrity. Uncomprehended, the mystery of pain in embodied power stood confronting the magic of the sea, and she quailed.

"Agonistes, Agonistes!" she panted, "now I find your name: it is Agonistes!"

But while he did not answer, her old light came to her for reading the tense inquiry of his eyes. Did they demand acknowledgment of her defeat and his supremacy? No, she would not own that; he should not know.

"And have you feared to keep what you got of the sea? And have you flung it away, as I counselled when last you beheld me?"

The strong, haggard face never altered for contest. He asked slowly:

"Was it a vision of Diadyomene that rose up to the waves through the shadow of a fisher's boat?"

With an effort she set her eyes at his defiantly.

"It was not I. I? For what cause?"

"He called you."

"I come for no man's call."

Against her will her eyes fell.

"Look at me, Diadyomene; for an evil dream haunts me, and your eyes have got it hid."

"An evil dream!"

She laughed, but her breath came quick as again their looks encountered.

What she met in the steadfast grey eyes brought terror gathering to her own. She shuddered and covered her face.

142

"An evil dream haunts *me,* and *your* eyes have got it hid."

He watched, dazed, and muttered: "You—you."

"What is it?—what is it?" she cried. "Why have you brought it with you out of season? It is like an air that I cannot breathe. Take it away!"

Never before had she shown so human a weakness, nor had she ever shown so womanly fair. Her clear eyes dilated, her whole face quivered, and for an instant a shadow of vague wistfulness crossed her fear. Her lover's heart beat free of dreams, for a passion of tenderness responded to her need.

"Ah, Diadyomene, no! Can you so dream it, when, to keep all evil from you, I would, God willing, enter hell?"

"May be," she whispered, "it is what you call hell I enter, every year once, when my dream comes."

Appalled he heard. "You shall not, Diadyomene, you shall not! Come to me, call me, and what heart of man can brave, by my soul I will, and keep you safe."

She found his eyes again, within them only love, and she rallied.

"It is only a dream," she said. "And yet to escape it I would give up many choice moments of glorious sea life."

She eyed him hard, and clenched her hands. "I would give up," she said, "the strongest desire my heart now holds; ay, in the dear moment of its fulfilment, I would give up even that, if so a certain night of the year might pass ever dreamless and untroubled."

"So would not I! though I think my dream cannot be less terrible than yours; though I know my desire cannot be less dear. Diadyomene, what is the desire of your heart?"

She would not say; and she meant with her downcast, shy eyes to mislead him. But in vain: too humble was he to presume.

"Diadyomene, what is your dream?"

"I cannot tell," she said, "for it passes so that my brain holds but an echo of it, and my heart dread. And what remains of it cannot be told, for words are too poor and feeble to express it."

He saw her thinking, sighing, and shuddering.

"How near is its coming?" he asked, and but half heeding she told, counting by the terms of the moon.

"Agonistes, how I know not, my deep, strong love of the sea grows somewhat faint when the hour draws near to dream; and the land, the poor, hard, unsatisfying land, grows some degrees dearer. Ah! but I loathe it after, when my life again beats strong and true with the pulse of the deep. Keep you far from me then, lest I hate you—yes, even you—hate you to death."

"Rather bid me here, to watch out the night with you."

"I forbid it!" she said, suddenly fierce and wary. "Take heed! Wilful, deliberate trespass against my express will shall find no pity, no pardon."

Quick she saw that, intemperate, she had startled her prey; therefore she amended, smiling sadly.

"See you how those diverse tides sway me even now. Agonistes, were you not of the land—did you share the sea—then may be—ah, ah—

"I will try to tell you. An awful sense of desolation falls, for I feel dry earth underfoot, and thin air, and I hear the sea moaning for me, but turn where I will I cannot see nor reach it: it lies beyond a lost path, and the glories, blisses, and strengths it gives me wither and die. And then horrors of the land close round me.

"What are they? I know not; they whirl past me so that their speed conceals them; yet, as streaks, are they hideous and ghastly. And I hear fearful sounds of speech, but not one distinct, articulate word. And in my dream I know that if any one stays, stands, confronts me, to be seen fully in the eyes and heard out clear from the din, all my joy of the sea would lie dead for ever, and the very way back would vanish."

Christian had his own incomparable vision of the magic of the sea to oppose and ponder.

"Ah! you cannot comprehend, for I tell of it by way of the senses, and they are without, but this is within: in my veins, my breath, my fibres of life. It is I—me."

"I can, ah! I can."

"Yet the dear heart of the sea holds me fast through all; with imperious kindness it seizes my will when my love grows slackest, and draws me out of the shallows; and down, and down I drift, like weed."

"Diadyomene, have you never defied your fear, and kept from sleep, and kept from the sea?"

Her voice sank. "If I did—my dream might—come true.

"Agonistes, what I saw in your eyes was—I doubted—my dream—coming true.

"No; I will not look again."

Christian's voice was as low and shaken as hers. "What was there?" he said.

Again and again she gathered her breath for speech, yet at last was scarce audible.

"A horror—a living human body—tortured with fire and scourge—flayed."

She lifted one glance and took the imprint of a strange tranced face, bloodless as death, void of speculation. Prone she sank to the edge of the altar rock, for such passions leapt up and grappled in desperate conflict as dissolved her strength under exquisite throes.

She never raised her head, till, after long wrestle, malice—strong, full-grown malice—recovered and stood up triumphant over all. And not one word all that while had come from her lover.

There lay he, his bright head low within reach of her hand. His tranquil ease, his quiet breath, flouted her before she saw that his eyes were closed in real sleep. His eyes were closed.

She sprang up, stung, willing to kill; her wicked heart laughed, gratified then with the doings of men.

How grand the creature lay!

She stood to feast her eyes on the doomed body. The placid composure of the sleeper, of serene countenance, of slack limbs, touched her as excellent comedy. But it exasperated her also to the verge of a shrieking finish.

She ached with a savage thirst in all her members; feet and hands and lips parched in imperious desires to trample, to smite, to bite her resentful hatred into the piece of flesh that mocked her control. The quiet sway of life within his ribs provoked her, with each slow breath he drew, to rend it from him.

She turned away hastily from temptation to so meagre a revenge; for his spirit must first be crushed and broken and rent, justly to compensate for insolent offence. "He cannot escape, for his heart is in my hand already," she said.

Ripples of jasper and beryl closed over her swift descent and shimmered to smooth. Lone in these splendid fittings for sepulture lay recumbent a make of earth meet to accomplish its void destiny.

Ripples of jasper and beryl broke from her slow ascent as a reflex current swept her back.

The mask of sleep lay over his face; though she peered intent, it would yield nothing, nothing. A want and a dread that struggled together for birth troubled the cold sea nature. Strong they thrust towards the light, as her mind recalled the intolerable speech of his eyes and his altered face. So near she bent that the warmth of his breath reached her lips. She shrank back, quivering, and crouched, rocked with passionate sighs.

"But I hate, I hate!" she moaned; for a contrary impulse bade her lay upon his breast her hand, and on his lips hers, and dare all her asking from his eyes. A disloyal hand went out and hovered over his heart. She plucked it back, aware of a desperate peril, vague, awful, alluring to destruction, like a precipice yawning under night.

His hair was yellow-brown, matching the mellow sands of the undersea; it ran into crisp waves, and over the brow curved up to crest like a breaker that stayed unbroken. No such hair did the sea grow—no hair, no head, that often her hand had so wanted to handle; ay, graciously—at first—to hold the crispness, to break the crest; and ever because she dared not did fierceness for tearing arise. So slight an inclination, ungratified, extended to vast dimensions, and possessed her entire. And she called it hate. How long, how long, she complained, shall I bear with this thirst? Yet if long, as long shall the quenching be. He shall but abandon his soul, and no doubt shall restrain me from touching as I will.

She covered her face from the light of day, for she contemplated an amazement to nature: deadly hate enfolded in the arms of strong love.

When the tide brimmed up and kissed him awake, Diadyomene was away.

Another manner of Diadyomene vexed her lover's next coming: she was mockery incarnate, and unkind; for she would not condescend to his limitations, nor forsake a golden spongy nest two fathoms and more below breath. Yet her laughter and her eyes summoned him down, and he, poor fool, displayed before her derision his deficiency, slow to learn that untiring submission to humiliation would win no gracious reward at last. And the young witch was as slow to learn that no exasperation she could contrive would sting him into amorous close for mastery.

Christian was no tempered saint. Diadyomene gained a barren, bitter victory, for he fled.

At sundown a monitress, mounting the night tower, by a loophole of the stair looking down on the great rock saints, spied a figure kneeling devoutly. When the moon rose late the same kept vigil still. In the wan of dawn the same, overtaken by sleep, lay low against the feet of St. Margaret.

Though Christian slept, he heard the deep bell voices of the three. Articulate they grew, and entered the human soul with reproof and exhortation and promise. He woke; and intrepid rose to face the unruly clamours of nature, for the sake of the cast soul of that most beautiful body, Diadyomene.

Vain was the encounter and the passionate spiritual wooing. Diadyomene would not hear, at heart fiercely jealous because no such ardent entreaty had all her beauty and charms ever evoked. She was angered when he would not take dismissal.

"Never, never," she said, "has any creature of the sea thwarted me so and lived; and you, you dare! Hear now. There, and there, and there, stand yet your silly inscriptions. Cancel them, for earnest that never again shall mention of those monstrous impossible three trouble my ear."

"No."

"Hear yet. Cancel them, and here, perpetual and irrevocable, shall right of freedom be yours, and welcome. Leave them intact, and I swear you shall not get hence scatheless."

"Can you mean this, Diadyomene?"

"Ah, so I because I relented once, you presume. See, and if those three can deliver you whole, them will I worship with you."

And it came to pass that Christian carried home the best member that he possessed broken, for fulfilment of Diadyomene's promise.

He doubted she had divined a profane desire, and covertly rewarded it.

CHAPTER XI

One there was who watched Christian with curious intentness, who, when the plight of the Alien staled on general interest, was singular by persistent advances: his old rival, Philip. Elder by two years, the tyrant of Christian's early day had he been; between them drawn battle raged while the one had yet advantage by a head, soon to alter when the other came stepping up from the ranks of boyhood to match with men, and to win final supremacy at every point. Latent challenge had not worn out of meeting glances even before Rhoda's coming accentuated an antagonism based primarily on temperament and type. When the world turned upon Christian, Philip's forwardness was accountable enough; when the world veered, his position might fairly have been backward.

And truly slowest he was to get conviction of the perfect cure that had befallen the alien. Though for proof he drew near, venturous to tempt a sparkle out of the quenched firebrand, his closest approach could discover none; nay, all lively mislike and jealousy seemed gone with the missing core; old remembered heats kept but indifferent life, and every trace of arrogance had vanished quite. To such an one Philip could be generous at no great cost were it not for Rhoda's preference.

In a character of but poor stuff some strands of good quality ran hid, and a love-liking for the shy, fierce, young girl was strengthening into better worth under reverses. That Christian stood first in her regard he knew well, for she made it abundantly clear, with a courage and frankness that brought comment. "Not maidenly!" retorted Philip to his mother, "then is maidendom the sorrier." He came to respect even the innocent vice in her that woke ever to affront him. That his passion could survive rages of vanity, often and deep wounded, proved its vitality and worth.

Slowly also and fitfully Philip came to think that Christian was no rival lover; that he never did, that now he never would, regard Rhoda as more than a sister. For his own gain he might be generous; yet among meaner motives stood an honest endeavour to deserve well of the girl who loved Christian, overbearing old antipathies; nor should it be to his demerit that he was unconstrained by any touch of compunction: an amended version of Christian, harmless, luckless, well-disposed, forbade any such disrespect to past measures.

While many wondered that he should be so considerate of the alien, Rhoda hardened her heart. Even greater than unquenchable resentment was her distress of grief and shame because Christian was tamed. Unwittingly, Philip himself afforded demonstration. No wonder his aim miscarried, and he had ground to complain bitterly of signal injustice.

Once, at twilight, as Rhoda turned towards the quay, looking for Christian and his rent nets, Philip stayed her, refusing rebuff, and sought to turn her home again with an awkward lie. She caught him out and stared. Then sudden terror started her past him, and winged her along the shore towards men clustering thick. But Philip was speedy, overtook her, and in desperation held her by main force.

"Rhoda," he entreated, "you must not go. It is not Christian, I say. It is not Christian."

She was struggling with all her might, beating at him, biting at his hands.

"I will go, I will! Christian, Christian! Let me go! Ah, coward!"

"It is not Christian," and he named another to pacify her. "Not Christian."

She did not believe him; as he had caught her she had heard a cry that maddened her so that her brain could take hold of no reason. She was sure that Christian was being done to death after some horrible fashion.

No; thank God, no. She saw him suddenly safe and free; and she fell to sobbing and trembling pitifully, so that Philip without offence for a moment held her in his arms. She saw him coming, one high, fair head conspicuous above the rest; she saw him looking aside, turning aside, when instinctively she knew that what he beheld was a thief bound and beaten according to the custom and law of the fishers. As he halted, overlooking the circle, she read by nods exchange of question and answer. And then on he came again. One or two turned and looked after him: that she noted.

She was moaning and rocking for pain, though she did not know it; she was white and cold, for fear so held her heart's blood that not even the agony of shame she felt for Christian could urge any to her face. She tried to go forward, but only got free from Philip to find she could barely stand, and must hold by the sea-wall. So Christian's face came near to be read, and lo! it was utterly blank: no anger, no pain, no shame, altered it by a line; but the lips were grey, and as he set eyes on Philip quickly he crossed himself. Then he saw Rhoda, and oh! the comfort to her of his strong, quiet grasp, and his eyes, and his voice.

Throbbing yet from Rhoda's warm weight, struck with vivid misdoubt and fear of the alien, Philip forgot control, and the natural man looked out for one moment with glance of hot challenge at his born rival. He met no response: Christian regarded him with resolute mild eyes, without jealousy, or resentment, or any perplexity, till he grew confounded and a little ashamed.

"Take me home," entreated Rhoda; and Christian, without a question or a comment, took her hand to lead. For one dreadful moment, breathless to Rhoda, he looked back and stood. Against his palm hers lay listening: it was mute, to her nerved apprehension telling nothing. Then home.

What could the loon mean with his signing? thought Philip, shaken by a doubt. Nothing, nothing—blank madness. Nevertheless, his sudden, shameful fear of the Alien did not soon lie down to sleep again.

A further proving awaited Christian and Philip. To Giles came Rhoda.

"He says—Philip," she began, choking, "that except he—he—shall excel in the contests to-day, Christian will be wanted for saving to our fleet its lead on the coast. Oh, he must not!—he shall not! And he said, with his hateful airs, that he would do his best—to spare Christian. And he said, if he failed at that, he could yet promise that none should offend Christian with impunity while he stood by—he—he." There a wretched laugh sobbed and strangled her.

"I said our Christian would not—no—not for love, nor fear, nor profit, for he hinted that. I said: with what face dare such asking approach? what part has he with the fleet? Never goes he aboard any boat, and never a soul comes aboard his, neither do any dredge alongside him and his ill-luck. The Alien they call him ever. Him—him their best, their very best, having used worse than the lowest outcast, they desire as their champion at need. Are devils so vile and shameless? Oh! he must not. Forbid it you, and he will not disobey."

The old man shook his head.

"He is no child—even now. He will look at me with those eyes of his, and ask why—and then am I done."

Later, Rhoda ventured down to Christian, mending his dredge on the quay, and persuaded him away. In vain; for some waylaid him, and there in her hearing got his promise, in swimming and rowing to do his best for the credit of the fleet. Rhoda dared only press his hand and look entreaty while his answer hung. A dazed look came and passed. Afterwards, his face of mild inquiry daunted remonstrance, as Giles foretold.

Philip fetched him away eventually, but had not even the favour of a look from Rhoda. She kept down her head, biting back tears and words of rage and grief.

"I think he means well—does Philip," sighed Giles unhappily.

Lois said bitterly: "Like Samson blind, he goes to make sport for the Philistines."

Rhoda broke into passionate weeping.

"Ah, ah!" she cried, "it is unbearable. At every turn strangers I saw—who have come and heard—who will see, and our Christian will hear—alone, all alone. Oh, would that I were a brother to stand by him! Philip mean well! He prides himself on it, he parades it as a virtue, and to himself pretends that he does not hate. But once, he forgot, and looked—and I saw—hate—hate and fear; And I know, though he do contrary, that his blood will dance for joy at any affront to Christian. I know—and he takes Christian out to show!"

Giles got on his feet.

"If I am ever to tread the old quay, it may well be to-day."

The remonstrance of Lois lacked vigour. He took help of Rhoda's shoulder the length of the downward street, and then shambled off alone to Christian's protection.

One, two, three hours passed, and twilight. Then back they came, Christian's ample strength charged with the old man's weight. Giles swore within his beard in his way that the women knew.

"He takes his way for no asking or need of mine," he declared gruffly; "and he might use his strength to better purpose."

"Christian outdone!"

"No," Christian said, "I think not. No, none say so."

He stretched wearily, sighed, and, laying his head down on his arms, slept profoundly. They exchanged woful looks.

"Poor lad, poor lad!" said the old man brokenly.

"Ah, yes; he bested the lot: in rowing hardly, in swimming easily. Oh, don't ask! it was pretty bad. Bad! Oh, good Lord, but it makes one man sweat again to look back on it.

"Oh! God damn their greedy eyes! Yet some few of our lot turned fair ashamed of their own handiwork; and when one brute of the Islands said—no matter what, but his own fellows muttered shame—and Philip would have struck him, yonder poor fool knocked up his arm quick.

"Yes, Philip, girl! and I tell you I saw no hate: and he looked long and close too."

Stirless in sleep, Christian offered remonstrance to nerves that quivered under the halting tale.

"The worst? no, the worst was after the young fools in their cups got heady. And in the end—well, the end of all was that Philip floored his man. And that should have been Christian's business, and he would not stir, though I nudged him to be up and at such foul jests. 'I have heard nothing unfit,' he says. And I wished I were underground. I never want to foot the .quay again. Poor lad! ay, and poor spirit! the very man of him has got flawed."

"No," said Lois painfully, "however it came he did worthily, up to his name."

Giles closed his mouth, but shook his head mournfully, and Rhoda drew to him.

This fell when late gales were closing the season to the coral fishers. Little more than a week after, Christian came back with his broken arm.

Then want came looming straight ahead. Every due was paid, but none knew by what hard stinting, for resolute pride uttered no plea, and hid every sign. That the waning life of Giles should suffer from no lack, the others fared the harder. A haggard Christian, befitting a chastened lot, drew no comment; and if Rhoda grew a little pale, and Lois shrunk and grey, known cares they had for allowance, barring any guess at scant bread.

The hardest of trials to a willing, strong man met Christian when, re-knit and sound, he offered for work and found that no man would hire him. His strange ill-luck cut him off from fellowship, so strong was the suspicion that a malignant influence had marked him down jealously. The only one to withstand the general verdict, to link him in, to per-suade some favour to his hands, was the unrewarded Philip, whose best endeavour but won for him few, and brief, and ill-paid spells of labour. A many there were who would not take his services at a gift, and he knew it. Refuse, stranded out of touch of the human tide, he hung idle on the quay, through shortening days from morn to night, resolutely pa-tient of the leaden hours and of the degradation on his famous strength.

Lois foresaw that bitter need might drive him away at last, but as yet she could not bid him go, for Giles was slowly dying.

CHAPTER XII

Philip sought out Christian secretly, to hint that on a venture three gold pieces might be his. Christian understood him well enough.

In the veiled language of the coast, a venture signified honourable service for brave men, though the law of the land held otherwise, and rewarded it as felony. A well-knit League carried on far and near a contraband trade in the lives of proscribed men, and even the scrupulous honesty of Christian brought no reluctance to engage.

"When, and with whom?" he asked.

"To-morrow, you and I," said Philip, and watched him anxiously.

"Then are you of the League?" said Christian indifferently, nettling the other, still in the young pride of a desired association. The Alien at his best, he knew, would never have been reckoned fit; for though he excelled in strength, he lacked head.

"You and I together," he said, "are fairly equal to any other three, and so can our gains be the larger."

Yet Christian would not readily close on the rich relief. He fixed on the other a thoughtful eye, pondering a question of fairness that might not be imparted. Philip flushed a little.

"I am answerable to the League," he said nervously; "and though from outsiders we exact oaths, I will take it upon me to accept as sufficient your bare word for good faith and secrecy."

This was no more than Christian's credit had established; for from boyhood, under the strict schooling of Lois, he had kept to his word as sacredly as others to their oaths, and from pride and a scruple had ever refused to be sworn.

Long seemed the pause and the trying scrutiny before Christian sighed and said, "So be it."

"And secrecy?"

"I promise secrecy."

"And you will not refuse a strict promise to obey orders—mine?"

A vague foreboding warned Christian to stay, but reason could not sufficiently uphold it against his dire need of the gold. He promised.

"I take it," said Philip carelessly, "that your boat would be the easier to handle. Mine is over heavy for two."

"I cannot risk what is not wholly mine."

"The League makes good all loss. And remember," he looked away, and his voice had a strange note, "if we do not come back—for long—or ever—the League sees to it that our folk do not want."

Christian looked at him hard.

"Agreed," he said first; and then, "You think that likely?"

"A venture is a venture; and, well, I may say that two ventures have miscarried, so many and brisk are the chasers; and I know of some who have fought shy of this one. I volunteered," he said with pride.

So they went their ways, Philip bidding his conscience lie still and mute, Christian questioning his.

Save Giles, never had any man put out in that boat with the Alien. As the two slid out under early night, Philip looked at him, wondering if his wits were sound enough to tell him this, himself misliking the instance overmuch now. The sea was black and sullen, and the wind chill; Christian, silent and indifferent, was no heartening mate; and the shadow of night brought out a lurid streak in the venture that viewed under daylight had been but dull and faint.

The stealthy boat crept on till midnight; now and then from the cusp of a bay floated out the faint cry of a quail. Then thrice it sounded, when the boat swooped in, touched, and with a third aboard, sprang away swift as a fishing gull.

About to the west, then, Christian steered as Philip gave word; still west and west. He did not scan the stranger with natural interest, nor had he yet asked one question on their goings, though they were stretching for a coast known to him by fatal influence. When the very roar of evil waters sounded, and through it the first expostulation of a buoy bell, Philip's scrutiny could still detect no reluctance.

Oh! fain now would he see a touch of human infirmity for fellowship; night had entered his blood, and shocks of horrid fear coursed; too stark and dreadfully mute was the figure at the helm for him to be void of apprehension. And the terrors of the sinister place, that his venture was to set at nought, according to a daylight mind, came beating in against unstable defences, entered, and took possession.

Christian stooped over the gunwale, peering into the dark water. At that, Philip's hand went searching hurriedly about the bow, and that he sought was missing. He braced himself and approached the Alien.

"Christian, has she never a twig of rowan at her bows?"

The face that turned he could not see to read. "No," was the curt answer, and shaken through, he drew off with doubled thumbs.

Too late now he doubted Christian to be no tool for handling with impunity. And worse he dreaded, out of a dark teeming with possibilities, dreadful to human flesh and human spirit. His hair rose, and he flung prayers to the hierarchy of heaven, but chiefly to those three—St. Mary, St. Margaret, and St. Faith. Comfort it was to draw to the side of one who abode, as he himself, within the limits of the five human senses. The quiet voice of the Adventurer rallied him.

"What goes wrong?"

"We bear no rowan, nor leaf, nor berry."

"Rowan! for protection against evil spirits?"

"Ah! name them not. Not here and now. Rather turn your thumbs against them, and watch him."

"Him! your chosen mate?"

"God forgive me, and help us—yes. Sir, I tell you, laughter here is more than folly—it is wickedness. No, I will not be questioned how and why. There—look there!"

He grasped the sceptic's arm and pointed; Christian again had suddenly leaned down to peer over the boat's side.

"What does he see?"

Philip's teeth chattered. "God knows, I dare not think."

He crowded sail recklessly, and the boat leapt along, quivering like a thing in fear. At speed they fled on further west, till the Sinister buoys were all passed by, and the Land's End drew up and turned behind them. Then Philip, with a heart lighter by some degrees, hove to, close furled, to wait and watch through the chill, long hours, till nearing dawn turned them back to the safe desolation of the evil place.

Daylight better than dark speech declared the three to each other. The Adventurer considered well the men charged with his life and fortunes. Of a splendid make they were, both above the common in stature and strength, and well favoured in singular contrast. A practised student of his kind could read lines of weakness, and some feminine virtues also, in the dark, oval face with luminous, fine eyes, and a mouth too fully perfect

for a man, and could read on the face from the resolute north a square
threat of obstinacy showing from the bones out, and daring and truth in the
grey eyes, deep set, and from brow to chin every imprint of integrity.
Both faces were set and haggard, and their eyes encountered with a
sombre disaffection that augured but ill for success. Strife was latent.

Christian's glance rested on the Adventurer, unhooded to the morning light, and he guessed him, and knew him by silver mane and black
brows an old lion-lord of a famous herd. The ray of recognition was
caught and weighed. "He has not been trusted, yet his looks are fit," ran
the old man's thoughts. He weighed Philip, whose features twitched,
whose hands were nervous, who eyed his fellow with an uncertain
glance, wavering at a return impassive as stone. Without hesitation he
questioned for clearance.

"Is all well—so far?"

"Ay—so far?"

"At your discretion I would hear how our chances lie, and on what
side peril. To a landsman we carry on in an aimless fashion."

Philip looked at him straight enough, then furtively towards Christian. The stranger dropped his voice.

"Is danger yonder?"

Philip did not answer him, and strengthened in misdoubt, he spoke
with a note of authority.

"I would know your plans."

"You shall," said Philip, but still he looked at Christian, and found it
hard to begin. He took heart of wine.

"Hearken—you also, Christian.

"Sir, my undertaking is to put you aboard a foreigner, due to pass
with her consorts off the Land's End, may be this day, or to-morrow at
latest, whose part is but to contrive so that darkness may cover this bit of
contraband trade.

"Your flight discovered will for sure have brought an embargo on all
the coast. Not a sail will be out, but chasers on the watch. Ashore now,
not a chance were possible; but we took wing betimes; and here may we
bide under daylight, and at night make again for the Land's End to
watch our chance."

"Go on. This contrivance is too incredibly bald to suffice. How, then, when presently a patrol sails round yonder head?"

"May Heaven forfend!"

"Heaven! are you mad? Is all our security to be the grant by Heaven of a miracle?"

"First, sir, I will tell you that we are like enough to be unharried; for it cannot be in mortal reckoning that we should dare here, since this place is a death-trap to be given wide berth in winter gales."

"The very place to seek men fugitive and desperate."

"By your leave, sir, I came into this venture as a volunteer, and not from desperation.

"The special danger of these coasts you do not know. Our winter storms, sudden and fierce, strike here at their hardest. Learned men say that high ranges leagues off over sea make a funnel to set them here. We fishers have another way of thinking—no matter what. But 'tis wide known that there is no record of any boat caught in a winter burst within sound of these breakers living to boast of it."

"Is, then, the favour of Heaven also to be engaged to preserve from storm as from chase?"

Philip, tongue and throat, was dry, and he drank again deeply.

"You tell me of risks that I cannot bring myself to believe a volunteer would engage; not though, as I hear, he doubled his price."

Wine and resentment mounted a flush.

"You do ill, sir, to fleer at a man who for your service risks freedom, life—ay, more than life—but that you would not believe; for you laughed, under night even, you laughed!"

"By heavens! every look of a death-trap comes out on your own showing; and except you show me the key to unlock it, I myself will hazard the forcing; I and your mate yonder, who well I see is not in your confidence, whose face tells that he has no liking for you and your doings."

Christian turned away and made no response.

"For God's sake, sir," whispered Philip then, "have patience, or you ruin all!"

"Let be that wine and speak out."

"Drink you, Christian."

He refused. Philip fetched breath for a plunge.

"Bear me out, Christian, when I say that one there is who can do what none other living can—and will."

Christian waited with a face of stone.

"Who can carry us safe through the reefs. Christian—this—you promised—you must undertake this.

"Look you, we may never be driven to it; a far ship could not easily make us out against this broken background.

"Christian, not another soul knows or shall know. Sir, you can tell him that the League had not even a guess. I stood out for that.

"You asked nothing. Had you but cared to ask, I would have told you earlier. You may have guessed; you cannot deny you are able. Sir, he is; and when I asked his services, he promised—without reserve he promised.

"Christian, you never have failed of your word; all your life that has been your pride, and so have I relied on it—a man's life relies on it."

Christian kept an averted face, and stared down into the water.

"You can—I know you can!"

"I can."

"And you will—to your promise I trusted."

"I promised, and I will."

Philip grasped his hand in cordial gratitude; Christian suffered it, but his face was sullen. The Adventurer saw sweat standing on the brow of each, so that he wondered at what were behind.

Philip turned with a brightened eye.

"Now, sir, you may see that our chances are not so desperate, since, from storm or chase, we can put to safe haven beyond the reefs, to wait or dodge; or at worst, to get ashore and take to the hills—a put back, but to you a good exchange for four walls. Only I have a thing to ask of you, sir, come good or ill: that you will never breathe to a soul of this way of escape."

The Adventurer eyed him with something of distrust still, while he fingered his beard thoughtfully and smiled, half sneering.

"I understand—you would preserve a monopoly, and continue a good trade. But it looks to me that you have done some cheating by your mate, that might make him decline partnership and seek his own market."

"By heavens! you are over ready with your imputations!" said Philip, angry. "The Alien there is welcome to make what profit he can for me. Never with my goodwill shall I be here again. For why I undertook it, I had my own good reasons, which concern you not at all. But I will tell you that I know not of another man who would dare partnership with the Alien—ay, ask him, and he will not deny it; or who would put body and soul in jeopardy in this place."

The Adventurer turned to Christian, smiling, courting friendly intelligence.

"You, it appears, have put body and soul in jeopardy, and know the place; and body and soul are none the worse."

Without any answer, Christian looked at him, and colour ebbed from his face. Philip touched for warning, and with lifted finger indicated the want, half guessed already by that fixed, blank gaze.

"Answer only at your pleasure, but for my soul's salvation I do desire to know what threats it here."

For the moment Philip did not suspect derision. Discreetly he told of the fatal tradition, that the settled conviction of generations had brought men fatally to uphold and abet. So much of reason he had discovered for himself, and he desired that Christian should hear.

The work was taken out of his hands by a skilled master. The reverend superstition was subjected to all the disintegrating forces that human scepticism can range; and with cold reason, logic, and analogy, went such charm of courteous tolerance, and wit, and wise and simple exposition, as tempered the mordant touch of lurking ridicule. He was but for pastime, trying his practised touch upon two young fools. Half scared, half fascinated and admiring, Philip responded; Christian stayed sullen and silent.

CHAPTER XIII

At its nearest lay the Isle Sinister under noon. The Adventurer sighed for the land as, cold and uneasy, he couched for needful sleep. Philip lay stretched beside him, Christian, according to his own preference, taking the first watch. Out of new bravado, Philip passed on to Christian a muttered question: Could he now carry them in and land them on the very Isle?

Like a bolt came Christian's answer: "Drowned and damned both shall you be before I will."

Philip rose up, startled by the answer and the unexpected intimacy it acknowledged. But the voice had been of level quiet, and the Alien's face showed no anger. The Adventurer watched with a sardonic smile; and Philip, forcing a show of unconcern that he did not feel, muttered a word of madness and dropped back. For a while resurgent terrors thwarted sleep; but the quiet breathing of his neighbour, the quiet out-look of the Alien, told on his shaken nerves, and slumber overtook him. Christian stayed waking alone.

Ah! the relief. He stood up to take free, deep breath, and stretched his great limbs. Long, intently, with shaded eyes, he stared towards the Isle Sinister. Ah! nothing, and well nothing. Could she trust that he meditated no trespass? that he would allow none? Could she deem that he offered no insane resentment against her severity? A sea-gull flapped close past his head, but was mute.

He turned and looked down on the sleepers, and his face, illegible for many a day, showed bitter resentment and scorn. Shamefully had he been beguiled, trapped, bound by a promise; and wanton goading had not lacked, all but intolerable. Fools! their lives were in his hand; and he was awake. Awake, as for months he had not been; his pulses were leaping to full heart-beats, there was stir in his brain; and therewith, dislike and contempt exciting, the keen human passion of hate lay torpid no longer; it moved, it threatened to run riot.

Who dare claim loyal service from him? Philip! One boat had been familiar with these reefs: somewhere in the past murder rested una-venged. Philip!

161

In the deep water that the boat shadowed a darkness slid, catching his eye. He peered, but it was gone. Before, and not once only, had an impression seized him, by deliberate sight not verified, that a sinister attendance lurked below. Now unconstrained he could watch.

Great dread possessed him. Storm and chase were light perils, not to be compared with her displeasure, her mere displeasure, irrespective of how she might exert it. With heavy grief had he borne late estrangement, and her severe chastisement of offence. Were his limbs but for his own service, lightly, so soon as they were able, had he risked them again to worship his love and seek grace. Alas! she could not know that loyal, and strong, and tender his devotion held; she would but see an insolent and base return, meriting final condemnation. Helpless rages of grief urged him to break from all bonds, and plunge headlong to engage her wrath or her mercy. He cast on the sleepers then a thought, with ugly mirth, mocking the control of his old enemy in his heart.

How would she take the forfeit! With her rocks and waves she had broken him once, and the surrender of all his bones to them in despair he had firmly contemplated; but human flesh and spirit shrank from horrors unknown, that she might summon for vengeance. Could he but see what lurked below.

Spite of the ripe mutiny in him he minded his watch, and swept the horizon momently with due attention. The day altered as the slow hours dragged: a thin film travelled up the clear sky; the sun took a faint double halo, while the sea darkened to a heavy purple. He knew the signs: small chance was there now of a stormless night. Not two hours of full daylight were left when below the sun rose a sail. His hopes and fears took little hold on it, for as yet it was but a speck; and he knew that before it could close darkness would be upon them, and belike storm also.

With a desperate remedy before his eyes a devil's word was in his ears: the League makes good all loss. Foul play? Nay, but had not the League by Philip played him foul first, with injury not to be made good. And those for whose sake he had owed regard for his wretched life would be bettered by his loss.

When Philip rose up from sleep a blackness stood upon the distant sea, threatening the sun; the chill wind had dropped, but a heavy, sullen swell insisted of a far-off tyranny advancing. To him no sail showed, but

Christian flung him word of it, and his sinking heart caught at high hope.

Then, since their vigil was soon to pass, Philip dared greatly; for he bade Christian sleep, set hand himself to sail and tiller, glided in past the buoys, and rocked at trespass.

"It is safer so, should the haze part," he said, but his voice shook.

The Alien said never a word; each looked the other hard in the eyes, paling.

"The League makes good all loss," said Philip, low. "And if so be that only some forgery of a loss can cover a fair claim, you may count on my—what you will—as you please."

Christian refused hearing. Flung down for unattainable sleep he lay stretched, covering his head to inspect by the light of darkness his wrongs, and Philip's treason, that left to him nothing but a choice of transgression.

The blackness stood higher and crept on. The sun was captured, shorn, disgraced, and sent bald on his way; a narrow streak of red bleeding upon the waters died slowly; all else was slate-black. Above the gloom of the cliffs the sky showed blanched, clear and pale. Ghostly white the sea-birds rose and fell. The tide was rising, deepening the note of the surf; between the warders white columns leapt up with great gasps.

It was Rhoda's name that Philip whispered over, to strengthen his heart at the perilous outlook. The make of his love had a certain pride in overbearing such weak scruples as a tough conscience permitted. Half he feared that the Alien's poor wits had yet not recognised the only path left open by a skilful provision; for there he lay motionless, with the slow breath of untroubled sleep. He would not fear him; with Rhoda's name, with hope on the unseen sail, he fortified his heart.

In the deep water unshadowed by the boat a darkness slid, catching his eye. He peered, but it was gone. His heart stood in his throat; a palsy of terror shook him. Oh speak, speak, St. Mary, St. Margaret, St. Faith, help a poor body—a poor soul!

When he could stir he headed about, and slunk away for the open, out of the accursed region. A draught of wine steadied him somewhat, and softly overstepping Christian he roused the Adventurer, to get comfort of human speech. He told of the coming storm, he told of the coming sail, but of that other thing he said nothing. Yet presently the Adventurer asked why he shook. "It is for cold," and he drank again. And presently asked, what did he look for over the side? "A shark's fin," he said, "that I thought I saw," and he drank again.

At their feet Christian lay motionless, heeding nothing outside his darkness. Yet presently the Adventurer said further: "He sleeps. From what disquiet should you eye him so?"

"If you list you shall know of his past," muttered Philip. His speech was a little thick.

From the coming from the sea of the alien child he started, and rambled on, with fact and fiction very inextricably mingled; but the hearer could make out the main truth of the blasting of a proud young life, and pitied, and was minded now to make large allowance for any misdemeanour.

From their feet Christian rose, and without a look removed to the bows. They were stricken to silence.

Suddenly Philip clutched the other, staring down. Both saw and blanched, though what they glimpsed gave to them no shape for a name. It was gone.

"What is it?"

"No rowan! not a leaf."

At that the old man mastered his nerves and laughed scorn in his beard. Philip cast a scared look towards Christian.

"Last night," he whispered, "he looked over the side. I saw him—twice—it was for this."

"What is it?"

"You saw. That was his familiar."

"Now look you," returned the other with grave sarcasm, "that is a creature I have seen never, and would gladly. You, if you be skilled as a fisher, catch me that familiar, and I will pay you in gold; or in broad silver if you win me but a fair sight."

Philip, ashy white, crossed himself. "Heaven keep us! The one bait were a human soul."

Not with all his art and wisdom could the Adventurer now reinstate the earlier hardihood of his companion. Against a supplement by wine he protested.

"Sir," said Philip, sullen, "I have braved enough for you and my conscience, and more. Longer here I will not bide; no, not for any price. We go to meet our fortune yonder of friend or foe."

The Adventurer looked at him and smiled. "You miscount. Should I and he yonder, the Alien, be of another mind, your course may be ordered otherwise."

Taken in his own toils, Philip glared in wrath and fear, sundered from a common cause, an adversary.

From the shrouded sea grew a roar; Christian sprang up; the darkness swayed forward, broke, and flew shredded; a line of racing waves leapt upon them as with icy stroke the squall passed. Through the broken vapours a rim of sun showed on the horizon; and there full west beat a tall three-master; a second was standing nearer; of a third a sway of mist withheld certainty. Here rose hope wellnigh clear of doubt.

But the mists spread down again with twilight adding. The House Monitory woke and spoke far behind as they went to windward. Now Christian steered.

Again was he aware of a stealthy threat moving below, and again looking he could nothing define. He was seen of both: the Adventurer came boldly to his side, and Philip dare not bide aloof. They peered, and he would not.

For an intolerable moment he forbore them, gripping the tiller hard.

"There is it!" said the old man. "What say you is the creature? Your mate has named it—your familiar," and he laughed.

Even then Christian forbore still, though the stress of long hours of repressed passion culminated in a weight of frantic anger and loathing, cruel to bear.

Then Philip lied, denying his words, and Christian knew that he lied; his crafty wits disturbed by wine, reverse, and fear, he blundered, protesting overmuch.

Said the Adventurer grimly: "Now my offer holds good for silver or gold; be you man enough to back your words, you who would give me the lie?"

Without tackle men take fish by flamelight, spearing; and thus fell the wording of Philip's menace, as, reeling between fear and resentment on either hand, he cried wildly:

"I care not—though, by heavens! a famous take may come of it. We have but to try fire."

Christian gripped him, very death in his face and in his strength; swayed him from his feet; gripped the harder .for his struggles, till the ribs of the poor wretch gave, and cracked within his arms; with a great heave had him shoulder high; with another could have flung him overboard. And did not.

On the finest verge of overpoise he held, swung round with a slackening hold, and dropped him like a cast bale to the bottom of the boat. Then he caught the tiller and clung to it with the strength of a drowning man.

Philip lay groaning, broken and wrung in body and mind. He realised a dreadful truth: for one brief second he had seen in Christian's eyes fierce, eager hatred; clear, reasonable, for informed by most comprehensive memory; mad he was, but out of no deficiency; mad, with never a blank of mind to disallow vengeance; as cunning and as strong he was as ever madness could make a man; unmasked, a human devil.

The Adventurer lifted him and felt his bones, himself half stunned and bleeding, for he had been flung heavily from unpractised balance, as suddenly the boat lurched and careened in the wallop of the sea.

The menace of an extreme peril closed their difference, compelling fellowship. They counselled and agreed together with a grasp and a nod and few words. Philip fumbled for his knife, unclasped, and showed it. "Our lives or his. Have you?" "Better," returned the other, and had out a long dagger-knife sheathed, that he loosened to lie free for instant use. "It has done service before. Can you stand? are you able?" It was darkening so that sight could inform them but little concerning the Alien.

Christian was regarding them not at all. From head to foot he was trembling, so that he had ado to stand upright and keep the boat straight. Not from restraint his lips were bitten and his breath laboured hard: quick revulsion had cast him down, so passion-spent, conscience-stricken, and ashamed, that scarcely had he virtue left for the face of a man.

Their advance strung him, for he saw the significant reserve of each right hand. That his misdeed justified any extreme he knew, not conscious in his sore compunction of any right to resist even for his life. He waited without protest, but neither offered to strike.

Reason bade for quick despatch—very little would have provoked it; but not Philip at his worst could conduct a brutal butchery, when conviction dawned that a human creature stood at their mercy by his own mere resolute submission. With names of coward and devil he struck him first, but they did not stir him to affording warrant. The Adventurer took up the word.

"Brutal coward, or madman, which you be, answer for your deed; confess you are a traitor paid and approved."

He shook his head.

"Why else have you now half murdered your fellow? Verily are you an alien through and through, for no man born on these shores would so basely betray a trust."

"Nor I," he got out, and rather wished they would strike with their hands.

"You lie!" said his accuser; "or robbery, or murder, or treachery you intend—or all. Own your worst; try it; this time openly, fairly: your brute strength upon two who are not your match: on your mate damaged from your foul handling: on an old man, whose gold you have taken, the trust of whose life you have accepted."

He could not attempt a protest, though his heart was like to break enforced to silence. The other advanced in temerity with an order.

"You have a knife. Give it up."

He obeyed without a word. Then the two made no reserve, but with a show of bare steel proved his temper. He did not lift a hand.

Lois might come to hear of his transgression: she would never know how hard it was to atone, because they dawdled so cruelly, because he knew they would bungle so cruelly: he did not think either had force to drive a blade home at a stroke.

The Adventurer paused. Here without madness was a guilty wretch cowed at detection, abject as a wolf in a pit!

"We would not your blood on our hands, yet to no oath of yours may our lives trust."

"I would not offer it."

"Only as the wild beast you showed yourself, look to be kept bound."

Such putting to shame was simply just, but oh! hard.

"I may not withstand you," he said, hardly, steadily, "but ah, sir! ah, Philip, suffer me! If this night I am to go to my account, I do greatly require that, through my default, the lives of two men may not drop in the loaded scale."

To them the plea rang strained and false.

"We choose our risk; against treachery of the skies will we rather provide."

He surrendered his hands to the Adventurer. Philip took the helm, but the miserable culprit winced to hear how the strain brought from him a sob of distress. The old man did his best under direction for shortening sail; but while yet this was doing, again the ominous roar sounded and grew, and a squall caught them unready.

The light boat quivered in every plank as she reared against the heavy charge; sheets of water flew over, blinding. Christian heard from the helm a shriek of pain and despair, and at that, frantic, such an access of strength swelled in him, that suddenly his bonds parted like thread, and he caught the restive tiller out of Philip's incompetent hold. There could be no further question of him whom by a miracle Heaven had thus graced in strength for their service. And for their lives they needed to bale. Christian blessed the cruel, fierce elements.

Far ahead heaved lights, revealed on the blown seas: far, so far. Right in their teeth drove the promised gale, with intermittent bursts of sleet and hail. Upon bodies brine-wet the icy wind cut like a knife. Twin lights sprang, low down, giving the wanted signal; bore down, then stood away: the appointed ship followed after her consorts, not daring, with a gale behind, to near the cruelest coast known.

Struggling on under a mere stitch of canvas, the wind resenting even that, clutching it, threatening to tear out the mast, they went reeling and shuddering on to their desperate fortune. For hours the long endeavour lasted, with gain on the double lights by such slow degrees as mocked at final achievement.

Except that his hands were like to freeze out of use Christian cared marvellously little for outer miseries. To him all too short was the span of life left for retrieving one guilty minute; no future could he look for to live it down, so certain had he become that this night death was hard after him.

Two stars reeling, kind, bright stars, shone life for others though not for him. Perhaps for him, he wanted to believe; some coward drop in his blood tried to cheat reason and conscience. Why not for him? Could his doom be so heavy as to sink that great bulk with its scores of souls? And though now he should freely release others of his peril, who would ever count it to him for righteousness, to soften the reproach that would lie against his name so long as ever it were remembered?

The cold touched his brain. Surely he had died before, long ago, out of all this pain and distress. Waves heaved gigantically; spray dashed hard in his face; he shrank humanly, knowing he was not fit to die; she was coming through the sea bringing life. No, ah! not now. She was lurking in the sea holding death.

"Madness and treason are not in him."

"He is a devil," said Philip, "a very devil. See! Go you now, and feign to persuade for abandoning the boat, and shipping together."

"That will I in all good faith," and he went and came again.

"First he refused outright; then he said, when the moment came we should know as well as he."

"I knew it, I knew it," chattered Philip, "oh, a devil he is! Sir, you will see me out of his hands. I know what he intends: on the instant you quit the boat he casts off and has me at his mercy, he and that thing below. I am no coward, and it ill becomes you to hint it; and I fear death no more than any sinner must, no clean, straight death.

"Sir, his putting out of life was long and bloody: I saw it; death by inches. And he looked at me with infernal hatred then; the very same I saw in his eyes but now. Why should he check at sudden murder, but for a fouler revenge. You cannot judge as I. You have not seen him day after day. Treacherously he accepts friendship; he feigns to be witless; and all the while this hell-fire is hidden out of sight. You do not know how he has been denied opportunity, till rashly I offered it.

"O sir, quit of him this once, I am quit of him for ever! No, I mean no villainy against him, but—but—it happens—there is every inducement for him to choose that he and his boat never be seen of us again. Drown? no, he never was born to drown. The devil sees to his own.

"It is true—true. You saw the Thing yourself. Also, did he not refuse an oath? So has he all his life. Now know I: there are certain words he for his contract may not utter."

When tall masts rocked above, and voices hailed, and a rope shot across, again the Adventurer pressed Christian hard with precious human kindness. Men big and fair-haired were shouting, knocking at his heart strangely. Most foolish and absurd came a longing just once before he died to be warm and dry again, just once. He shook his head.

Philip kept off, nor by word or sign offered the forgiveness he ached after, but hasted to pass first. Then the other followed; he loosed the rope; it leapt away. The last face he saw gleaming above him was Philip's, with its enmity and a ghastly drawn smile of relief: never to be seen of him again.

How long would her vengeance delay? The vast anger of the sea leaped and roared round him, snatching, striking. An hour passed, and he was still afloat, though the mast was gone; and near another, and he was still afloat, but by clinging to an upward keel. In cruel extremity, then, he cried the name of Diadyomene, with a prayer for merciful despatch, and again her name, and again.

Diadyomene heard. The waves ran ridged with light that flickered and leaped like dim white flame. Phosphor fires edged the keel; a trailing rope was revealed as a luminous streak. He got it round his body, and his hands were eased.

Up from below surged a dark, snaky coil, streaming with pale flakes of fire; it looped him horribly; a second length and a third flung over him; a fourth overhung, feeling in air. A loathsome knot worked upon the planks, spread, and rooted there. He plucked an arm free, and his neck was circled instead. His knife he had not: barehanded he fought, frenzied by loathing of the foul monster, the foulest the sea breeds.

Before his eyes rose the sea's fairest, towered above him on the rush of a wave, sank to his level. Terrible was her face of anger, and cruel, for she smiled. She flung out a gesture of condemnation and scorn, that flashed flakes of light off shoulder and hair. She called him "traitor," and bade him die; and he, frantic, tore away the throttled coil at his throat, and got out, "Forgive."

Like challenge and defiance she hurled then her offer of mercy: "Stretch, then, your hand to me—on my lips and my breast swear, give up your soul: then I forgive."

She heard the death agony of a man cried then. Ceasing to struggle, his throat was enwound again; both arms were fast: he cried to his God to resume his soul, and to take it straight out of his body and out of hell.

Away she turned with teeth clenched and furious eyes; then, writhing, she returned, reached out, with one finger touched, and the foul creature shrank, relaxed, drew coil by coil away, dropped, and was gone. Diadyomene flashed away.

When the night and the trouble of the storm were past, not a ship afloat was scatheless. From one that crawled disabled, a boat was spied, drifting keel upward, with the body of a man hanging across it, whose bright hair shone in the early sun, making a swarter race wonder. Against all conjecture life proved to be in him yet. And what unimaginable death had been at him? What garland was this on his throat: blossoms of blood under the skin? When he was recovered to speech he would not say. Good christian men, what could they think? His boat was righted, and with scant charity he was hustled back into it; none of these, suddenly eager to be quit of him, wishing him God-speed.

Under cover of night he crawled up to his home, dreading in his guilt to face the dear, stern eyes of his mother. Ah! no, he entered to no questioning and little heed: the two women sat stricken with sorrow; not for him: in the room beyond Giles lay dead.

So Christian's three gold pieces buried Giles with such decent honour as Lois could desire.

CHAPTER XIV

Christian's misdoing was not to pass unregarded.

A woman turned upon Rhoda passing with a mutter so like a curse that the girl's surprise struck her to a pause. It was Philip's mother who faced her, glowering hate.

"What have you done with my boy?"

"I?" said Rhoda, with widening eyes, though she blushed.

"You—smooth-faced chit—yes, you! Oh, keep those fine eyes and that colour to take in men, for me they will not! I can see through you! I know you, and the games you are playing!"

"What then?" flashed Rhoda. "You accuse me? Of what? and by what right?"

"Right! The right of a mother whose son you have driven away."

"He is nothing to me—never will be—never—nothing!"

"I know it. I know it well, and I told him so: nothing! 'Tis only your vanity to have at your heels the properest lad and the bravest of the place."

"He!" cried Rhoda, in disdain.

"Ay, I know how your fancy has run, against natural liking for the dark-haired and dark-eyed of your own race; your vagary goes after fair hair and grey eyes. Well, see for all your sly offers that great blond dolt gapes and gapes over your bait, never closing to it. That northern blood is half brine."

Rhoda stood speechless; her anger, shame, and pain transcended blushes, and she changed to dead white.

"And you pick out one who can love like a man, who fires at a word or a look, and him you delight to stab and torment with your cruel tongue, while you use him for your ends. Shameless! You have dropped yourself into his arms even, so to heat the Alien from his fishes' blood. May I live to see you put to shame of some man!"

"He said—oh, vile—of me! Cur, cur!"

"'Tis I that can read between the lines, not he, poor blind fool! Miscall him! ay, you have got the trick. You may bring up faults against him—some do; but I tell you no man will do greatly amiss who still goes to his old mother and opens his heart to her."

Rhoda's breath caught like a sob at that, for there unknowingly went a stroke at Christian. She gathered herself together for bitter onslaught, for outraged pride and indignation drove out compunction, drove out any mercy. Out it all shrivelled at a blasting thought that stopped her very heart. Mute she stood, white, shuddering, staring. Then she got out a whisper.

"When did he go—tell me? Since—my uncle died—or—before?"

"Well enough you know 'twas before—"

Rhoda turned and fled homeward, fleet as terror, though her knees went slack and her brain reeled. She drew bolts before her dreadful incoherent whispers welled out to Lois.

"Where he went she did not know, did not guess, never thought it was on a planned venture. None would think of that, or think that two alone would suffice, or dream of Christian—I had thought that strange—you too. And we know Christian went on a venture, by the three gold pieces we know: and that could not have been alone, and he is not of the League. And I thought it had been with Philip; and I thought Philip meant kindness—perhaps for my sake, which vexed me. Oh, perhaps it was for my sake, and I was vexed! Yet see, none others guess it nor do conceive that any, in any cause, would go hand in hand with our Christian. And none would greatly mark his goings and comings—Christian's—for unreason has so chartered his ways. Then, though both were away that same day, not even his mother had noted it. And oh! think of Christian in these days! Has sorrow only been heavy at his heart? And a hurt on his throat he would not show. And oh!" she said, "and oh!" she said, and failed and tried again, "oh! his *knife—he has not his knife.*"

The love and faith of Lois sprang up against belief.

"Child, child! what do you dare to say—to think? Would you hint that Christian—my boy Christian—has done murder?

"No, no, never! No, never, never! I would stake my life—my soul—that it was fair fight!"

Lois looked at her and said a cruel thing: "You are no helpmeet for him. Thank God! you are not his wife!"

Rhoda quivered at that, and found it a saying hard to forgive. Her heart swelled to refute it, and might not for maidenhood. Long ago she would have had Christian rise up to avenge himself terribly; her pride had suffered from the poor temper she saw in his. Now, though he had exceeded the measure of her vague desire, he stood fair and high in her estimation, illuminated, not blackened by the crime she imputed. Against all the world, against his mother, she was at one with him. Was there any other who desired and deserved the nearest and dearest claim, that she had renounced.

A wedge of silence drove between them. The character of the mother's stern virtue dawned upon Rhoda, appalling her: for the salvation of her son's soul she might bid him accept the full penalty of his crime—even that. A horror of such monstrous righteousness took the girl. She stole to unbolt the door and away to warn Christian, when a whisper stayed her.

"I failed him. I thought then only of my man, and I had no prayers for my boy. Ah, Christian, Christian!"

Doubt had entered. Lois knelt and prayed.

Rhoda wavered. Her estimate or the world's, the partial or the vindictive, shrank to their due proportions, as Lois thus set Christian's crime before the eye of Heaven. She wavered, turned, and fell kneeling, clinging and weeping, convicted of the vain presumption that would keep Christian from the hands of his God.

She was bidden away when Lois caught a sound of Christian.

His mother held him by the window for the first word.

"Christian, where is Philip?"

His startled eyes were a stab to her soul; the tide that crimsoned his very brow checked hers at her heart. He failed of answering, and guilt weighed down his head. She rallied on an inspiration that greatest crimes blanch, never redden, and "You have not killed him?" was a question of little doubt.

"No, thank God! no!" he said, and she saw that he shook.

Then he tried to out with the whole worst truth, but he needed to labour for breath before he could say with a catch: "I meant to—for one moment."

To see a dear face stricken so! Do the damned fare worse? More dreadful than any reproach was her turning away with wrung hands. She returned to question.

"Then where is he?"

"I cannot tell. He left me. He would not—he was afraid."

"What had you done? You had harmed him?"

"Yes," he said, and told how.

"What had he done to anger you? Had he struck first?"

"No."

"You had quarrelled?"

"No."

"Had you no excuse?" she said.

He hesitated. Could she know and understand all, there might be some pity with her condemnation, there would be some tempering of her distress.

"I can make none," he had to answer.

When next she spoke: "Then it was old hate," she said, and after a minute he answered "Yes" to that.

So she had to realise that for months, according to her gospel, he had been a murderer at heart; and her assurance of a merciful blank of mind and memory tottered, threatening a downfall that would prove the dear son of her hope of a rotten build. She tested his memory.

"I asked a promise of you once, and you gave it."

"Yes," he said, and, do what he would, "I have broken it" got mangled wretchedly in his throat.

"Your promise! Is it believable? You could—you!"

"O mother! If God forgot me!"

Her heart smote her because her prayers had deserted him then.

"Oh, peace!" she said, "and do not add blasphemy, nor seek to juggle with God."

She did not spare him, and deeply she searched his conscience. Self-convicted already he was, yet his guilt looked freshly hideous worded by her, as look wounds, known to the senses of night, discovered by the eye of day.

For a whole dreadful hour Rhoda listened to the murmur of voices. Then they ceased, and Lois came. "Thank God, child!" was all she needed to say.

"Heaven forgive me! Can you? can he? Let me go to him—I must. Ah me!—can he forgive me?"

Lois held the door and turned her. "He has nothing to forgive," she said, and her face frightened questions.

From among some poor hoards Lois drew out a tiny cross of gold. It was Christian's, sole relic left of his young unknown life. As a little lad he had played with it and lost it, and Lois finding it had taken it into keeping. Now she took it to him.

"I will ask no renewal of a broken promise—no. I want no hard thing of you, only this: when temptation to deadly sin is overbearing, before you yield, unfasten this and fling it from you into the sea. You will? Christian, answer—say, 'I will.'"

"What worth has any word of mine?" he said in his despair; but her arms were round his neck fixing the knot, and stayed to clasp, but her rare terrible sobs rose as she cried, "Oh, God help you, my son!" and "I will, I will!" flew strong to assure her that that word would never have to be fulfilled.

Near was the time that would put him to the test, and he knew it. A day passed and a day passed, out of eternity into eternity, and the moon filled up to Diadyomene's account.

"Rhoda," he said, "do you know what day this is?"

"Christmas Eve."

"Yes—but to my mother—her child was born—"

"Yes," said Rhoda hurriedly, and bent her head: she for the first time knew her own birthday.

"Listen, Rhoda! She has aged and weakened so; the day and night of prayer and fasting she has now begun I fear may outdo her strength. Will you keep ever at hand to listen and be careful of her?"

"And you?" asked Rhoda.

"I may not stay. I cannot."

She flashed a look of amazed indignation, for instinctively she knew that he would be leaving his mother to seek the strange-named woman, and such filial misconduct in him was hardly credible. No kind word or look would Rhoda grant him. He never felt the lack: his mother's blessing he did greatly desire, but he dared not intrude on the day of her mourning to ask it.

Short was the day and long the way, but over soon by some hours was he footing it. The singular incidence of the day encouraged belief that a special mercy of Heaven was ordering his goings for the comforting of a long sorrow. Ah! God grant her a soul from the sea, and ah! God grant it by me for a token. All his steps were taken to prayer, and the least thing he asked of his God was that, though his sins were so heavy, he might not die till he had seen that salvation. His head and his heart told him that if he failed in his high endeavour he must surely perish.

Over the wold came a harsh call, and again till he answered and stayed. He was making for waste stretches, gashed athwart by long gullies preventing any fair paths. Already, though but half a league forward, tracks had grown rough and uncertain. The voice came from a mudded hollow, where a loaded cart stuck fast, an old horse and an old man striving with it in vain. Though loath to be hindered, Christian turned aside to give help.

He was not graciously welcomed. The old man scowled, and swore under his breath. "The Alien, deuce take it, he will not serve!"

But he stared, and words failed when Christian promptly laid hand on the load, saying, "Here's bad balancing, Gaffer; we had best uncord first and set it right."

"Ay, it shifted. Have it that way, if so you can and will. My two boys did the cording, and two fools they be."

He sidled away, muttering wonderful oaths as curiously he watched the Alien's tackling. The load was a tree brought down by the recent gale; protruding roots clawed the mud behind; piled branches nodded to the fore, orange-red berries bright as coral dangling there. Christian's great strength made light of the work, and soon the cart went crawling out of the mire. He snapped off a twig to scrape the mud from his shins, and the gaffer's mutter then caught his ear.

"He's done it—sure! Be danged if I reckoned he could. Well, well, some be liars!"

"In your best days, Gaffer, you might have done as much."

The old face wrinkled with a sour grin. "'Twas said you couldn't abide the rowan."

"Why?"

"Well, I never asked. May be they lie who swear that never a twig of the rowan goes in your boat. Some have taken to say so."

"None, true enough. What then?" said Christian, and he noticed that the man had thrust a bunch of berries into his belt.

"Well, there, 'tis not I that can give the reason."

"Can you think mine the only boat that goes without that garnish?"

"I swear the only one."

Christian did not know how on his very account a prevalent custom had gained ground. He brought out a string of names.

"Why, most of those from this very tree have had takings. 'Tis an ill wind that blows nowhere; for I reckon now to get a good price off this timber—ay, to the last scrap, and 'tis you I owe some thanks for that. So, look you, I have a mind, after I have made my profit, to open out of your doing here with me and take the laugh. Hey? Ah! it seems to me that some of your wits are left, so may be all I heard tell of was lies, when 'twas said you had had games with the Evil One, and had lost to him both wits and soul."

Christian said slowly, "You thought I had no soul?"

"Never thought at all; why should I? Let fools think; I see. You, I see, but now handle the rowan freely, and pass it to and fro, as never could you have done had your soul known unholy tampering."

Christian stood stock-still, with an unseeing stare, till the old man called back to him, "Come on, just to lend a hand up this pitch." Then he ran after, and so eagerly bore, that one spoke he broke.

On the level he said, strangely breathless, "Now I want payment."

"What! A great hulking fellow can't go two steps out of his way and lift a hand for one with old age in his bones but he asks payment!"

"Yes," said Christian, "and for the love of God, give me the payment I shall ask."

"No promise, but what's your asking?"

"Give me berries of the rowan."

With his sour grin the old fellow muttered, "Well, well, no wits after all!" as he plucked some bunches and chucked them across.

"More! more! and oh! quick; I lose time. See, fill up my cap."

"All you can't have. My brats have been promised their handfuls, and want you may."

When all that entreaty could get he had, Christian parted at a run, and the way he took was home.

Rhoda wondered, seeing him pass the window. Presently, laying aside resentment, she went out to seek him in the linhay. The door resisted her hand.

"Christian," she called, and after his answer, "Come in. What are you about? Bring in your work; there is fire still."

He said "No" so forcibly, that she went away aggrieved, and a little curious.

All was very quiet; of Lois she heard and saw nothing, and Christian made no noise at all. She wondered if he too were engaged in prayer; she wondered if she ought also to be so devoted.

From the window she saw two figures on the road, and watched them idly. They neared, and from the opposite approach came two others. All four were known to her by sight, though hailing from some distance; they were kin to Philip; two were father and son, two were brothers. At the gate they stood, and turned in.

Rhoda's heart dropped as she guessed their errand. To her a word from Christian were enough; but what solemnest oath, what evidence short of Philip's self, would convince these?

They were knocking, while still her countenance was out of command; and when they asked for Christian, her wits were so troubled, that she said lamely, "It is Christmas Eve; can you want him now?"

"Wait then—I will go—wait here, and he will come."

When she passed out and turned the wall, she knew by the sound of feet that two had started to go about the contrary way to make against any escape. At the linhay door she knocked, again getting an impatient answer.

"Christian, come out, or let me in. You must."

He came out and closed the door, keeping his hand upon it while she told.

"I cannot come. Go, say I cannot come; I will not!" and desperately impatient his hand beat upon the door.

"You must," she said, and her white face and shaking voice went far to convince him. "I think you must. O Christian, don't you know why they come?"

He looked at her blankly.

"To ask after Philip."

His face burned red, and he stood dumfoundered.

"You know? From my mother?"

"Yes," she said. "No," she said. "I thought that first, and told her. Oh! why did she not tell you all when she would not let me confess? Yes, I thought that, and O wretch that I was! I thought no blame either. Now hate me, and never forgive me."

He also said, "I have nothing to forgive"; and half audibly he groaned, "Ah, Christ! is there no forgiveness of sins?"

Footsteps made them turn to see two rounding the linhay; and again, footsteps behind brought two after Rhoda, impatient of delay. None of the four from that moment judged Christian to be innocent, nor Rhoda wholly ignorant: their looks so bespoke guilt and apprehension.

Some touch of resentment at the intolerant intrusion set Christian's head high, and his eyes were not to be daunted as he measured each for strength of will and strength of body. He knew them for the pick of Philip's kin; all were of the League.

"Say why you come," said Christian.

"Bid me stay," whispered Rhoda, though she saw that her presence hindered a ready answer; but Christian bade her go, and reluctantly she withdrew.

Out of earshot she went, but no further than to the gate. There she leaned, and tried to keep her face averted, but against resolution now and then her head would turn to better her heart. Uncloaked, in the cold she shivered, and from apprehension.

"Concerning our kinsman Philip," began the eldest.

His colour went and came for witness against him.

"Speak low," he said, glancing at a near window, "lest my mother hear," and at that a second score went down against his innocence.

"You put to sea with him; you came back alone. Where is he?"

In his haste Christian answered to more than was asked.

"Alive he was when I saw him last. Where he now is I know little as you."

The youngest put in a word. "Alive! But was any plank under him? Will you take your oath that he was alive and safe, and unhurt by you?"

At that red guilt flew over his face, for he could not.

Another turn of words might give him a chance, but he had no skill to play for it. The imposition of an oath he might not resent with his old high claim: a promise had been broken, though they knew not, and his head sank for shame. That, with his brief pause, sealed conviction.

One muttered, "Now I would not believe him though he swore"; but the other three frowned silence upon him, the spokesman saying, "We do require an oath before we ask further."

No protest did he offer to hinder a quick despatch. He uttered the form prescribed, though conscience and pride alike took deep wounds of it. Afterwards it was told against him how his countenance worked, as for the first time an oath had been forced upon him.

"Now be speedy," said Christian, "for I have little leisure or list to bide."

At that crass speech something of grim smiling hardly kept to concealment.

"Is Philip alive?"

"Yes," he said, "if he be not dead," an answer that angered them. "God knows"; then he said, "I have no cause to think him dead."

"You saw him last alive and like to live?"

"More like to live than I."

"Where, then, did you leave him?"

"I may not say. I am pledged to silence."

"How pledged? To whom?"

"To Philip."

"Ay, we know; but we all are of the League."

"None were excepted; 'not to a soul,' he said."

"He, speaking for the League, meant to not a soul beside."

"I mean to the League no less. So I think did he."

A poor satisfaction was in standing to his word against those who compelled him to an oath.

"Crack-brained devil—"

"Lower!" Christian said, glancing anxiously up at the window.

"This is no case for foolery or brag. Out of you we must have the whole truth, lief or loath."

His stubborn face said no. To no man on earth could he tell the whole truth, nor, were that possible, would it be believed; less than the whole doomsday truth could scarce make his own outrageous act comprehensible.

"Philip may tell you, but not I," he said witlessly. And as he spoke and looked at these four, it came upon him that he might not long out-live Philip's telling of the tale, if only by reason of that lurking thing un-certainly seen. He clapped his hand upon the hidden cross, as a perilous flash told how less cause had set down a record that might not bear the light. So close was he ever to the mouth of hell.

Live temper faded from his face, and it settled to the old blank mildness that had been lifting somewhat of late days.

"Is he so mad?"

"No, he shams."

"Leave fooling, and speak straight in a matter of life and death."

"Oh! more—more than life and death. For the love of God, make an end, and take a final answer. I will tell no more; nor would the most I know further you to Philip."

The comment of a vigorous curse checked him there.

"Hear me out. If you need but to know how a venture went, I can tell you: well. If you have other need of him that does not brook delay, I can but offer to serve you to my best, for following and bringing him again; whatever be the risk, I owe that to him and you. Only this day I must have to myself. I must, though I pay for it with the rest of my life."

That preposterous offer took away breath. Then an oath yelping high with derision above anger brought Christian to entreat for his mother's quiet.

"Let us in here, then," said one, and reached to the latch behind him.

Christian struck up his arm. "No!" he said, and barred the way.

Instantly, moved by a prompt suspicion, the four sprang out ready steel and swung one way, ringing him in. At that, Christian realised his desperate case. He blanched, and sweat started. "For life and death!" he said hoarsely. "O my God, my God!"

Rhoda shot in between, and, voiceless from fear and speed, clung to Christian, presuming her weakness to turn offence.

"Cowards!" she panted, "four against one, and he empty-handed. What—why? Christian?"

"You would do well to counsel your madman to give way and let us pass, if he care greatly for the quiet of any there within."

Christian yielded. He lifted the latch and thrust the door open, standing aside that they might pass him by; but two linked arm with him, walked him in, and held him a prisoner. He did not offer to resist. Rhoda pressed after him close; the last to enter closed and bolted the door.

Puzzled silence fell. Not a corner of the bare place could harbour suspicion. Some tools were ranged against the walls; twine and canvas and common oddments lay there, a small enough show of garden store, and of fuel a pile pitifully low. A stool overthrown told of Christian's last hasty rising; on a bench lay his cap, half filled with scarlet berries, and strung berries were spread beside. Four blank countenances were turned upon him, whose looks were sullen and guilty like a criminal's taken in the act. Rhoda, bewildered, owned to her sinking heart that here showed such vagary of his wits as passed her reckoning.

"You were best away, Rhoda."

"I will not go," she said, "except I be thrust out."

None urged for that rough kindness now, having gone so far; her presence might even turn to account, for it must lie with the Alien to spare her distress.

The prisoner took up question.

"The League has charged you to be judges?"

"Yes."

"To give sentence?"

"Yes."

"To execute it?"

"Yes."

Christian grew as white as a coward; he went on steadily nevertheless.

"You are charged to do murder."

"To do justice."

"Without any proof that Philip is dead."

"Lack of proof that he is alive comes to the same as the case stands."

No lie would now avail of Philip lost overboard. In the stress of clear thinking for his life he felt relief that he could not be so tempted to damn his fair cause before Heaven.

"He will return," he muttered, "but too late, for me too late."

"Christian, they dare not," gasped Rhoda; "no, you dare not, for

Philip will return to confound you. Should he return—too late—then may God have no mercy on your souls."

Christian said "Amen" to that.

The spokesman turned to Rhoda.

"You speak positively: can you bear witness in his favour?"

"I know nothing—nothing."

"Yet have you shown singular quickness of apprehension."

She looked piteously at Christian, galled by remorse.

"Oh me! Must I say?"

"Why not? None here will blame you. I cannot."

So Rhoda faltered out how she too had entertained a wicked suspicion.

"What evidence then routed it?"

"His."

"His evidence?"

"His denial."

Her sincerity was beyond question; her simplicity commanded respect; no ingenuity could have spoken better to his credit. Yet all was vain.

"Bare denial may not suffice for us, when furthermore without valid cause he has refused any clear statement to satisfy a reasonable demand, and quibbled and defied."

"Give me a moment's grace," pleaded Christian, "to make sure if I can go no further."

He might take his time; but little he needed to gain conviction for despair; for he saw how inevitably answer would beget question point by point, till, again at bay, having traversed ground bristling with hostile indications, he must stand at yet worse disadvantage.

Before his eyes, one, fingering in mere impatience, took hold of the strung berries; at a rough twitch some scattered. Christian, exasperated, plucked for a free hand, and a tightened grip set him struggling for one instant with the natural indignation of young blood at rude constraint. So well dreaded was his strength, that on a misconstruction of his aim, every tool that might serve as a weapon was caught up and thrust hastily from the window, while more of the rowan danced down. Balked the Alien seemed, resisting no longer, and sweating, shaking, choking, with eyes miserably wet with rage. But Rhoda, who had watched his face, turned, and gathering all the berries loose and strung, laid them safe from handling.

"God bless you, dear!" he said; and so she knew that she had guessed right, and so she could not doubt but his wits had fallen again to their old infirmity.

He had ended patience and grace when a gleam of hope came.

"It must be within your knowledge," he said, "who last saw him with me."

"Yes."

"Then this I may say—he and Philip went together when we parted company."

"That too we had thought to be possible."

Christian recognised an ominous note, and the hostile faces he saw more dark and grim.

"Speak out!" he cried; "what is it you think?" Yet half he knew; yet quite he knew. "Speak out! Do you dare think I have betrayed them?"

"We have little doubt. Traitor, thrice over traitor, the League's account with you is overdue."

He laughed out savagely.

"Now, devils that you are you show, that bring a false accusation, since well you know that once only have I been on a venture."

"Well we know how two ventures before failed—well-planned ventures. Now we know how you have played the fool and the spy together. Two times have you been gone, no man knew where; over a day gone, and not at sea. Will you say now where you went?"

He despaired, and did not answer, while Rhoda's glance wavered consciously. At last he said:

"Though I myself can make no defence, in due time I cannot fail to be cleared—of murder and treason. I cannot wait. This day I want; I must be free on any terms. No terms? But hear! I claim judgment instantly, this hour. Men, you dare not give it. Then I claim the judgment of God. I will fight it out. Choose your place and pick your man,—nay, any two. What? Cowards! three, all four together, but forgo your knives or lend me one."

"Fight you may, but the place shall be here, and the odds against you, as you see."

The door was fast, and the six within stood close in the limited space; he was held at disadvantage, and weaponless, against choice men prepared. Also he cared for two women.

"Oh!" he cried, shaken and white with fury, "I must, I must have one day. With what but my life may I purchase? Is it cheap, think you? As you hope for heaven by mercy, deal with me. Only one day! By this hour to-morrow, if I breathe, I surrender. I will swear to it by any form you will. Make harder conditions, and I take them. All my life-days after would I engage to set this day free. What more can a man offer than his life for lending or ending?"

His face and voice were so dreadful to Rhoda's heart, that she could not brook the limits of reason.

"Mine! Christian, you have mine. You will not refuse; you will let him go, for I will be his surety."

"This is folly."

"It is not. Is it not enough? I—life—honour, in pledge for him. O Christian, you cannot gainsay, else you dishonour your own purpose."

"We are plain men who are dealing for justice. An innocent girl cannot be substitute for a traitor all but proved, whom, moreover, the League needs for a better information."

Still Rhoda tried protests.

"Girl, are you out of your senses too? dishonest too? Can you state any circumstance to justify this urgency for a day's grace? Failing that, well we can guess what he would do with it. It is somewhat barefaced."

Christian checked her answering, and owned defeat.

"Give over now," he said. "An hour have I wasted fighting over losing ground. You have gained all along, and I know it. In every way you have the advantage. Say now, what will you do with it?"

"You surrender?"

"No. By your force, not by my will, shall liberty go. Quit words and be doing. No: what then?"

"Consider that the odds are against your taking boat alive were a hint out of your foul dealing with the League. Yet if you promise resistance we have no choice but to hale you an open prisoner. Have you a mind to face stones?"

Rhoda's scared looks drew one to assure her, that were Christian free from guilt, his cause could not miscarry at their hands, unless by his own intemperance; therefore should she persuade him to voluntary submission. He groaned in miserable despair.

"I yield, but only till these stringent conditions be passed. Dispose with me as you will, and I submit—yes, absolutely—yes; but for a time only. A limited term; for one half-hour? More I will not, and look you after. I cannot surrender my will to be free this day."

Likely enough it was out of pity for the girl that his offer was taken. Against suspicion of some reservation he was constrained to swear faith under dictation; also the order of his going was ruled minutely, with warning that the lifting of a hand unallowed would be instantly fatal. "Be doing—be doing quickly," he said, and the bolt was drawn.

Christian turned to stay Rhoda, who came following, and the four men, with fine consideration, passed out first, letting the door swing to on the unhappy pair. Their eyes met, poor souls, with miserable consciousness that a barrier of reserve thwarted solace.

"Keep heart, dear," he said; and bravely tearless she echoed him.

"But, oh!" she said, "be patient, and not rash, for the sake of those who love you."

"O Rhoda, Rhoda! you do not know. I have a work this night. I think—I know it was meant for me. By Heaven, I think. My own sins have risen up against me now. They thwart. Hell itself striving against me has advantage by them. There must be some way. But I cannot see it. There must be! Oh! I cannot be condemned through turning back on an amended hope. So Heaven-sent I blessed it. No way—no way!"

Muttering, he reached over to the rowan and absently fingered it, while Rhoda urged on him what she knew of reason. He turned on her a musing look.

"Rhoda, will you help me?"

"Oh, tell me to: never ask."

"Take the rowan, and finish what I was about."

She broke down at last, and turned away in such a passion of sobbing as owned desertion of hope.

"Rhoda! You desert me, Rhoda!" in so broken a voice he said, that against all sense she cried: "But I will! Yes, yes; trust me, I will!" and could not after retract when she saw his face.

"I am not mad," he said; "look at me: I am not." And with that she knew not how to reconcile evidence.

"Be speedy against my return."

"Is it possible? How?" she whispered.

"As God wills, I cannot know; but some way will show, must show."

Again she entreated against temerity, and for answer he taught her of a lonely spot, asking her to carry the threaded rowan there, and to wait his coming. "If I do not come," he said, "I shall be—"

"Not dead!" she breathed.

"Oh, damned and dead," he said.

"It cannot be. No. Yet, O Christian, should any harm befall you, avenged you shall be. Yes. No law can serve us here efficient against the tyranny of the League; but if in all the land high places of justice be, there will I go, and there denounce the practice of such outrage and wrong. Those four, they shall not escape from account. For that I will live—ay, even hazard living—I know."

"You will not," ordered Christian; "for I myself freely have served the League, and have taken payment. And these four mean to deal justly; and I have no right to complain."

A hint of impatience sounded against the door, and Christian, with a last word enjoining secrecy, turned and lifted the latch. A forlorn sob complained. He caught both her hands in his.

"Dear heart, dear hands, a farewell were misdoubt," he said, and on brow and hands he crossed her. "A human soul shall bless your faithful doing."

He loosed and left her. She saw the door's blank exchange for him; she heard the brisk departure of feet; away fled the spurious confidence she had caught in his presence, and desolate and despairing, blind and choked with grief, she cursed her own folly and bewailed his.

When she took up her lunatic task the red berries like told beads registered one by one prayer too like imprecation, for sure she was that the strange-named woman stirred at the heart of this coil. In heats of exasperation she longed to scatter and crush the rowan; yet the thread crept on steadily through her hands, inch by inch, till that misery was over.

Then it pleased her grief to bring out her own best scarf for enfolding. "So I further him to her," she said; "so I fashion some love-token between them." As soft-foot she went for it, outside a fastened door she stood to listen. She heard the low mutter of petition, and jealous resentment sprang up against a monopoly by the dead of the benefit of prayer, so wanted by the living.

As she stood, a patch of calm sea shone into her eyes through a narrow light; and from the frame, small as a beetle, moved a boat rowing across. Five men she counted, and she made out that the second rower was the biggest. So had he entirely surrendered. All hopeless she turned away to fulfil her promise.

At that moment Christian was speaking.

"I take it, the time is now up."

By a mile of engirding sea the prospect of escape looked so vain that one joined assent with a fleer. Placid as the sea's calm was the Alien's countenance, and he pulled on steadily. The leader from the helm leaned forward to regard him fixedly, finding his tranquillity consonant only with imperfect wits.

"You think better of resistance, nevertheless?"

"Truly I do," he answered. "I think better of resistance now," and in his eyes was no reading of resentment or anxiety.

His glance turned with his thoughts to distinguish the roof that covered his mother and Rhoda. Dear heart, cried his, do your part and I will mine.

Rhoda by then was doing after her own thought and liking. Though fasting herself, poor child, that on the morrow the board might be the better spread, for Christian she was lavish. Wine she took that Giles had not lived to drink; of griddle cakes the best she chose, and also of figs from those she summertime ago had gathered and dried. Then she wound the silly rowan in brown moss, knotted it up in her scarf, and cloaked herself, and went out on her fool's errand.

Some miles to the west, on the edge of waste, stood a landmark of three trees, and near by, off the path, a furze-stack. Thither by devious ways of caution came Rhoda on the first wane of daylight, and having done all, faced the drear without heart, crouching into shelter of the furze.

Poorly clad for such a vigil, thin from days of want, fasting, exhausted by excitement and grief, she had no strength left to bear bravely any further trial. Though Christian's desperate emphasis stood out to bar despair, she told herself his coming was impossible, and her spirit quailed in utter cowardice as she realised her own outlook. She was afraid of the night, and her engagement had taken no limit of time. Should the dreaded ice-wind of the season rise, there were peril to life; but her heart died under a worse terror, that increased as waste and tree bulked large and shapeless under drawing dark. For was it not the Eve of Christmas, when the strict limitations of nature were so relaxed that things inanimate could quit station, and very beasts speak like men, and naked spirits be clothed with form. Her mortal senses were averse. With desperate desire for relief she scanned the large through the longest hour of her life.

Night was in the valleys, but on the uplands twilight still, when against the sky a runner came. He, dear saviour.

But his footsteps made no sound; but he showed too white. Doubt of agony that this was not he in human flesh froze her, till he came and stood, and not seeing her close crouched, uttered his heart in a sound dreadful to hear.

"Here, here!" cried Rhoda, and had her hands on him before her eyes had fairly realised him. He was mostly naked.

Coatless, shirtless, unshod, his breeks and his hair clung damp, showing by what way he had come free. She held him, and laughed and sobbed.

"You have it?" he said. "Give it here—give it."

"This also—this first. Drink—eat."

"No; I cannot stay."

"You shall—you must," she urged. "Do you owe me nothing? What, never a word?"

He declined impatience to her better counsel; and when he had got the rowan and belted it safe, to the praise of her providence he drank eagerly and ate.

Rhoda spied a dark streak on his shoulder. "You are hurt—oh!"

"Only skin-deep. Salt water stanched it."

"And what of them? Christian, what have you done?" she asked with apprehension.

"Yes; I have a charge for you. Oh, their skins are whole all. Can you step on with me a pace? You will not be afraid?"

She looked at the wan south-west, and the sable heath, and the stark trees; but she could answer now: "No," stoutly and truly, and shiver for fear only. He withheld his pace for her, she stretched to a stride for him.

"Well done, I know," she said, "but tell me how."

He gave a meagre tale, but many a detail she heard later to fill it out. It was easy doing according to Christian, when time and place suited, to beat out a rib of the boat, to stand his ground for a moment while the sea accomplished for him, then to drop overboard when blades struck too quick and close. The boat went down, he said, near three miles from shore.

"O Christian! are any drowned?"

"No, no. I had done my best by them. You know how the Tortoises lie. We were well within a furlong of them. I got there first, and was doffed and ready when they came, waiting to offer them fair; Rhoda, you will carry word of this that some fellows may go to take them off."

"Not I," she said vindictively; "let them wear the night there for due quittance."

"No. They might be perished. And 'twas I counselled them not to attempt the shore, and said I could send word of their plight; and I meant it honestly, though the fools grew so mad at that, that they took to stoning."

When, later, Rhoda heard the tale more fully, it showed elements of incongruous comedy; later still, she heard it grown into monstrous proportions, when the name of the Tortoises was put aside, and the place was known as the Devil's Rocks thenceforward. The Alien's feats that day, his mighty stroke staving the boat, his swimming of marvellous speed, his confidence and temerity, were not passed on to his credit: adverse was the interpretation, and he never lived it down.

"Tell me, Christian, where you will be, and how we are to get news of you till you dare return."

"Dare return! If I be not dead, that will I to-morrow."

She cried out against such insanity.

"You must not. It is wicked with a foolhardy parade to torment us—your mother."

"Have no fear, dear. If I come again, it will be with joy, bearing my sheaves."

She could put an interpretation on his words that loaded her heart.

"Rhoda, dear sister, I owe you much this day, and now I will ask for one thing more."

She said "Yes," though foreboding ordeal. It was a minute before he spoke.

"Will you pray for us?"

Poor heart, how could she? Anything but that.

"What worth are the prayers of such an one as I? Desire rather your mother's prayers."

"She for another cause will be praying the night through. Will you do as much for us?"

He stopped her, for she did not speak, and held her by the shoulders, trying to see her face to get answered.

"O Rhoda, will you not pray for us?"

She made her answer singular. "I will pray for thee"; but his greater want overcame her into ending: "and—for Diadyomene."

He stood stock-still and gripped her hard when that name came, but he asked nothing. "I will, I will," she whispered; and then he kissed her brow and said: "God bless you." She flung her arms round his neck without reserve; her cheek lay against his bare breast, and because she felt a cross there she dared to turn her lips and kiss. He gathered her to close embrace, so that swept from her feet she lay in his arms rapt for one precious instant from all the world.

When he had set her on her feet, when he had blessed her many times, she clung to him still, heaving great sobs, till he had to pluck away her hands.

"Yes, go," she said. "I will pray for you both," and down she knelt straightway.

"God be with you."

"God be with you."

He passed from her into the darkness, away from sorrows she knew to some unknown. Rhoda, flung prostrate, wept bitterly, rending her heart for the getting of very prayer for that unknown woman, her bane.

Too little thought Christian, though he loved her well, of her who so faithfully went on his bidding, trudging wearily on to make good his word, kneeling afterwards through the long hours in prayer that was martyrdom. If the value of prayer lie in the cost, hers that night greatly should avail.

CHAPTER XV

Late knocking came importunate to the House Monitory. One went to the wicket and looked out. Her light, convulsed, for an instant abetted a delusion that he who stood knocking outside was Christ Himself with the signs of His Passion: unclothed was the man she saw, bloodstained, both head and hands. Then she noted fair hair, and had to believe that this haggard man was one with the brave-faced boy of earliest summer. He clung to the ledge for support; so spent was he that a word was hard to compass.

"For the love of God," he said, "you who are watchers to-night pray for a human soul in sore need."

She would vouch for that; she would summon one with authority to vouch for more.

When she carried word within: "'Tis the same," said one, "who twice has left fish at the gate, who slept once at the feet of St. Margaret."

To the wicket went the head monitress, and, moved to compassion by the sight of his great distress, she gave him good assurance that not the five watchers only, but one and all, should watch and pray for him that night, and she asked his name for the ordering of prayer.

"Not mine!" he said. "I ask your prayers for another whose need is mine. Pray for her by the name Diadyomene."

He unfastened the cross from his neck and gave it.

"This is a pledge," he said, "I would lay out of my weak keeping for St. Mary, St. Margaret, and St. Faith to hold for me, lest to-night I should desire I had it, to be rid of it finally according to promise."

He had not made himself intelligible; clearer utterance was beyond him.

"No matter!" he said. "Take it—keep it—till I come again."

He knotted the empty string again to his neck, and, commended to God, went his way.

Now when these two, little later, asked of each other, "What was the strange name he gave?" neither could remember it. But they said "God knows," and prayed for that nameless soul.

Somehow Christian got down the cliffs to the shore, as somehow he had come all the way. Little wonder head and hands showed bloody: every member was bruised and torn, for he had stumbled and gone headlong a score of times in his desperate speed over craggy tracks, where daylight goings needed to be wary. Scarcely could hoofed creatures have come whole-foot, and he, though of hardy unshod practice, brought from that way not an inch sound under tread. An uncertain moon had favoured him at worst passes, else had he fallen to certain destruction.

He stood at the sea's edge and paused to get breath and courage. To his shame, he was deficient in fortitude: the salt of the wet shingle bit his feet so cruelly, that he shrank at the prospect of intensified pain through all the innumerable wounds he bore. He saw exposed a pitiful, unstable wretch, with a body drained of strength and nerve, and a spirit servile to base instances. In desperate spite he plunged and swam.

He had ever waited for an outgoing tide; he had ever taken a daylight tide; now for his sins he had night and the flood against him. But still the moon blessed him. Delusions beset him that pains of his body came from the very teeth of sea-creatures, too fierce and many for him to cope with, crowding, dragging, gnawing hard at his life. For ease a passive moment and a little painful, airless sobbing would suffice: soonest, best. And had the pale moon darkened, he had gone under as at a supreme command, to such depravity and destitution were come his vital instincts. But, her light holding him alive, by hard degrees he won his way, till, for the last time, he stood upon the Isle Sinister.

But when he had made his way through the narrow gorge, and trod sand, the moon was dark, and night fell upon his heart. He dared not call, and neither sight nor sound granted him assurance of Diadyomene's presence. Wanting her footprints to tell she had passed in, he feared lest he should be barring her very entrance. He fell down and prayed, being without resource.

And Lois was praying, and Rhoda with bitter tears, and the House Monitory with the ring of its bells. Very faint was the moan of the sea in their ears.

Slowly, slowly, the blessed moon stepped out, and lifted him up and delivered to his sight the track of light feet set from seaward—one track only. In haste, by the wavering light of the moon, he laid out the threaded rowan and weighted one end against the rock. The whole length extended came short of the further wall by about two feet.

He rallied from the momentary shock, resolving that he himself could stand in the gap to bar passage.

No form nor motion could he discern within his range as in slow scrutiny his eyes sought her from side to side. He lighted on despair; the entrance to the cavern had escaped his providence.

In the dark he went to the low arch, and felt about the sand inch by inch for the dint of her feet. Naught could he find. Yet what did it profit him that she had not yet passed? To drop prone on the sand was his poor conclusion, abandoned to despair.

He was but cast back on the morning's portion, then of fair sufficiency, but now oh! meagre, meagre, compared to the ripe hope that had come of nourishment strange and opportune as manna from heaven. Then had he incurred to no purpose expense of blood and sweat and anguish of body and mind, nay, brought to the crucial hour such an appalling deficiency.

To contest a human soul with powers of darkness required perfect steadfastness of will and faith; lost, lost, with mere self-control lost in a useless barter that left him now a clod of effete manhood, with just life enough for groaning pain. Before conflict was he vanquished. Diadyomene need but come with a word of anger or derision to break him into childish sobbings.

Yet driven to last extremity, such man's strength as remained to him might prevail in sanctified violence for the winning of a soul. He would hold her by the feet; his hands were bloody, but he would hold her by the feet; should he have to cling round her, he would not hurt; meek and gentle could he be, though fury should set her to such savage handling as a woman's strength may compass.

To win a human soul? O wretched piece of clay, not that! The mere thought of contact with Diadyomene, close contact with her, cool, soft, naked there in the cold dark, swept the bright delirium of sea-magic over him again, stung his blood to a burning fever, set him writhing as pain had never. At the fiery blast, in this nadir hour the place of pure love was assaulted and taken by base lust; his desire was most strong, not for the winning of a human soul, but for the wicked winning of a human body, ay, maugre her will—any way.

Yet, oh for the fair way of her favour! Had she not allowed him very gracious hints?—"lay your hand upon my breast, set your lips to mine." Thrice she had said it—once when a touch on her hand had brought magical vision, once at her kindest, once at her cruelest. Though her command was against him, though her anger might not be overpast, a hope kindled that dread of the dark hour of her fate might urge her to his arms, there to find such gladness and consolation as might leave no place for horror to come into possession.

"And give up your soul." Thrice too had that been said. He was loath to give it remembrance, but it entered, whenever faint bells tolled on his ear it entered.

Very strangely, while good and evil fought equal-handed for his will, he perceived that his body had risen to hands and knees, and was going forward very fitly like a beast. All round the cold dark began to burn. A boulder lay athwart his course, and then very strangely he was aware that his arms had fastened round it with convulsive strength, and brow and breast were wounded against it. He could not take possession to end this disgraceful treason; all that was left to him was to rescue integrity at least by undoing the knot at his neck.

Then prevailed the blessed guile of Lois. The trivial exaction brought her son face to face with her, with her sorrows, with her prayers, and the mere communion of love set him praying frantically, and so brought him to himself again.

> We beseech, we beseech, we beseech:
> Lord God for my unbaptized!
> Dear Christ for Christian's Diadyomene!
> Blessed Trinity and all Saints for a nameless soul in sore need!

Vile, vile indeed, were he to desert a holy alliance.

There where the token had lain on his breast cross-edges of the boulder were wounding, and strange human nature turning ravenous to any gross substitution of fires, seized with wild energy on the ecstasy of pain, till the rock cut to the bone, while the whole boulder seemed to stir. In nowise might the cross be cast aside: it was kept against his will in holy ward; it was printed indelibly in his flesh.

The very boulder had stirred. Then hope rose up as a tyrant, for he had fallen spent again. Spirit was weak and flesh was weak, and it were task hard out of measure to heave that boulder from its bed and set it up to block the low entrance; and useless, when at a sight or a sound Diadyomene were away fleet foot to the sea.

And yet he felt about, set feet and shoulder for an arch of strength, and strained with great hefts; and again the mass seemed to stir. He dropped down, trenched painfully round, and tried again till his sinews cracked. Nor in vain: with a reluctant sob its bed of sand gave up the stubborn rock, and as it rolled endlong a devil that had urged excuse went from Christian. Foot after foot he fought that dreadful weight along the sand, right up to the cleft, right across the cleft he forced it. Not yet had he done enough; for he could feel that as the boulder lay, there was space for a slim body to press across and win the cavern. To better the barrier by a few poor inches, this way and that he wrung his wearied body and broke flesh; and to no purpose. "Except my bones break, I will." He grappled strenuously; a little give responded. He set his feet closer in, and lifted again mightily, and the boulder shifted, poised onward to settle.

Who struck? Death.

Nerveless, he swayed with the rock, on a motion its own weight consummated, agape, transfixed by the wonder of living still.

Fresh, horrible pain seized him by foot and ankle, casting him down to tear up the sand, to bite the sand, lest in agony he should go shrieking like a woman.

He writhed round to strike in the dark at the senseless mass, in the madness of terror and pain deeming the boulder itself had moved with malignant intelligence, not merely according to the preponderate laws that lift the world. To him the presence of infernal powers was manifest in this agent. In foul warfare they held him fast by the heel, and mocked the impotent spirit within the bonds of flesh. The dark grew pregnant with evil beings as he struggled to swooning.

Pray for us, faithful hearts, pray! In the name of the Father, the Son, and the Holy Ghost, for her service! Then he prevailed, and out of the teeth of hell he wrenched his heel.

Broken, crippled, strengthless, Christian crawled over the sand to the spot where he would die. Indistinguishable in the dark was the furrow he left stained till the tide should come: long before daylight broke the tide would come up to smooth and whiten it. He knew he was dying, and, touching the ended rowan, rendered thanks that it was to be there. All was nearly over, pain and a foolish, arrogant hope on which he had staked his life: presently, when he was dead, Diadyomene would come, to overstep his body, eluding there the toils. He misliked the thought that her feet might go red from treading him, and he stretched about weakly for briny hollows along the rock to cleanse the hot, slow oozing that chilled and stiffened into long stripes.

Why should he be gasping still, as breathless as after his hardest race, as after his mightiest heft? He required breath to help endurance of thirst and exorbitant pain; air could he gasp in, deep and free, and yet he wanted for more.

Why he should be dying, and how, Christian did not know. Life's centre had been stricken mortally quicker than a lightning-flash, too subtly for the brain to register any pain, so unmistakably he wondered only he was yet alive. From breath to breath he awaited another touch and a final, yet nothing lacked for vital order save air, air, more air. At short, merciful intervals he drifted out of the range of any pain.

On this his third death he did not so very greatly shrink from passing out of the body to stand before the face of his Maker. He could not take up any meaning for prayer. He was discarded from service; perfect justice had tried him, judged him, and condemned him as unfit. It was bitter for him; but review of his finishing span of life, its sin, failure, impotence, brought him to acquiescence. "Thine is the kingdom, and the power, and the glory" was all he had of prayer.

The apprehension of each human principle was straitened, by darkness about him, by pain in strong possession, by recognition of death closing in. As visitants to his heart from some far-distant sphere came Rhoda, Lois, Diadyomene; they vanished away; he could not keep them close—not even Diadyomene. "Dear love, my love!"

Through the dark she came.

He rose to his knees, aware of a moving glimmer of grey, nearing, near. At her swift, beautiful pace she made for the sea. Suddenly she stood. He heard the catch of her breath; swiftly the dim oval of her face was turned to him; then away. She swayed back a step; she swayed forward; hung a moment at poise upright; reeled aside, and fled back into the dark.

Then Christian found he had yet strong faculty for life. He had retained small certainty that she had not long passed him by; speculation had fallen faint. Lo! she was here, controlled, and he not dead. He could pray, for her and for a little life, passionately.

A low, bitter cry quivered through the dark to his heart. Diadyomene had fled for a way of escape, and found it barred. Soft rapids were her feet; she came speeding full to leap past. In vain; with a cry she flung up her arms, revulsed irresistibly, swerved, and stood stone-still. She moaned out long, agonised sighs; she seemed to turn away in pride, ignoring him; she seemed to face him again, not defiant. He saw her hands outstretched in appeal. "What have you done?" she said; "what have you done?" and then the woful complaint was changed to wilder: "What have I done? what have I done?"

He did not dare to speak, nor had he the breath. He was weeping for her. But she, not seeing, was stirred to wrath and fear by a silence so cruel. To her height she rose above the gasping, crouched shape, and her voice rang hard and clear.

"Stand away. Once you trespassed, and I forgave you fully; twice, and I spared you; this third time—get you gone quickly, and find yourself some easy death before it be out of reach."

Still he did not answer. Her fear outdid her anger, and she stooped her pride.

"Only be kind and true, and let me go," she implored, and knelt low as he. "I let you take my secret, and you turn it against me treacherously. You plan a shameful snare, you, you, whom I counted true as the sun. To you, a bold, graceless stranger, I granted life at the first; to you I gave the liberty of my dearest haunt. Be just, and leave me free in my own. Have pity, and let me go. Woe and horror are coming upon me to take me, awake and astray from the comfort of the sea." She moaned and sighed piteously.

His tears fell like rain for grief of his doings, for bitter grief that he might not comfort her.

Because of a base alloy that had altered sacred love he had to fear. He turned away his head, panting and shaking, for pain and thirst made almost unendurable a temptation to stretch out his hand to hers, by the magic of her touch to lose himself till death in a blissful swoon.

Her wail had in it the note of a deserted child and of a desolate woman.

"I am crying to you for pity and help, and you turn away; I, who in the sea am regnant. But late you cried to me when no mercy and pardon were due, and I let you live. And if then I judged you unheard and wrongly, and if I condemned a breach of faith over harshly, here kneeling I pray you to forgive—I, who never bid vainly, never ask vainly, of any living creature but of you."

Christian only was weeping; Diadyomene shed no tear, though her voice quivered piteously.

"Ah, my sea, my sea! Hark how it moans to me, and cannot reach me! My birds fail me, nestling afar—that you considered when you came by night. Undo, undo your cruel work, and I will reproach you never."

His silence appalled her. "Why should you do this?" she cried. "What would you have of me? A ransom? Name it. The wealth of the sea is mine to give; the magic of the sea is mine. To all seas, to all sea-creatures, you shall bear a charmed life henceforward, only let me go."

He sobbed, "But I die, I die!" but so brokenly that the words failed at her ears.

"Hear me," she said; "I make no reservation. Ask what you will, and nothing, nothing I can grant will I refuse—only quickly let me go."

She was crouched before him, with her face downward and hidden, as she moaned, and moaned surrender. Presently she half lifted, and her voice was at a lovely break between grief and gladness.

"Fool, dear ignorant fool, Diadyomenos, are you blind? You have come to me often; have I ever looked unglad? Have I wearied of you soon? Have I failed you? Could you read into that no favour from me, Diadyomene, who have the sea to range? Can you wrong so my grace to you in the past as to plan an extortion? Ah, foolish, needless, empty wrong! Your eyes have been fair to me when they said what your tongue would not. Speak now fair words, since I cannot read your eyes. Dear hands, reach out for mine, take them and draw me out of the snare, and with gladness and shame own it needless, as with gladness and pride will I."

So vile a wretch she took him to be! and the bitterness was that he might not disclaim. For a moment he had fallen to that baseness; it might be that only because life was going out of him so fast was he past such purpose now. A stupid "No, no," was all he could bring out.

She sprang up at a bound, driven to fury. She longed to strike with mere woman strength, yet she dared not a contact, lest hers be the disadvantage. With a shriek she fled back into the dark, and he heard the dreadful wailing cries wheeling away. Desperately he prayed for himself and for her; for his pain and an agony of pity were almost more than he could bear.

Suddenly she came upon him and stood close. Her tone was changed.

"At last," she said, "miserable creature, you shall know the truth. You love me. I know it well; I have known it long. And with all my strength—I—hate you. Not for this night's treachery and insolence only; from the first I hated you; and hatred has grown since more bitter-strong, till your one life and body seemed all too little to stay it. Ah! the love I read in your eyes has been sweet sustenance. So I waited and waited only for this: for love of me to take deep hold of your heart, to be dearer than life, before I plucked it up by the roots; and to laugh in your face as I did it, knowing it worse than any death. Oh! it should have been by daylight. I would like to see your face and your eyes now, and watch your great body writhe—I think it does! Why, laugh I must.

"Can you fathom my hate by its doings? You stood here first, glad, proud, strong in your youth; but a few short weeks, and I had turned all to ruin. Yes, I—I—only was your bane, though I but watched, and laughed, and whispered beneath my waters, and let you be for the handling of your fellows. Truly my hate has worked subtly and well, and even beyond device; it has reached beyond you: an old man treads the quay no more, and a girl comes down to it grown pale and heavy-eyed, and a woman ageing and greyer every time. Think and know! You never shall see them again; for a brief moment you check and defy me, but the entrance of the tide shall bring you your death.

"Now, I the while will plan the worst death I may. You think you have faced that once already? Fool! from to-morrow's dawn till sunset I will teach you better. The foulest creature of the deep shall take you again and hold you helpless—but that is nothing: for swarms shall come up from the sea, and from twilight to twilight they shall eat you alive. They shall gnaw the flesh from your limbs; they shall pierce to the bone; they shall drill you through and rummage your entrails. And with them shall enter the brine to drench you with anguish. And I, beside you, with my fingers in your hair, will watch all day, and have a care to lift your head above the tide; and I will flick off the sea-lice and the crays from your face and your eyes, to leave them whole and clear and legible to my hate at the last. And at the very last I will lay my face down against yours, and out of very pure hate will kiss you once—will kiss you more than once, and will not tire because you will so quicken with loathing. Even in the death agony I mean you to know my fingers in your hair. Ha! Agonistes.

"And now you wish you had died on that moonlit, warm night long ago: and me it gladdens to think I did not then cut you off from the life to follow after, more bitter than many quick deaths. And you wish I had finished you outright in the late storm, that so you might have died blissfully ignorant of the whole truth: and I spared you only that you should not escape a better torture that I had contrived.

"Ah! it has been a long delight to fool you, to play my game with flawless skill. As I choose a wear of pearls, so chose I graces of love for adornment. Am I not perfect now? What have I said of hatred and love? No, no, all that is false. Because you scorn the sea-life so dear to me, I try to keep hatred; but it may not abide when you stand before me and I look in your eyes—oh! slay it, slay it quite with the touch of your lips. My love!" her voice fell softly: "My love, my love, my love, my love!" She was chasing the word along all the ranges of derision.

She stood no more than a pace from him, a flexile figure that poised and swung, to provoke the wild beast in him to spring. Christian never stirred nor spoke.

"Would the moon but shine! I mean to watch you when you die, but I think a better sight your face would be now than then. How well it pleases me your eyes are grey! Can grey eyes serve as well to show hate as love? Ay, I shall laugh at that: to see in them hate, hate like my own; but impotent hate, not like mine. It hardly has dawned yet, I guess, but it will; and presently be so strong that the dearest joy left would be to have your hand on my throat to finish my life. Do you think I fear? I dare you, defy you! Ha! Agonistes."

He did not come hurling upon her; he did not by word or sign acknowledge her taunts.

"Why, the night of my dread goes blithely as never before. There is no bane left in it. I have found an antidote."

She forced a laugh, but it went wild, strangled, and fell broken. Again she fled back into the dark, and, like a prisoned bird, circled frantic for the sea that she could not reach. Far from Christian, she halted and panted low: "Not yet have I failed, dear sea. Though love may not prevail, nor hate, yet shall my song."

Though the incoming tide sounded near, echo still carried the tolling of the bells. For the knell of that passing soul fittest names they bore out of all the Communion of Saints. St. Mary! bitter dregs had his life to drain; St. Margaret! his pearl of the sea was lost in deep waters; St. Faith! utter darkness was about, and desperate striving could find no light of Heaven; his life, his love, his God forsook, rejected, disowned him.

Loss or fear could not touch him any more, for not one hope, one joy remained. From the cruel havoc, calm, passionless wonder distilled, and new proportions rose as his past came before him to be measured anew: so tolerable looked the worst of inflictions, a passing wrong, forgivable, forgettable; so sorry looked the best endurance, a wretched contortion, defacing, deforming. Against Diadyomene not one throb of passion stirred: she had broken his heart outright, so that it had not true faculty of life for any new growth. Strangely, to his wonder, under this her doing, the old derangement passed away, and the way of loving-kindness to all men showed clear. Too late! Never in this life could he meet his fellows with good, quiet blood, and frank eyes, and wholesome laughter, unafraid, simply acknowledging all records, free, candid, scrutable.

He began even before death to resolve to impersonality; he surveyed the perverse obstinacy of vitality that would not quit its old habitation, though fierce pain was in possession; and he could wonder at the wretched body heaving, tortured by a double thirst for air, for water, when so short a time would render it mere quiet earth, soon to unshape.

Out of the darkness rang her voice, noting beauty wordless, and sunlit seas glanced through the nights: the magic of the sea was upon him.

Brief sweetness! the bright sound faltered, broke. O blackness and pain! The far, slow knell struck in.

Again, up welled the buoyant voice, poised and floated exquisitely, mounted and shrilled frantically sweet, caught up the failing senses from the death sweats, and launched them on a magic flood of emotion, through racing sprays, and winds vivid and strong of the brine.

Gone, ah! gone; for a wailing cry came, and then thwart silence suddenly, and flung him back to the dominion of black anguish.

And again and again, high-noted, above the tramp of the nearing tide, that perfect voice flew to delicious melody; and promise of words strengthened the enchantment; and yet, and yet, a cry and a silence stabbed and bled the spell she would fashion.

Perfect achievement came. Up rose a measure transcending in rapture all forgone, and flawless, unfaltering, consummate, leaped on and on, rhythm by rhythm, clear-syllabled for conquest.

> "Where silver shallows hold back the sea,
> Under the bend of the great land's knee,
> And the gleaming gulls go nestled and free.
>
> Where the tide runs down in the round of the bay,
> There in the rings where the mermen play,
> On ribs and shallows their footprints lay.
>
> In liquid speech they laughed and sung,
> Under the rocks, till the rout outswung,
> Called from the echoing cave its tongue.
>
> They were away with the glimmering seas:
> Off with the twilight, off with the breeze,
> Wave-weeds fell from their glancing knees;
>
> Robes laid by, which the hollowed spars
> Held and hid, while the wet sand-bars
> Failed of the sunlight and filled with stars.
>
> Sea-mists rose for a dream, but when
> Mists wore faint in the sunlight, then
> Lo, the sea with its dancing men.

Spume and swirl spun under their feet;
Sparkle and flash, for the runners were fleet;
Over them climbed the day to its heat.

And the day drew a draught of the tide-winds strong,
As a singer the breath to be rendered song,
As a child the life that will last so long."

Christian had fallen prone.

While she sang, so potent was the magic, he lusted to live. Sentient only to the desires she kindled, out of account lay the dead heart, and the broken strength, and the body so shattered within and without, that wonder was it yet could hold a man's life. Pain was excluded by a great sensual joy of living.

Her song manned the mirage of her delight, and straightway he was passionate for life. Never before had she acknowledged the sea-fellowship to occasion the ravenous ache of jealousy. She sang of the mermen, and they rose before him visionary at the spell, with vigorous hair and frolic eyes, very men, lithe and sinewy for the chase and capture of their feminine fairest in amorous play. Life was one fire burning for the hot war of nature's males, as through the riot, whirling with the song, he eyed challenge and promise of a splendid wrestle with strong, hard limbs; and the liquid, exquisite voice was a call to him to speed in and win, nor suffer the wanton sea-brood to prevail.

It was then that his body fell, face forward, never to rise again.

On sang Diadyomene, not knowing that a power stronger than her magic, stronger than his will, kept him from her feet. On she sang, herself possessed, uttering not with her own will more than magic. What alien element underlay the spell she would deliver? what lurking revelation to be dreaded, to be desired, hid beneath? Her voice was caught back again, and yet again, to repeat the finish:

"As a singer the breath to be rendered song,
As a child the life that will last so long—
As a child—"

Then bell notes fell in a chime. She lifted her head; they rang, she hearkened, motionless, wordless.

It was midnight, and joy for the birth of Christ thrilled the world. No spell could hold. Christian must resume the throes of death.

The cold and the tide were merciful to shorten. His limbs were stone-cold and dead already, past motion, past pain. Against his side the foremost lap of the tide told. It licked and bit along his body, flanks, breast, throat, touched his cheek. Astray against his face he felt the thread of rowan. It kissed along cheek, along brow, and swung wide and away.

"Christ, Christ, ah! Christ."

He turned his head and drank of the brine, and drank and drank to slake the rage of thirst. The drawing of breath made hindrance: not for long. The last draughts he took were somewhat sharp and painful, but they quenched his thirst. He was entirely satisfied.

> "We beseech, we beseech; we beseech:
> Lord God for my unbaptized!
> Dear Christ for Christian's Diadyomene!
> Blessed Trinity and all Saints for a nameless soul in sore need!"

CHAPTER XVI

Through all creation went the divine breath of renunciation. Joy for the birth of Christ rang on; and motionless, wordless, Diadyomene hearkened, released from the magic of the sea.

Dawned a vision remote, but strangely distinct, of a small life comprehending two dear figures—one most dear; and thereto a small, beautiful pain responded. A tale flashed across and across, gaining coherence, giving it: the tale of a loved and lost child, long years ago lost to the sea; loved still. Perfect grew the interweaving; the substance of the two became one.

Joy for the birth of Christ was abroad, thrilling all planes of existence with the divine breath of renunciation. In the soul of Diadyomene, waked from its long trance, love was alive; a finite, individual love, chief centred on one dearest to remembrance. The beautiful pain grew large, and the cold heart that the sea-life had filled and satisfied was yearning for share in another life long forgone. A small divine instinct, following ignorantly in the wake of that great celestial love that hundreds of years ago stooped to the sorrow of life, urged her to renounce the ample strengths and joys of the sea, and to satisfy a piteous want, were it by repression of energies, by eschewing full flavours of sense, by the draining of her young life. The soul of true womanhood in this child for the cherishing of her mother waxed mature.

Motionless, wordless, she hearkened while separate bells cadenced; when again they fell to their wonted unison, the sea-bred woman knew that a soul was hers, and that it claimed dominion.

> "We beseech, we beseech, we beseech:
> Lord God for my unbaptized!
> Dear Christ for Christian's Diadyomene!
> Blessed Trinity and all Saints for a nameless soul in sore need!"

Diadyomene flung out vacant arms, and moaned a dear name, for years unuttered. Across the long interval of sea-life her spirit leaned to own the filial heart of childhood. Clear to her as a yesterday came back that broken fragment of earlier life,—bright, partial, inadequate, quaintly minute, as impression had gone into a happy, foolish infant. Not a memory had traversed the ground since to blur a detail, though now the adult faculties could apprehend distortion, the beautiful vagarious distortion that can live in a brain over toddling feet.

Recent song caught colour; reflected it.

"As a woman the breath to be rendered song,
As a child the life that will last so long."

From deep roots under dense forgetfulness the song had drawn up truth to blossom in perfect form. Before the eager wonder of the child the sea had revealed its secret of men shapes, who had beckoned, and laughed, and tempted her with promise and play, till she stretched out her arms to their glee, till she ran in their circles, till, breathless, she thirsted and drank of their offering, and so passed.

So tempered was her cold sea body that no ice-wind ever started a shiver. Now one came, for the mother might not recognise her child, for the child might be grown unworthy of her mother's love.

There was one to succour: Christian. What had she done? There was one to blast her, too foul for any love: Christian.

Her hideous doings rushed back upon her with conviction of guilt; an old sense revived; she shrank and cowered, bowed to the ground by an agony of shame.

Lo! the moon bared her face and looked.

Diadyomene rose to her knees; with a steady will she rose to her feet and went to suffer her full penalties.

Her portion of shame was dreadful to bear; her bold avowal of love for Christian, her atrocious wording of hate intervolved to double disgrace. Then neither passion had been entirely feigned; now she knew that love swayed her alone, turning her to a worship of the man. No bitterer penance could she conceive than with confession to him to strip heart and soul naked as her body; this only could extend it: should his large generosity keep under his loathing and contempt, and order him to deal gently for her help according to pity. No way could he remit her dues.

As she went to meet his face, she lifted her gaze up the slant moon-beams, looking piteous, despairing appeal for darkness to come back and cover her. Wisps of cloud made only a poor pretence. She met the tide unhindered, and stood; she looked, no man was there; she wailed "Christian, Christian," and no voice answered. With relief for the lengthened shadows below the rocks, she made for the very spot where he had knelt; it was far overpassed by the tide. Ankle deep she trod: knee deep. She sets her foot upon a man's hand, leaps, stumbles on his body to a fall: Christian dead lies under her embrace.

Supreme justice had measured her due.

The placid clay had returned to an old allegiance, and weltered with the tide according to the joint ordering of earth and moon. The living creature would not acknowledge that right dominion, most desperately would withstand it. She stooped her shoulder beneath the low head, and heaved it up above the tide: the air did but insist that it lay dead-still. With all her slender feminine strength put out for speed, she girthed, she held, she upbore the inert weight afloat for moonlighted shallows. There her knee up-staying, her frantic hands prevailing over the prone figure, the dead face fell revealed. No hope could appeal against that witness.

A strange grey had replaced the ruddy tan of life, darker than the usual pallor of the dead. That, and the slack jaw, and the fixed, half-shut eyes, a new and terrible aspect gave to the head, dear and sacred above all on earth to the stricken creature beholding.

For a long moment appalled she gazed, knowing yet but one fathom of her misery: just her loss, her mere great loss past repair. Then moaning feebly, her arms went round again to draw it close. Her smooth palms gliding over the body told of flawed surfaces, bidding her eyes leave the face to read new scores: on the breast a deep rent, on the shoulder another, and further more and more wherever a hand went. Along one arm she stretched hers, and lifted it up to the light of the moon. Beside the tense, slender limb, gleaming white, that other showed massive, inert, grey-hued, with darker breaks. The hand hanging heavy was a dark horror to see.

Shadows invaded, for the moon was foundering on the rocks.

Across her shoulders she drew the heavy burden, strove to rise upright to bear it, tottered, fell, and then dragged on with elbows and knees as the waves resigned to her the full load. Heavy knees furrowed the sand beside hers, heavy arms trailed; the awful, cold face drooped and swayed from her shoulder as she moved; now and again it touched her cheek.

Withdrawn from the fatal sea, what gain had she? The last spark of life was long extinct, and she knew it; yet a folly very human set her seeking Christian's self in the shell that was left, scanning it, handling it, calling upon deaf ears, drawing the wet head against her breast. Cold, cold was her breast; the sea-magic had bred out all heat from her heart.

She pressed the dripping hair; she stooped and kissed her dead lover on the lips. It was then her iniquity struck home with merciless rigour complete. "I will lay my face down against yours, and out of very pure hate will kiss you once. Even in the death-agony I mean you to know my fingers in your hair."

The wretched soul writhed as the hideous words rose up against her to damn. They were alive with every tone and laugh; they would live stinging and eating out her heart until she died.

And after death?

"Christian! Christian!"

The agonised cry now was no effort to waken deaf ears; it called after Christian himself, gone past reach of her remorse into unknown night. Gone deliberately, to be finally quit of so abhorred a creature? In mute witness the quiet body lay to vindicate Christian: too broken it was, too darkly grey for any death self-willed.

Then she could look upon the blank face no more, for the moon passed quite away. Then the stretching tide came lapping and fawning, soon to sway the dead weight she held. She was not worthy to look upon clay so sacred, she was not worthy to touch it, she who in wanton moods had inclined to a splendid male, nor recognised in him a nobler version of love. No spark of profane passion could remain after she had kissed the cold, dead face.

The dreadful cry of a soul's despair broke the vacant air with the name of Christian. Many times his name, and no other word. The desolation of great agony was hers: no creature of the sea could bring her any comfort now; no creature under heaven; for the one on earth to whom her child's heart yearned was the one on earth she least dared face with her awful load of guilt.

Nothing could atone for what she had done: life could never give scope, nor death. Were this that she held Christian himself, able to see and hear, her passionate remorse could conceive no dearer impossibility than at his feet to fall, with supplication, with absolute confession delivering the love and worship of her heart before him: to be spurned by his inevitable hate. The inexorable indifference of the dead was a juster, a more terrible, recompense.

Yet a more terrible conception woke from a growing discernment of Christian's utter abstraction from the mortal shape, that so long had represented him to her, and so well. This his body had ceased from suffering and endurance, yet the very self of Christian might bear with him unassuaged the wounds and aches her malice had compassed. Hate would heal, would sear, at least; but oh! if he had not quit him of a tyrannous love, then bruised and bleeding he carried with him still a living pain of her infliction. She dared not confidently reckon her vileness against the capacity of his extravagant love. She dared not. Her full punishment reached home to her at last.

Her ignorant mortal senses strained to pierce the impenetrable mystery that had wrapt Christian to an infinite remoteness. For his relief, not for her own, would she present to him her agonies of love and remorse: him stanched, averse: him bleeding, tender; to gratify, to satisfy, to plenish any want.

Tempests of despair raged through that undisciplined soul. Every hope was cut off, every joy was extinct. The sweet attraction of loving service, the pride and glory of despotic rule, were not for her, an exile from the one, and from the other abdicating. In all the world there was no place for her but this, between sea and land, with a hold on a dead illusion of Christian, with vain, frantic crying after his reality.

She did not know, whelmed in gulfs of sin and grief and despair, she did not know how divine a dawn brooded over the waste. From the long-lost past clear echoes swept of childish prayers, to blend as an undercurrent with that message her lover had so tried to deliver, that she had repelled as hideous and grotesque. She used no conscious memory, nor followed any coherent thought, but, consonant with the first instinct of her fresh awakened soul, that longing for her mother's sake to make renunciation, consonant with Christian's finished achievement—his striving, suffering, enduring even death for her unworthy sake—was this incoherent impression of a divinity vastly, vaguely suffering in exemplary extreme out of great compassion and love to mankind, thence accrediting suffering as the divinest force that can move the world. Her also it had vanquished.

The tide had turned; it pressed her gently to resume her old way to the deeps. The drift of another tide took her.

Out of her futile striving for direct communion with Christian grew a sense that the sole possibility left to her was to yield body and soul to his will in strict possession, and to follow that guidance. In her great misery and helpless desolation a how and a whither with quailing beset her going. Lo! the first step was sure, because it entailed a heartrending renunciation.

Ah! desperately dear was this, Christian's body, to her mortal apprehension of him. She held it very closely with an access of love and worship such as appertains to vacant shrines. O woe to part from it, to lay it aside and leave it to final obliteration!

Suddenly she wept. This near, definite distress, so humanly common, broke up the fountain of her tears so many a year sealed. To a creature long of the cold sea breeding tears were scalding to the heart.

Moaning, weeping, yet a little while she failed to forgo that embrace of pure worship and untainted love. Worthy of reverence that piece of clay was, for its loyal alliance with a high soul; wonderful as a noble and true representative; very sacred from the record of devotion scored deep, so fatally deep.

She wept, she wept as though weeping could cease from her never. Could the deep draught of sea-magic in tears be distilled, void of it should she be long before daybreak come.

The shallowing run of the tide drove her to resign the dead weight that exceeded her strength to uphold. Weeping, heartwrung, she bent her to replace her own will by Christian's! So first she gave away the dead body to final peace, and laid it down for ever in its destined sepulchre, and thereafter went alone into unfamiliar darkness to grope blind among strange worlds for the ways of Christian's countenance.

> We beseech, we beseech, we beseech:
> Lord God for my unbaptized!
> Dear Christ for Christian's Diadyomene!
> Blessed Trinity and all Saints for a nameless soul in sore need!

CHAPTER XVII

Some four days after Rhoda heard what more befell before that night was out. The chief monitress told her.

"We were watching all," she said, "and praying according to that promise I had made for a nameless soul in sore need, whose name, Diadyomene, you have restored to us. The dull roar of the sea came in swells of sound, filled as often with an illusion of voices; angry voices they sounded then. This I say that you may understand how a cry like a human creature in distress could pass unregarded at first. Again and again it came more distinctly, till we were startled into suspicion that a feeble knocking was close by at the lych door of our chapel. One went at my bidding to look out. Back she fled, with terror white as death: 'God and His saints guard,' she said, 'that without is not of flesh and blood!'

"I and another took her light and went to the door, and before unclosing I asked in the name of God who was there. No answer came but a sound of bitter sobbing. Then I looked out, and verily doubted also if what I looked on were indeed flesh and blood. Upon the threshold crouched a slender woman-shape, naked. I flung wide the door and touched her: she was cold as marble, colder, I dreaded, than any creature of life could be. Then did she raise her head to show the fairest and saddest face I have ever beheld. Her eyes were full of tears fast falling, and oh! the wild, hunted, despairing look they had. 'Christian, Christian!' she wailed. None knew of any such name.

"We lifted her up and led her in and covered her hastily. Her dark hair was all drenched; recent wet had not dried from her skin. A few flakes of snow had been drifting down; I noticed some that lay on her shoulders: they did not melt there. Cold as a marble statue she was, and as white, and of as beautiful a form as any that man has fashioned, and but for her sobbing and that one cry of 'Christian,' one could think as dumb.

"I would have led her to comfort and warmth and food, but she would not: from touch and question she shrank bewildered and scared; as though the cloak we had wrapped about her were irksome, she slipped it off once and again, unashamed of nakedness. Still her tears

214

fell like rain, and heavy sobs shook her. But as the great bells struck overhead, she caught in sudden breath and held it while the air throbbed, and thereafter broke out with her cry: 'Christian, Christian!'

"I bade all kneel and pray, that if this were indeed one of God's creatures, wisdom might be given us to deal with her for her welfare. In great perplexity I prayed, and some fear. I think it was that utter coldness of a living body that appalled me most.

"One spoke from her knees. 'The name of Christ is in her utterance; no creature outcast from salvation could frame any such word.' Then I said: 'I will take upon me to offer her instant baptism. That may be her need that she cannot perfectly utter.' She did not seem to hear one word when I spoke to her; I could see her mind was all too unknit for comprehension; she only cried out as before. But when I turned towards the altar and took her by the hand, she followed me unresisting.

"So, right before the altar we brought her, and made her kneel among us all. All our font was a stoup of holy water held at hand. Then I prayed aloud as God gave me the grace. She ceased to weep; she caught my hand in hers; I know she heard. In the name of the blessed Trinity I baptized her, but signed no cross; too suddenly she rose upright; she flung up her arms with one deep sigh. I caught a dead body from falling.

"God knows what she was."

The speaker fell to prayer. Presently Rhoda said: "How did you name her?"

"I named her Margaret."

Rhoda whispered: "She was Diadyomene."

Then she covered her face with her hands, lest the grave eyes should read over deep.

"What else?" she said, "tell all."

"When the grace of God had prevailed over our doubt and dismay, we did not dread to consider the dead countenance. It was fairer even than in life; serene as any sleeping child; death looked then like a singular favour.

"We closed her eyes and folded her hands, and laid her out before the altar, and resumed prayer for the one nameless and another Margaret.

"And no more we knew of whence she came than this: that by daybreak a powder of drying brine frosted her dark hair, and the hollows of her ears were white with salt."

"So," said Rhoda, "might come one cast ashore from a wreck."

"We took measures, indeed, to know if that could be; but out of all the search we sent about not a sign nor a clue came. If she were indeed that one Diadyomene, we may only look to know more when the young man Christian shall come again."

Rhoda turned her face to the wall when she answered very low: "He will not come again. Well I know he will never come again."

Then her breathing shortened convulsively, and past restraint her grief broke out into terrible weeping.

The dark-robed monitress knelt in prayer beside her. That pious heart was wise and loving, and saw that no human aid could comfort this lorn girl fallen upon her care. When Rhoda was spent and still, she spoke:

"My child, if, indeed, we can no more pray God to keep that brave young life from sin and death, yet may we pray that his soul may win to peace and rest under the mercy of heaven. Nay, there is no need that you too should rise for kneeling. Lie down, lie down, for your body is over spent. Kneel before God in spirit."

There was long silence, and both prayed, till Rhoda faltered to the betrayal of her unregenerate heart: "Was she so very fair indeed? Where is she laid? Take me—oh, let me once look upon her face."

"It may not be. She lies a day buried, there without among our own dead—although—God only knows what she was."

Rhoda again would rise.

"Yet take me there. Night-time? Ah yes, night, night that will never pass."

At daybreak she stood, alone at her desire, beside a new-made grave, and knew that the body of Diadyomene lay beneath, and knew hardly less surely, that somewhere beneath the sea she overlooked the body of Christian lay. Nearest the sea was the grave on the wind-blown, barren cliff. No flower could bloom there ever, only close dun turf grew. Below stretched the broken, unquiet sea, fretted with rock and surf, deep chanting of the wind and moon. One white sea-bird was wheeling and pitching restlessly to and fro.

She turned her eyes to the land far east for the thought of Lois. Over there a winter dawn flushes into rose, kindles bright and brighter, and a ruddy burnish takes the edges of flat cloud. Lo! the sun, and the grey sea has flecks of red gold and the sea-bird gleams. She cannot face it.

Rhoda knelt down by the grave to pray. Presently she was lying face downward along the turf, and she whispered to the one lying face upward below.

"Ah! Diadyomene, ah! Margaret. God help me truly to forgive you for what you have done.

"I have tried. Because he asked it, I have torn out my heart praying for you.

"You fair thing! you were fairer than I, but you did not love him so well as I.

"Ah! ah! would it were I who lay down there under the quiet shelter of the turf; would it were you who lived, able to set up his honour and make his name fair before all men!

"Ah! ah! a dark rebuke the mystery of your life has brought; and the mystery of your death eats it in.

"Can you bear to be so silent, so silent, nor deliver a little word?

"When you rise, Diadyomene, when the dead from the sea rise, speak loud, speak very loud, for all to hear.

"He loved you! He loved you!"

The sod above the face of Diadyomene was steeped with the piercing tears of Rhoda. "He loved you!" came many times as she sobbed.

Blind with tears, she rose, she turned from the grave; blind with tears, she stood overlooking the sea; sun and shine made all a glimmering haze to her. She turned from those desirable spaces for burial to stumble her blind way back to the needs of the living.

It was late, after sunset, that Rhoda, faint and weary, dragged into sight of the light of home. In the darkness a voice named her, struck her still. "Philip's voice!"

Groping for her in the dark, he touched her arm. Energy she had to strike off his hand and start away, but it failed when she stumbled and fell heavily; for then Philip without repulse helped her to her feet, and as she staggered a little, stunned, would have her rest a moment, and found the bank, and stripped off his coat for her seating. She said, "No, no," but she yielded.

"You thought me dead?" he asked.

She sat dumb and stupid, worn out in body and mind.

"Do you hold *me* to blame?"

Still she did not speak.

"Rhoda, O Rhoda, I cannot bear this! Has that devil Christian taught you?"

Rhoda rose up with an indignant cry. Then she steadied her voice and spoke.

"The name of Christian I love, honour, reverence, above all names on earth. You are not worthy even to utter it. Betake you, with your lies, your slanders, your suspicions, to others ready to suspect and slander and lie—not to me, who till I die can trust him utterly."

She turned and went. Philip stood.

"Is he dead?" he said to himself. "He is dead. He must be dead."

Awe and compassion alone possessed him. To his credit be it said, not one selfish consideration had a place then. Quick wits told him that Rhoda had inadvertently implied more than she would. He overtook her hastily.

"Hear me! I will not offend. I will not utter a word against him."

He spoke very gently, very humbly, because of his great compassion; and truly, Christian dead, it were not so hard to forgo rancour. But Rhoda went on.

"You must hear what I come to tell you before you reach home. Do you think I have been watching and praying for your return these hours, only to gird at Christian? For his mother's sake I came, and to warn you—"

She stopped. "What is it? What is it? Say quick."

"Nothing that you fear—nothing I can name. Hear me out!

"Last night I came back, and told, in part, what had befallen me; and heard, in part, what had befallen Christian. To-day, one thrust in upon his mother, open-mouthed, with ugly hints. She came to me straight and asked for the whole truth. Rhoda, I swear I said nothing but bare truth, mere plain, unvarnished fact, without one extravagant word; but her face went grey and stony as she heard—oh! grey and stony it went; and when I asked her to forgive me—I did, Rhoda, though what wrong had I done?—she answered with her speech gone suddenly imperfect."

Rhoda pressed forward, then stopped again—

"What did you tell her? I must know that."

Philip hesitated: "Then against Christian I must speak in substance, however I choose my words."

"Go on—go on!"

So Philip told, as justly and truly as he could, all he might.

"Was this," put in Rhoda, "off the Isle Sinister?"

"Yes."

She heard all the tale: of Christian's sullen mood; of the dark something attending below, that he knew, that he watched; of his unfinished attempt at murder.

"That we knew," she said.

Told in the dark by one who had lived through them, nearly died through them, whose voice yet acknowledged the terror of them,—circumstances were these of no vague indication to Rhoda. The reality of that dark implication stirred her hair, chilled her blood, loosened her joints; yet her faith in Christian did not fall.

But no word had she to say to refute the dreadful accusation; no word for Philip; no word for an adverse world. And what word for his mother? Her heart died within her.

The most signal evidence sufficient for her own white trust was a kiss, a close embrace, hard upon the naming of Diadyomene. She had no shame to withhold it; but too likely, under his mother's eye, discount would offer were maiden blood quick to her face when she urged her tale.

She knew that an ominous hum was against Christian, because he had struck, and swum, and escaped as no other man could; she guessed how the roar went now because of Philip's evidence. How inconsiderable the wrong of it all was, outdone if one injurious doubt his mother's heart entertain.

To hatred and to love an equal disregard death opposed. No menace could disturb, no need could disturb the absolute repose Christian had entered. She envied his heart its quiet in an unknown grave.

"Be a little kind, Rhoda; be only just; say I was not to blame."

She could not heed.

"Why do you hate me so? For your sake I freely forgive Christian all he has done; for your sake I would have been his friend, his brother, in spite of all. O Rhoda, what can I do?"

"Let be," she said, "for you can undo nothing now. If I saw you kneeling—no, not before me—but contrite, praying: 'God be merciful to me, for by thought and word and deed I have sinned against the noblest, the worthiest,' then, then only, far from hate, I think I could almost love."

No indignation was aflame with the words; the weary voice was so sad and so hopeless as to assure Philip she spoke of one dead.

"All I can do now is to pray God to keep me from cursing you and the world for your working of a cruel wrong that can never be ended." Her voice pitched up on a strain. "Oh, leave me, leave me, lest I have not grace enough to bear with you!"

Philip, daring no more, stood and heard the hasty, uneven steps further and die. His eyes were full of tears; his heart ached with love and pity for Rhoda in her sorrow and desolation, that he could do nothing to relieve—nothing, because her infatuation so extravagantly required.

Rhoda braced her heart for its work, reached to the latch, and stood face to face with Lois. The trial began with the meeting of their eyes; Rhoda stood it bravely, yielding no ground.

"Is he dead?" muttered Lois.

"None can tell us." She faltered, and began to tremble, for the eyes of Lois were dreadful to bear; dreadful too was her voice, hoarse and imperfect.

"Is he worse than dead?"

"No! Never—never think it."

Lois forbore awhile with wonderful stoicism. She set Rhoda in her own chair; the turf-covered embers she broke into a blaze to be prodigal of warmth; there was skilly waiting hot; there was water. She drew off Rhoda's shoes, and bathed her feet, swollen and sore; she enforced food.

Though she would not yet ask further, the sight of her face, grey and stony indeed, the touch of her hands, trembling over much, were imperative to Rhoda's heart, demanding what final truth she could give.

"Child, if you need sleep, I can bear to wait."

"I could not," said Rhoda. "No."

She looked up into the tearless, sleepless eyes; she clasped the poor shaking hands; and her heart rose in worship of the virtues of that stern, patient soul.

As the tale began they were face to face; but before long Rhoda had slipped from her seat, to speak with her head against his mother's knees.

"I will tell you all now. I must, for I think I am no longer bound to silence, and, indeed, I could not bear it longer—I alone."

"And you promised, if I would let you go unquestioned away."

"I did, thinking I went to fathom a mystery. Ah, no! so deep and dark I find it to be, the wit of man, I think, will never sound it. But your faith and love can wing above it. Mine have—and yours, oh!—can, will, must."

"Ah, Christian! Child, where is my Christian? His face would tell me briefly all I most would know."

"You have listened to an ugly tale. I know—I know—I have seen Philip. You must not consider it yet, till you have heard all. I own it not out of accord with the rest, that reason just shudders and fails at; but through all the dark of this unfathomable mystery my eyes can discern the passing of our Christian white and blameless."

"Your eyes!" moaned Lois.

Rhoda understood. She hid her face and could not speak. In her heart she cried out against this punishment as more than she deserved, and more than she could bear. No word that she could utter, no protest, no remorse, could cover a wrongful thing she had said for Lois to recall. So small the sin had looked then; so great now. She had spoken fairly of deadly sin just once, and now Lois could not rely on her for any right estimate, nor abide by her ways of regard.

"Ah, Christ!" she whispered in Christian's words, "is there no forgiveness of sins?"

Lois heard that, and it struck her to the heart.

Rhoda took up her burden again.

"Christian loved one Diadyomene. What she was I dare not think: she was shaped like a woman, very beautiful. Dead she is now; I have seen her new grave. God have mercy on her soul, if any soul she have.

"I have known this for long, for some months."

"He told—you!"

"No—yes. I heard her name from him only in the ravings of fever. He never thought I knew, till the very last: then I named her once; then he kissed me; then he went."

She turned back to the earliest evidence, telling in detail of Christian's mad course with her; then of his ravings that remained in her memory painfully distinct; she kept back nothing. Later she came to faltering for a moment till Lois urged:

"And he asked you to be his wife?"

"Yes."

"And because of this knowledge you refused him?"

"Yes. And he kissed me for joy of that nay-saying. On the very morrow he went—do you remember? It was to her. I knew it."

"O Rhoda, you might have saved him, and you did not!"

Rhoda raised her head and looked her wonder, for Christian's sake, with resentment.

"God smote one," she said, "whose hand presumed to steady His ark."

"O child, have you nothing to show to clear him?"

"Wait, wait! There is much yet to tell."

Then she sped on the last day with its load for record, and, scrupulously exact, gave words, tones, looks: his first going and return; the coming of Philip's kinsmen; that strange vagary of the rowan berries that he had won her to a bet. Lois had come upon a garbled version of Christian's escape; Rhoda gave her his own, brief and direct.

"Was it Christian—man alive!—that came to you?"

"It was. It was. He ate and drank."

Of their last meeting and parting she told, without reserve, unashamed, even to her kissing the cross on his breast.

Was ever maiden heart so candid of its passion for a man, and he alive? Too single-hearted was Rhoda to know how much of the truth exhaled from her words. Without real perception Lois drew it in; she grew very still; even her hands were still. Verily it had got to this: that to hear her dearest were dead, merely dead, could be the only better tale to come.

"Then," said Rhoda, "the morrow came and closed, and I would not believe he could have kept his promise to be dead; and a day and a day followed; and I dared tell you nothing, seeing I might not tell you all. Then I thought that in such extremity for your sake I did right to discover all I could of his secret; at least I would know if she, Diadyomene, were one vowed as I guessed in the House Monitory.

"Now I know, though I would not own it then, that deep in my heart was a terrible dread that if my guess were good, no death, but a guilty transaction had taken our Christian from us. Ah! how could I? after, for his asking, I had prayed for her.

"Now, though the truth lies still remote, beyond any guess of mine; though I heard of a thing—God only knows how she came by her life or her death—lacking evidence, ay, or against evidence, we yet owe him trust in the dark, never to doubt of his living worthily—if—he be not—dead worthily. Ah, ah! which I cannot tell you.

"I went to the House Monitory and knocked. So stupid and weak I was, for longer and harder than I looked for had the way been, and my dread had grown so very great, that when the wicket opened I had no word to say, and just stared at the face that showed, looking to read an answer there without ever a question. I got no more sense than to say: 'Of your charity pray for one Diadyomene.'

"I saw startled recognition of the name. Like a coward, a fool, in sudden terror of further knowledge, I loosed the sill and turned to run in escape from it. I fell into blackness. Afterwards I was told I had fainted.

"They had me in before I came to myself. Ah! kind souls they were. A monitress knelt at either side, and one held my head. When memory came back, I looked from one to the other, and dared not ask for what must come. There was whispering apart that scared me. Then one came to me. 'My child,' she said, 'we will pray without question if you will; yet if you may, tell us who is this Diadyomene?' I thought my senses had not come back to me. They would have let me be, but I would not have it then. 'Who is she?' I said; 'do not know, I came to you to ask.' 'We do not know.' Bewildered, I turned to the one who had opened to me. 'But you know; I saw it in your face when I named her.' 'The name I knew, nothing more; and that I had heard but once, and my memory had let it escape.' 'Where had you heard it? Who knows?' I said. 'On Christmas Eve a man came, a young man, fair-haired.' 'Christian,' I said, 'that was Christian.' At that three faces started into an eager cluster. 'Christian!' they said, 'was his name Christian?' Then they told me that after night-fall he had come and named Diadyomene, and that before daybreak a woman, naked and very beautiful, had come wailing an only word, 'Christian.' But because of the hour of his coming I said no, it could not be he, for I had seen him too shortly before. And indeed it seemed to me past belief that any man could have come that way by night so speedily. So they gave detail: his hair was fair; his eyes grey; he was of great stature; he was unclothed, bleeding freshly, and, yes, they thought, gashed along the shoulder. 'But here is a sure token,' and with that they showed me that cross he had worn. 'This,' they said, 'he unloosed from his neck.'"

Never a word more Lois heard of that tale, though for near a minute Rhoda carried it forward. Then looking up, she saw a face like a mask, with features strained and eyes fixed, and sprang up in terror, vainly to strive at winning from the stricken senses token of the life they locked.

Was she guilty of this?

Never did she know. For the few days that sad life held on till it reached its term never a word came: not one fiducial word through the naming of Christian to exonerate Rhoda.

So Lois, too, had the comfort of death, and Rhoda only was left, through long life to go unenlightened, and still to go dauntless of the dark.

EPILOGUE

Tell us how an altered estimate grew after the passing of Christian, to end his reproach.

But his name came to be a byword of disgrace, his story a dark, grotesque legend among records of infamy.

Tell us how Rhoda lived to be happy.

But the pain and shame of his stigma her heart could never lay aside, though long years gave to patience and fortitude a likeness to serenity and strength. Where Christian had lived would she still abide all her days; and the poor reward of her constancy was in a tribute of silence concerning him that came to respect her presence.

Tell us how Philip ripened to iniquity and was cut off.

But a tiny germ of compunction, lurking somewhere in that barren conscience, quickened and grew under Rhoda's shadow, till, spite of the evidence of his own senses, spite of reason, spite of public judgment, he entertained a strange doubt, and to his world and its ridicule acknowledged it. Long years wore out Rhoda's suspicion of his sincerity; long years raised him in her esteem in exact proportion as he sank in his own.

Tell us how Rhoda never stooped to mate with one less worthy than her first love.

But a day came when the House Monitory gave her way to a grave with a little son against her breast; and she stood there to look out over the sea that hid the bones of Christian, and thanked her God for appointing her in His world a place as helpmeet for a weak soul, who by paths of humility sought after right worship. Then she wept.

Tell us in some figure of words how the soul of Christian entered for reward into the light of God's countenance.

At rest his body lay, and over it flowed the tides.

Tell us in some figure of words how the soul of Diadyomene, wan and shivering, found an unaltered love, with full comprehension and great compassion, her shelter in the light of God's countenance.

At rest her body lay, and over it sang the winds.

Tell us in some figure of words how Lois beheld these two hand in hand, and recognised the wonderful ways of God and His mercy in the light of His countenance.

At rest her body lay, and over it grasses grew.

We need no words to tell us that God did wipe away all tears from their eyes.

Surely, surely; for quietly in the grave the elements resumed their atoms.

The Drawn Arrow

The king lay hid in a hollow of the red sandhills. He watched the poisonous grey asp flicking through the burnt crouch-thorn, and the little long-legged rat nimble at the fray, and the tawny flatwing that is never still; and no other life showed astir within the round horizon. Red sand was all the world, overhung by a yellow sky; the sun swung up the dome to his highest pitch.

"The half of my kingdom would I give for one draught of water."

Not many days ago he had been on his throne, a great king, with peace at home and conquering armies abroad. Then rose the tribes ripened to revolt by a traitor half-brother; and treason had opened his gates, and fired his palace over his head; and treason had broken his ranks in the field, so that of his first army none outlived the day save himself and his armour-bearer. Now was he cut off from all relief, for his foes warded the river and held the desert wells, knowing that a few more hours must deliver him to death if not to them.

The king waited his armour-bearer and waited in vain. "He has found no water. He is dead by thirst. He is slain. He is taken." The face of his armour-bearer rose to mind, such a face as grows over a true brave heart. "No," thought the king, "he is not taken: he himself would take his knowledge of me out of reach of the tormentors: he is dead."

He drew out a wavy dagger, and tested it again on his sleeve that gave way like mist, on his palm that gave way like water. The studs of emerald gave a good grip; though he were weak as a child he could yet baulk his half-brother's hate of a promised satisfaction. "Me alive he shall not have to flay. No."

The anguish of thirst was terrible. It ached through every exhausted vein like fever, and like fever waxed and waned, stinging the brain into acute recognition of its scope, blanking it till the whole surrounding universe was impregnated with thirst, and a symbol.

Scents strangely strong took possession of his brain: the scent of a melon, the gold-laced melon that overhung the water-tank where as a boy he bathed; the scent of a woman, one bronze-dark woman; from a cup tinkling with mountain ice they drank together, and she struck him, the king, in lovely intoxication when the wine spilled into her bosom; the scent of sodden corn in the floods; the scent of camels by the summer wells; the scent of date-buds in the cool of dusk, when as a youth he stood at the ford, and saw across the water great manes stooped to lap. One draught bit keen from memory, quaffed on a day's chase, rank with bruised fennel; and another quaffed but late in the press of disastrous battle, tingeing red as he drank: it was the reek of his own blood he drew. And between all these and others came wafts of a far remembrance, a scent unrecognisable so long forgotten; it pervaded all others, it dominated all others, blossoming late from the remotest corner of the brain: it was the scent of his mother's milk.

The signal call of the restless flatwings gave a warning, and down in the trough of the sandhills he spied a figure coming. The king lay close in his lair, and pulled forward his screen of crouch-thorn. No faithful armour-bearer came here: this, by his fillet of yellow, was a man of the river hills, from a tribe of doubtful fidelity with claims to independence against him. Tough and spare he was, hairy, red as the sand; a goatskin was all his clothing, and his only weapon a staff headed with stone; a wallet and a gourd swung at his back.

At sight of the gourd the king's hand sought his dagger, and his thirst became a torment quite intolerable. Lo! the man halted not far off, sat him down on the red hillside, and loosed the thong of wallet and gourd. At that the king thrust away his screen; his sword he left, for his dagger was enough; he turned inwards the bezel of his signet-ring, as he stepped out on the crumbling, shelving sand.

Little rat and grey asp ceased fight and scudded, and the flatwing shrilled away. The hillman turned, looking up, and sprang to his feet; he held up his right hand in token of peace, but the king came on. Then he caught up his staff, poised and swung it, but dropped it again, and once more offered the sign of peace. And then the king stood and held up his right hand, for he was dizzy and weak, and he saw that the man was wary, hardy, agile, more than his match.

So the hillman said, "Come on in peace"; and as the king came close he read in him the extremes of drought, and took the gourd and offered it instantly. And the king drank, blessed him by all his gods, and gave it back to him half-drained. Also food the hillman offered; and there they sat down together and shared like brothers, of dates and a morsel of bread, and passed the gourd to and fro; but from the hillman's hand hardly did it pass any lighter, for he saw how great was the thirst of the other.

Naught knew the red man of the shaking of a kingdom. He shaded his eyes, and looked.

"Yonder ride horsemen."

Not a sign of them could the eyes of the king descry. "Belike a troop of wild ass," he said.

"Three days," said the hillman, "did I follow the wild ass southward, seeking a lost pair of mine who shun the bit and disown the slayer of the night lion."

"Even so would the hillmen by their king."

"Lions are the hillmen and not asses; let the king know!" And he added the loyal formula: "As the sun's be the king's reign."

Still he looked. "Northward go these. They are fighting men, and many. They head for the passage of the river."

He caught up wallet and gourd. "Do they think to take the pass of our hills?" he muttered. "Not with arms in their hands, though they should be of the royal army!"

"Stay!" said the king; and the man turned and looked sharply at him who spoke with authority in the desert of the red sandhills.

"Water and food have you given for no asking; add thereto a third boon, the sound of your name."

"I have not asked yours," said the hillmen sullenly.

"Harken! Go you to the hillmen, and warn them that till the king's army come they keep the pass of the hills against his enemies. In the presence of the king only shall you know my name; and ask you him then whatsoever boon you will and for my sake will he grant it."

"Give then a token."

"No token to bear lest you fall in with the king's enemies; for you the token of my hand and eye."

The king held up his right hand, took the other's held up likewise, and gripped it hard, and their eyes met and held till the hillmen was satisfied. Released he said: "My name is Speed."

He glanced down at his palm: a rayed disk was faintly indented from the signet. One more keen look he cast. "As the sun's be the king's reign!" he said, caught up his staff, and swung away along the trough of the red hills.

Soon he was out of sight, and the king could see no living thing but the asp and the rat and the flatwing. Northward hung a blur on the horizon, dust raised of the horse he could not discern.

Long hours trailed down the sky, and the king lay close, waiting for cover of night to amend his chances.

With the edge of dark came his faithful armour-bearer, burnt with thirst and despairing. Past speech, he gave to the king one poor plant of the water-cactus, his only gain. But the king bade him slake his own thirst with this, and live and listen. Then he told all that had passed between himself and the hillman.

The armour-bearer got his voice, and said, "O my lord, was this a hairy man, all red, hair and skin, small headed, long in the thigh?"

"Even so."

The armour-bearer smote his hands together.

"Oh, my lord, rise, haste and flee! the enemy have that man. He passed me, I hiding, though quick were his eyes; a nimble man and light in build, but going heavy and hard like a dog that runs mad. A misgiving I had then. And later, edging above the plain, I saw far off a chase, and my man running and doubling to win the farther side, and in the end ridden down and taken. Oh, my lord, he was taken alive!"

The king, without a word, took his sword and set forward. He pointed. "Yonder is the star of my birth; be that our guide, since reason can prefer no road."

On through the weary night they went as destiny led; slower and slower, for the armour-bearer flagged, then dropped, and the king sat and waited for light to show him his fate.

With one breath of dawn rose broad day.

"My star!" cried the king. "Look and live."

But the armour-bearer said hoarsely, "My lord, I cannot see."

"Yonder, in sight, is the river," said the king, "and my horse hold the bank, and the foot cross thick as locusts, and the battle joins on this side. From all quarters the foe gathers, with pickets streaming in, keeping the wells no longer."

"Water!" muttered the armour-bearer, and got on his feet, but reeled and could not see.

Yet, in the end, both he and the king got down from the hills to the next well, and laying their sleeves over the mud of it, drew in delicious moisture of life. Also the water-cactus grew there.

While battle raged on the river bank, and the fortune of the day hung, a cry rose up, "The king, the king!" and with it the thrill that foretells victory ran through the royal army. And the enemy broke and fled, smitten without swords by the cry.

Now when the fight was ended and the slaughter, the king, riding by the river through the camping ground of the vanquished, spied among the herd of prisoners fillets of yellow, and bethought him of Speed the hillman. At his bidding his armour-bearer went, and presently came again with a man under his hand.

"My lord, two women there bound wear the yellow. Too dazed are they for speech or for knowing friend from foe. But this man of the prisoners knows of a foul thing to tell."

Then the prisoner told over how the hillman had been taken and brought before the traitor brother; when, though he denied stoutly all knowledge of the fugitive king, his goings were held against him, and torture was ordained to make him speak. Yet still he denied stoutly, spite of all persuasion by steel and cord and fire. Then the traitor, knowing that an army drew near, and most eager for his brother's person, sent swift horsemen to the river hills, who by guile got from the tribe the mother and the sister; and he purposed to torture them also before the eyes of the hillman. But the day coming, and the battle, they were left bound in the camp.

"Where now is the hillman?" said the king.

"Yonder he lies in the river caves."

Awhile the king stood in thought; then he ordered that the mother and sister should be kept bound, and that none should speak with them, and he took his armour-bearer with him to the river caves.

"Go in," he said, "and see."

And the armour-bearer went, and came out the paler.

"It is the man. Go not in, my lord. Yes, my lord, he lives: his eyes are shut but he surely lives."

The king stood saying naught.

"My lord," said the armour-bearer, "the title of Most Faithful, ordained by you this day for my reward, I cannot hold. This poor hillman has the better claim."

"It is truth," said the king. "Great shall be his reward."

Then he turned to his guards and bade fetch the women.

"I have a mind," he said, "to try the man, and the greater shall be his reward."

And while his tent was pitching hard by he told his armour-bearer all that was to be done, and when the women came, put them in his hand for the doing, while he turned himself to the gathering of the captains.

So soon as the armour-bearer came again in at the tent the king bade for silence that he might speak.

"My lord, at the voices of the women he opened his eyes and sat, strong-alive yet. Oh, my lord, I got another with a stiffer throat than I to speak further. They, no less than he, doubted not the dead earnest of all; and they used all the power of woman-speech beseeching him for pity on himself and on them, and still he shook his head and denied that he had any knowledge of the king to deliver. Then that young woman, his sister, caught me by the knees beseeching pity of me, protesting that he knew nothing, for he would withhold nothing for the life of his mother and her, his sister, his twin sister. And yet when the order was given for her to be led away as to death, the hillman muttered something at her ear: 'As the sun's be the king's reign,' I thought it to be. And the young woman looked him in the eyes, and kissed him, and with no word more, went out straight. Then was brought in a human heart fresh killed, and put into his hand as his sister's heart, with the heat and the beat of it still there. And he holds the heart and looks at his mother, and still he shakes his head."

"Great shall be his reward," said the king. "And the mother?"

"Oh, my lord, pardon!" said the armour-bearer, kneeling. "I have carried your command no further. Had you witnessed you could desire no further trial. Oh, my lord, spare him more."

"Go," said the king in anger, "and obey." And the armour-bearer went.

When he came again tears were running down to his beard.

"Oh, my lord, I was born of woman. She uncovered the breast to her son; she was taken out struggling and crying to him to save her. And a second heart was brought in and put hot into his hand. And he sits there, holding in his blistered hands those two hearts that he takes to be his sister's and his mother's, and now one and now the other he holds against his breast to keep it warm, and he mutters over them, and all he says is: 'As the sun's be the king's reign.'"

"It is enough," said the king. "Great shall be his reward."

Then by order, Speed the hillman was cleansed and dressed with wine and oil; and a costly ointment the king gave, fit for the healing of blood royal.

Then on the next day the king had the hillman brought and set down in the tent where he lay. And he entered alone and closed the entrance, having on him the royal boss and the purple, and all the gear of the throne.

On the red man had been put a linen tunic to cover most of him, but with the aroma of the royal balm the smell of the torture came off him yet, and the look of torture lay dead on his face; and though the king in his splendour stood before him, the eyes of Speed the hillman stayed wide and blank without speculation, and when the king spoke to him by name they never moved.

Then the king, for a token, took what was left of the right hand of Speed in his own, and lifted it up, and fixed his eyes straight upon his and held so. And in a while the flesh he grasped quivered as the man's eyes wavered with sense; recognition swam into them; his hand answered feebly; a great straight grin came out; he drew a thirsty breath and laughed low in his throat. At the dreadful noise the king, loosing, stepped back, when Speed reached to the hem of his sleeve and touched it at his brow. "As the sun's be the king's reign," he muttered; and his head sank on his breast and his eyes settled.

Outside sounded the ringing of silver bells and the king uncovered the door of the tent, took Speed and set him there, and bade him look out.

Before the hillman's eyeballs came, at slow pace upon white asses housed with silver and blue, two women with fillets of yellow, and the gowns of the tribe under long veils of gold; and they held up their hands and called him by name, and brother and son. With a sound little and shrill like the voice of a bat Speed the hillman spun round twice, beat the air and fell flat.

Now the women were come and had bowed at the king's feet, and had taken up Speed upon their knees, and the king was fain with his own mouth to discover the circuits of his grace. But when a glimmer of recognition came with a shape of their names, yet the wells of joy lay all untouched, viewless and dark, the heart of the king so swelled with compassion that he had no voice to speak. He went out hastily, and calling his armour-bearer bade him go in and do the telling. "And when all things are made clear to Speed the hillman, bring him out hither, in the midst of all to me hither." And the armour-bearer was pale and shook as he went at the king's bidding.

Under a wide tented canopy of gold sat the king to deal out justice without mercy, and honours and rewards without stint. And many and many came before him, but not the armour-bearer with the man Speed, whose reward was to exceed all others; till the king, impatient, sent for the armour-bearer and questioned.

"My lord, all has been told, and his mother and his sister have told it after me, and he says nothing at all but their names. His eyes never leave them, and now to one and now to the other he thrusts his hand, and beneath the closing of the gown feels at the warm beating of the heart."

"Send home the women," cried the king, "and make straight his understanding."

So the armour-bearer went, and again the king waited in vain, and again sent.

"What of the man Speed? What says he?"

"My lord," said the armour-bearer, "he says nothing at all." The king stamped for anger.

"Is this your duty? Have you not made him to know yet?"

"He knows! he does know. Oh, my lord, my lord."

"Bring him here then," cried the king. And the armour-bearer lifted his arms and cried: "Oh, my lord, my lord!" and went.

Every eye turned for the coming of the man above all others proved loyal and true by transcendent trial. In the midst sat the king on a throne, his nobles and his captains standing thick on either hand, backed by the glittering line of his guard. Six chosen men stood by him, three and three on either side; two swordsmen with blade drawn and up; two bowmen with strung bow and the arrow notched ready on the string; two spearmen with stooped spear. Brought in by the armour-bearer before all these, the red man in the linen tunic, with the smell of torture and the face of dead torture, stood on his feet and lifted a patient inanimate gaze.

Then, smiling, the king rose up from his throne to honour the man. "Oh, faithful and true," he said, "great shall be your reward. No service of these the greatest in all my land has equalled yours. Turn your eyes and behold."

And Speed turned his head this way and that, and saw all heads bowed to the earth honouring him. Only the king and his six guards stood upright, and the armour-bearer who forgot to worship with his body.

"Hear first the recompense that a king gives unasked; then ask your boon, and by the word of one who drank with you in the desert, is it granted.

"Hear all ye the recompense that a king gives unasked.

"It is my will that henceforth and for ever the tribe of the hillmen be free of tribute and toll; and that they have beyond the river of the water-lands as far as their flocks can in a day travel.

"It is my will that the sister of Speed the hillman be taken to wife of what man he shall choose in all my land, barring only the blood royal.

"It is my will that the mother of Speed the hillman be entitled Honourable, and that he make choice of a city for her maintenance.

"Also I will that the yellow fillet be worn of the royal brides.

"And for you, oh, Speed, shall be herds of white asses, and lordship, and trumpets shall be blown for your entrance of a city, and no man, not of my house, shall have place before you. Also the fair virgins of my land shall be sought out for your choice. Also my half-brother who is taken shall be given alive into your hand, that you may strip off his kin to serve you with covering till yours be whole. And the title of Brother to the King shall be yours; and the name you shall bear shall be my name, so only you yield me the gift of your name in exchange."

Then the king took off the boss of gold and set it on the head of Speed, and on his neck a collar of gold, and on his finger the signet-ring; and he took off his mantle stiff with gold and with it clothed Speed the hillman, whose eyes had sunk and whose head had bent while these honours were laid upon him. And the majesty of grace was all the adornment left to the king's person, therefore the more did all heads worship towards him.

Then the hillman lifted his head and looked into the eyes of the gracious king a while; with full understanding he looked; with mild eyes and weary he looked; with eyes that never shifted he held the king as he took the boss from his head and laid it on the throne and likewise the collar of gold from his neck, and the signet-ring from his finger, and loosed the mantle and let it fall. And he turned, and from the presence of the king and his great ones went out softly upon the hot sand, and turned his face towards the river hills.

All men there looking on the king held breath; his breathing only, in the silence, was heard rattling.

"Shoot!" said the king. Quick, quick the bowstrings rang; an arrow sang out across the sand, stopped mute at the heart of Speed.

Quick, quick and frantic high tore out recall: too late. The voice of the king's agony never reached the heart of Speed. He clutched the sand once and died.

No man but the armour-bearer dared look in the king's face when he stood by the dead man. The arrow stood upright in his back quite still. His hands had all they could hold.

But it was the voice of a king's displeasure that said: "One arrow!"

The armour-bearer with his left hand held up another; held up his right hand: it was stricken through.

"Most faithful," said the King low, "bury you him—where he lies; you and none other."

He turned away with the face of a king, and the day went down on the last of the army winding away, and the armour-bearer alone smoothing the vacant sand half-way between the caves and the river.

But the king beheld the face of his most faithful armour-bearer never again.

Now when the king died, being of very great age and honours, and entered his chamber of silence for the last time, the new king, his son's son, according to custom entered also for the first time. And there for his reading on the walls with strong lines and fair colours was set out the record of the dead king's life from the star of his birth. And very long and splendid was the tale of his deeds and his conquests; and the woes that fell when his foes flourished because of the sleep of the gods were also set there and not diminished.

To the high-priest the young king said: "What means this arrow that stands in the heart of the king: with his foot on the neck of his half-brother he stands, and an arrow is in his heart; and never after find I him without it sticking there."

But the high-priest could not tell him, nor could any man; and the craftsmen who wrought the walls had not marked in those arrows.

In dull red were the arrows drawn, and in the last of them the line wavered. And the first arrow of all was lined beneath the feet of the king, and a red man giving him drink from a gourd in the desert.

Above the rest of the hillman and above the rest of the king the wind of centuries with equal wing has smoothed the vacant sand.

Laurence Housman's
Were-Wolf Illustrations

Melissa Purdue

*T*he *Were-Wolf* was published twice in the nineteenth century—the first time in 1890 in *Atalanta,* a popular girls' magazine, and the second in 1896 with John Lane's Bodley Head press. This edition uses the John Lane edition, which includes illustrations by Clemence's brother Laurence. The original *Atalanta* illustrations were by Everard Hopkins. Laurence Housman and Hopkins created distinctly different visual interpretations of Clemence Housman's story.

Laurence Housman studied at the Lambeth School of Art and the Royal College of Art. In addition to the woodcut engravings he did for *The Were-Wolf,* he also illustrated other nineteenth-century works such as Christina Rossetti's *Goblin Market and Other Poems,* Jane Barlow's *The End of Elfintown,* Percy Bysshe Shelley's *The Sensitive Plant,* and George Meredith's *Jump to Glory Jane.* Like his sister Clemence, he was active in the woman suffrage movement. Together with Alfred Pearse, they founded the Suffrage Atelier—a collective of artists who worked to enfranchise women. Everard Hopkins studied at the Slade School of Art. He was an assistant editor of *Pilot* and worked for years as an illustrator for *Punch* magazine. Hopkins also illustrated for other magazines and many books, including L. T. Meade's *The Children of Wilton Chase* and Alfred, Lord Tennyson's *The Princess.*

Rechelle Christie argues in "The Politics of Representation and Illustration in Clemence Housman's *The Were-Wolf*" that while the original images published with the story by Everard Hopkins reinforce conventional depictions of masculinity and femininity, "Laurence's images for *The Were-Wolf* in the Lane illustrated edition instigate a dialogue between image and text that reflects Clemence's passion for a community free from gender constraints and social hierarchies" (61). Likewise, Lorraine Janzen Kooistra points out that the final full-page image, in which Sweyn carries his dead brother with his arms outstretched and with a glowing cross in the background, "restores patriarchal order." This image marks the hypermasculine Sweyn as the hero of the story who has attempted to save his brother from the dangerous and alluring female monster. It is an interesting contrast to Housman's final image in which Sweyn is brought to his knees and Christian is portrayed as the "superior form of humanity by his androgynous blending of genders" (Kooistra). As an artist herself, having attended the South London School of Technical Art to learn wood engraving, Clemence would have been very aware of the impact of the visual messages accompanying her story. Thus, her decision to work with her brother to create new images for the John Lane edition is a telling one. Hopkins's images highlight the story's messages about Christian sacrifice and salvation and the dangers of the New Woman, whereas Housman's images stress the story's challenge to gender norms.

Works Cited

Christie, Rechelle. "The Politics of Representation and Illustration in Clemence Housman's *The Were-Wolf.*" *Housman Society Journal* 33 (2007): 54–67.

Kooistra, Lorraine Janzen. "Magazine and Book Illustrations for *The Were-Wolf.*" In *Clemence Housman's* The Were-Wolf. Edited by Lorraine Janzen Kooistra et al. COVE Editions, 2018.

Bibliography

The Were-Wolf. Atalanta 4 (Christmas 1890): 132–56. London: John Lane/The Bodley Head; Chicago: Way & Williams, 1896.

The Unknown Sea. London: Duckworth & Co., 1898.

"The Drawn Arrow." In Ernest Rhys and C. A. Dawson Scott, ed. *31 Stories by Thirty and One Authors.* New York: D. Appleton & Co., 1923. 314–26.

About S. T. Joshi

S. T. JOSHI is the author of *The Weird Tale* (1990), *H. P. Lovecraft: The Decline of the West* (1990), and *Unutterable Horror: A History of Supernatural Fiction* (2012). He has prepared corrected editions of H. P. Lovecraft's work for Arkham House and annotated editions of Lovecraft's stories for Penguin Classics. He has also prepared editions of Lovecraft's collected essays and poetry. His exhaustive biography, *H. P. Lovecraft: A Life* (1996), was expanded as *I Am Providence: The Life and Times of H. P. Lovecraft* (2010). He is the editor of the anthologies *American Supernatural Tales* (Penguin, 2007), *Black Wings* I-VI (PS Publishing, 2010, 2012, 2013), *A Mountain Walked: Great Tales of the Cthulhu Mythos* (Centipede Press, 2014), *The Madness of Cthulhu* (Titan Books, 2014–15), and *Searchers After Horror: New Tales of the Weird and Fantastic* (Fedogan & Bremer, 2014). He is the editor of the *Lovecraft Annual, Spectral Realms,* and *Penumbra* (all published by Hippocampus Press). Among his works of fiction are *The Recurring Doom: Tales of Mystery and Horror* (Sarnath Press, 2019) and *Something from Below* (PS Publishing, 2019).

CPSIA information can be obtained
at www.ICGtesting.com
Printed in the USA
BVHW041043170223
658745BV00008B/153